Getting Over It

Sapphire Falls, book six

Erin Nicholas

ISBN: 978-0-9863245-9-8

Editor: Heidi Moore
Cover artist: Valerie Tibbs
Copy edits: Kelli Collins
Digital formatting: Author E.M.S.
Print formatting: Kim Brooks

DEDICATION

It seems that my list of people to thank continues to grow...what an awesome thing!

To Nikoel and Kim, who talk me off of ledges weekly...even the ones I create in my imagination.

To Crystal, Shannon and Michele who said all the right things at the right time.

To Rhian who is my voice of reason.

To my family, who puts up with much and who shares in every success.

And to the town of Stromsburg, Nebraska, my mental model for Sapphire Falls. No place is perfect—unless you spent your childhood there with your grandparents. Then it gets pretty darned close.

CHAPTER ONE

It was a gorgeous summer day in Sapphire Falls.

The sky was a beautiful cloudless blue. There was a light breeze, birds sang sweetly from the trees and multicolored butterflies flitted among the pink, white and purple flowers in Hailey Conner's backyard flowerbed.

And she was going to kill someone today.

Namely the idiot who was mowing his lawn next door at six freaking a.m. on a Saturday morning.

Blurry eyed, she stomped to the window, shoved it up and leaned out.

He was mowing on this side of the house, but she couldn't see anything over the top of the tall wooden fence that surrounded her yard.

But he had bought the loudest mower she'd ever heard.

She had yet to catch even a glimpse of this new guy next door. It was so weird. She knew someone had bought the place because the for-sale sign was gone. She knew someone had moved in because she'd seen lights in the windows and heard pounding late at night. But when she'd gone over to introduce herself, no one had come to the door. Twice.

No one in town knew who it was. Not at the diner, the bakery or the bar. And if people there didn't know, *nobody* knew.

Except Delaney Callan. She had bought and renovated the house and had then sold it to whoever this was. Hailey only knew it was a man because Delaney's fiancé, Tucker, had slipped with that information last week. The new owner had *paid* Delaney to *not* tell anyone who he was. Who did that?

And who kept that secret anyway?

Delaney was new here. She didn't know that people didn't keep secrets in Sapphire Falls. Or that they especially didn't keep secrets from Hailey.

Hailey was the mayor, for God's sake. She should know what was going on in her town.

Particularly when it was going on right next door.

She leaned out farther, bracing her hands on the windowsill. Was he young, old, tall, short, fat, thin? It was driving her crazy.

But she couldn't see a thing.

Well, he was home now. Outside. He couldn't avoid her if she showed up in the yard he was mowing.

Suddenly wide awake, Hailey headed for the shower.

As she stripped out of her pajamas, she noticed the bright-pink sticky note on her bathroom mirror.

Ask Frank about the blue paint.

Dammit. She'd forgotten to do that yesterday. Especially with the sticky note on her *bathroom mirror* rather than somewhere useful like, oh, maybe her desk.

She kept the sticky notes and a pen in the bathroom though because thoughts and questions would come to her at very random times and her memory was, well, mostly nonexistent.

It was the same reason she kept sticky notes and pens in every room of her house.

She wrapped herself in a towel and headed for her desk in the spare bedroom. Might as well e-mail him now. She sent off a quick message to Frank, the primary maintenance man for the town, asking if there was enough blue paint to repaint the flower pots along the sidewalk on Main Street. She hit send, gave a satisfied sigh, and headed back for the bathroom.

She was stepping into the shower when she thought that maybe they should have the Boy Scouts and Girl Scouts help with the painting. They could then decorate the pots with their own artwork as well.

Hailey leaned over, grabbed a sticky note and wrote *Scouts painting* on the top sheet and stuck it to her bathroom mirror.

An hour and a half—and six more sticky notes and two more e-mails—later, Hailey was ready to go.

Looking at herself in the mirror, Hailey noted all of her positives the way Lena, her therapist, had instructed. The bodice of the dress accentuated her breasts without showing too much cleavage and the short skirt showed off her legs without making bending over dangerous. Her pedicure looked good, the tan she maintained with help from a tube of the best self-tanner on the market was perfect, and the highlights in her hair made her look as though she'd spent the summer at the beach.

Her positives most often had to do with her looks.

In spite of all of her other quirks—she really did prefer that word to "issues" or "flaws"—she was thankful she'd been blessed with beauty. She'd been the prettiest girl wherever she went, and she'd started putting extra effort behind it when she was about fourteen and realized that hair, makeup and clothes could take pretty to gorgeous...and gorgeous kept people at arm's length.

Women were often intimidated by her and men often thought she was out of their league. Thank God. Having people avoid getting close was easier than pushing them away.

But if someone decided to try to get closer, her bitchy, I'm-better-than-you attitude usually put them off quickly. There were very few who had stuck around in spite of all of that.

Hailey shook her head. No, she wasn't supposed to think about the negatives. She was supposed to catalog the things she liked about herself rather than listing the things that irritated her. Like her addiction to sticky notes, or the fact that she couldn't get ready and out of the house in less than an hour and a half because of all the distractions, or that she was only comfortable with *a lot* of personal space around her.

She applied lip gloss, ignored the sticky note hanging on the lamp on her bedside table, and went down to the kitchen. Where she had to ignore six more sticky notes.

Avoiding looking at the stack of colored folders and her planner on the table next to the cute plate of brownies, she picked up the treats and turned to leave the room. And hesitated.

She didn't want him to think she was inviting a friendship or regular coffee breaks together or anything. She'd lived next door to Betty Griffin for only a year before the woman passed away and the house had been empty since. Betty had been a very nice woman, but Hailey liked having an empty house next door. She didn't want a neighbor who was in her business and inviting himself over all the time. She had no intention of borrowing tools or loaning cups of sugar back and forth.

The brownies were probably the wrong signal to send.

The only reason she had the stupid things in the first place was because Ty Bennett had said something a few days ago about Hailey not being the type to bring brownies to a neighbor. And that was true. But it had irritated her that he knew it, so she'd picked the dumb things up from the bakery.

What any of this had to do with Ty, she couldn't explain. But he had this way of getting into her head and making her do things, say things, think things that she never would have otherwise.

And he knew it. Which made it all worse. He knew he got to her—and she didn't let *anyone* get to her. So somehow taking brownies to her neighbor had turned into a way to show Ty that he *didn't* know her that well.

As if he would ever find out.

That was how crazy he made her.

Hailey consciously banished additional thoughts of Ty from her mind and headed out the front door. She'd get this over with and then she could stop thinking about her neighbor, and Ty, and get back to her regularly scheduled Saturday.

She paused on her front porch to determine which side of the house her neighbor was mowing on at the moment.

But she heard nothing.

She frowned. No. He couldn't be done already.

But with a sigh, she acknowledged that it had been almost two hours since she'd first awakened.

Damn it. Damn her morning routine. Damn those sticky notes. Damn Ty for his idea about brownies.

Irked that she might have to wait even longer to meet the mystery man, she stomped down her front porch steps, over to his house and up the steps to his front door. She balanced the plate of brownies in one hand, rang the doorbell and pasted on a bright smile.

That faded second by second as no one came to the door.

Dammit. She'd missed him again.

She kicked the door in frustration and turned to leave.

Her foot hit the top step when she heard the door behind her open.

Yes!

She pivoted quickly, fake smile firmly in place, with one foot on the porch and one on the top step.

The move wobbled her in her high wedges and she felt herself tipping and the brownies sliding. She was about to end up on her butt on his porch with chocolate down the front of her when a strong, warm hand grasped her elbow and another grabbed the plate.

"I love making your knees weak, but let's not hurt anyone, okay?"

That voice. That deep, sexy, teasing voice…

She'd know it anywhere.

"You've got to be fucking kidding me." She glared up at Tyler Bennett as he helped her stand, get steady on her feet and up on the porch before letting go of her.

Except, he didn't let go of her.

He continued to hold her elbow. And stand way too close.

"What are *you* doing here?" she demanded.

Well, she'd meant to demand it. Her voice actually sounded a little breathless to her ears.

Probably from the near fall.

"Saving your...brownies," he said with a smile.

No, not *a* smile. *The* smile. The one that made her stomach flip.

The one he wasn't supposed to ever give her in Sapphire Falls.

She pulled her arm from his grip and stepped back. She smoothed her skirt, ran a hand over her hair and wet her lips. She'd known he was in town. She'd seen him just last week out at his brother's house. Where he'd mentioned the brownies. He'd been visiting a lot this summer, but she had stubbornly refused to ask him why.

Now she knew why he was in town this time. "You know the guy who bought this house." It wasn't a question.

Of course he did. In spite of living in Denver, Ty had an unreal amount of knowledge about Sapphire Falls and what went on here.

Ty nodded slowly. "I do."

She put her free hand on her hip. "And you didn't think to mention that to me any of the times I've talked about not knowing who was moving in next door to me?"

Dammit. They'd been together three weeks ago. They'd been *naked* together three weeks ago. And he hadn't thought about telling her he was friends with her new neighbor?

"I couldn't mention it," he said.

God, he looked good. Hailey tried not to be distracted by his lean, muscular body that swam, biked and ran for a living. But it was impossible. There was no way she couldn't think about how great he looked when her entire body felt as if it was straining toward him.

She distinctly remembered the day she'd admitted she was sexually attracted to him. He'd been wooing her with his sense of humor and his sweetness and the fact that he was, or at least had seemed to be, over the moon for *her* for two years in high school. But that night at the senior class party, she'd suddenly truly seen him physically. He'd climbed out of the river looking like a freaking god, in only a pair of swimming trunks. She'd watched the water trickle over every bump and ridge of hard muscle on his body as he'd come to stand right in front of her. When he'd reached past her for his towel, she'd been overwhelmed by the heat and by how big he suddenly seemed and how obviously comfortable he was nearly naked.

And now she knew every inch of his body and what that body was truly capable of. He was more slender than his brothers, but he was hard *everywhere* and had stamina that was truly mind-blowing. The man made a living with his body and it showed in everything he did. Yeah, there was no *not* being distracted by that.

Which was one of her big problems when he visited Sapphire Falls. He distracted her from *everything*.

He was in a simple T-shirt and jeans today and, having grown up around denim and cotton in all shapes and sizes, Hailey had to admit that blue jeans seemed made for showing off asses like Ty's, and T-shirts were meant to cling lovingly to wide shoulders and flat abs.

His hair was longer than usual and looked windblown—which fit a guy who spent most of his time outdoors. He also hadn't shaved today. It seemed that she shaved nearly every inch of her body, but she was a born-and-raised country girl, and scruff, tanned skin and big work-roughened hands did it for her.

She knew exactly how that scruff and those hands would feel rubbing over her—

"Hailey?"

She focused on his eyes. He was giving her a knowing grin.

She hated when he did that. When he *knew* things about her that she didn't want him to know. It made him smug. And it made her aware of the things he *didn't* know. The deal breakers. The reason she preferred ogling him and losing her mind over him in *Denver*.

She needed her mind and her pride when she was here in Sapphire Falls.

"Why couldn't you tell me?" she asked, thrilled to be able to remember what they'd been talking about. Seriously, she was standing on the porch of the neighbor she had been wondering about for weeks and she almost didn't remember that *he* was the topic of conversation. Pathetic. "He paid *you* not to say anything either?"

"Because it would have upset you and you would have caused problems for...him...moving in. He needed to get settled first."

It would have upset her? Why? Who the hell was this?

"So you decided to wait until he was all moved in to tell me that you know him?" she asked. "In spite of us..." They never talked about their affair while in Sapphire Falls. Ever. It was one of their rules. Okay, it was one of *her* rules. Actually, pretty much her only rule. She sighed. "Who is it?"

He chewed on the inside of his cheek, simply watching her as several seconds passed. She waited.

Finally, he seemed to make a decision. "Me."

She expected him to grin or go on and explain that he was house-sitting for her new neighbor until he could move in. Or something.

But he didn't say anything else.

Tyler Bennett teased her a lot. He gave her a hard time. He loved to rile her up just to rile her up.

But he didn't look like he was kidding now.

No.

Her stomach knotted, dread trickled through her, and she started shaking her head. No. *No.* Ty lived in Denver.

Tyler was a triathlete who competed on the international stage. He'd left home for Colorado right after high school to train. He'd been entering and placing in the top three in races all over the world ever since, including a silver medal in the Olympics.

But it wasn't gold, and he wasn't going to stop until he had one of those too.

His training and constant striving for that number-one spot kept him in Colorado. Talk about personal space. She had five hundred and two miles of personal space. Oh, sure, he thoroughly invaded that personal space the second she set foot in Denver—and she loved every minute of it. But then she could retreat back to Sapphire Falls and breathe deep and recover and live her life.

While he lived *his* life.

In *Denver.*

Seeing him for a weekend every couple of months was fine. And enough. Ty was…potent. When they were together, he took over her thoughts. He distracted her from everything else. He owned her. Which was fine for a couple of days, far from home and work, every once in a while. It was more than fine, actually. It was heaven.

But there weren't enough sticky notes and planners in the world to keep her on track and any kind of productive if Ty lived next door.

He could *not* live next door. That would be crazy. He loved their weekend indulgences as much as she did, but he'd also confessed that if she were around all the time, he'd never be able to focus fully on his training. She made him want to stay in bed all day and eat ice cream—off of her—and spend the day at the zoo and lie on the couch watching Netflix marathons and have sex on every available horizontal surface. And a couple of vertical ones.

They worked out together. She loved rock climbing and

zip lining and biking and running with him. But it was hardly at the level he needed to work out at to stay competitive.

His training wasn't just a hobby or a way to stay in shape. It was his *life*. It was the way he made a living, between the prizes and his endorsements. And his training happened in *Denver*.

"You?" she finally asked. "What do you mean?"

"I mean, I'm your new neighbor."

His grin was gone. His smugness was gone. In their place was a confident, direct gaze that told her he meant it. And that she was in big trouble.

This was not the teasing, fun-loving Ty who visited Sapphire Falls. This was the intense, I'm-in-charge Denver Ty who made her do things that…well, that she'd never do in Sapphire Falls.

That meant he wasn't kidding.

And that meant they had to break up. Or she had to move.

ৎ৯৵৶

"Well, now that's impossible," Hailey said after a stunned silence, in that cool, haughty tone she'd perfected in the ninth grade.

"Impossible?" Ty asked. "Why is that?"

He could smell her shampoo and body wash and his entire body tightened in response. She always smelled good. Even after a workout or a hike, he wanted to put his nose…pretty much all over her.

"Because you're not stupid," she said, lifting her chin. "You *act* like an idiot sometimes, but you're not actually dumb enough to move in next door to me without talking to me about it first."

No, not if he wanted everything to be civil between them.

But he didn't. *Not* being civil with Hailey was one of his favorite things in the world.

This woman frustrated the shit out of him. She pushed him away. She argued with him. She called him on his bullshit and wasn't impressed with his trophies and medals. She made him work for every smile, every moan, every yes.

And he fucking loved it.

It sounded crazy, he knew, but it was the competitor in him. He loved to win, but the sweetest victories were those that were hard-won.

He also loved adrenaline. Loved feeling it pumping through him, making him daring and strong. And no person got his adrenaline flowing like the good mayor of Sapphire Falls.

He hadn't expected her to be overjoyed by this at first. He knew that she loved their arrangement exactly as it was—miles and time in between them. But things had changed and he wanted more. He wanted *her*. She was going to have to deal with that.

"If I had told you, you would have cut me off," he said, keeping his tone light. "And you know I'd lie, cheat and steal to get my tongue on your—"

"You're right," she broke in. "I would have. Like I'm doing right now."

Her cheeks were flushed and Ty wasn't sure if it was anger, lust or a delicious combination of the two.

She started to turn away, but Ty anticipated her move and blocked her from the steps with his body.

She narrowed her eyes. "Get out of the way."

"Not until we talk about this."

"Okay, here's what I've got to say. If you live here, that means I don't get my weekend in Denver anymore, which means I don't get to eat at El Ranchero anymore, and I don't get to go skiing and I don't get to have massages from Meredith anymore. Basically, you're fucking everything up, and if you think you're ever going to have sex with me again after taking away my enchiladas, you're a dumbass."

She shoved him out of the way and started down the steps.

He knew the enchiladas were not her main concern, but taking her away from her favorite Mexican food would definitely be held against him. Not to mention Meredith's magic massages.

Of course, he was gambling on being more important to her than corn tortillas and cheese.

He really hoped he wasn't going to lose that bet. He couldn't be number three on her list behind lavender massage oil and the best red sauce in the US.

Ty started after her, but she suddenly stopped on the third step. He caught her by her shoulders to keep from plowing her over.

"We can still go skiing," he said.

She turned and looked up at him. "Not together, Ty. It's all over."

For a moment, he thought he saw her bottom lip quiver.

But, no. This was Hailey Conner. Her lower lip did lots of really nice things, but pouting was not one of them.

She lifted the plate of brownies she held. She'd brought brownies to her new neighbor. Ty started to grin.

Until she shoved the plate at him, brownies first, smashing them against his chest. "Welcome to the neighborhood."

Ty caught the plate as she spun away and stomped down the steps.

She was pissed.

He could work with that.

Hailey was a challenge, but she always had been. Riling her up and then wearing her down was some of the most fun Ty had in life. And he really needed some fun.

Things in his life over the past few months had been

pretty damned bleak. No one here, outside of his family, knew anything about it, of course. He was upbeat and cocky as ever as far as they were all concerned. Even Hailey. *Especially* Hailey. But ever since that fucking truck crossed the middle line and forced him and Bryan, his friend and riding partner, over the edge of the mountain, things had been rough.

He'd tried to stay positive for Bryan, who had spent weeks in a hospital bed and then rehab. But Ty had been in pain, restless, angry and frustrated in varying amounts almost constantly since then.

With the exception of Hailey's visits.

Since things had gone to hell five months before, she'd been to Denver twice. Part of him had wanted to confide in her. He'd even started to tell her on one occasion. But being with her had made him forget about the pain and the things he couldn't do and, in the end, he couldn't tell her. The pain and fear he felt when she *wasn't* there had actually made it even clearer that she was a bright spot in his life, and he needed more brightness. So he'd consciously kept the darkness out of their time together.

Instead of deep, revealing conversations, they argued about politics and pop culture and if cream or jelly was the best donut filling. They pushed each other to climb higher on the rock wall and to run farther on the indoor track. They even competed when doing word searches or playing chess.

And when she left, he felt it in everything. His house was quieter and didn't smell like coconut. He was bored to death by the word search and his workouts went back to being work.

It wouldn't be easy to convince her that he needed her full time, of course, but he was looking forward to that. He didn't like things that came easy. Anyone could do easy. It took a champion to stick with something in the face of opposition, hurdles...and one stubborn, pissed-off, gorgeous mayor.

The plate still against his chest, he followed her down the steps and across the grass between their houses.

Damn, she looked good walking away.

Or walking toward him. Or standing there. Or lying there...

"This isn't about enchiladas," he said.

"Those enchiladas are amazing."

"You haven't been driving eight hours for enchiladas."

"Well, you can't get enchiladas like that just anywhere."

Right. He climbed her porch steps behind her. "But everything else you love about coming to Denver you *can* get anywhere?"

She spun on him. "No. That's the thing, Ty. I can't zip line here. I can't hike in the mountains here. I can't see concerts in Red Rocks here. I love hanging out with you in Denver and now you've messed it all up."

She'd said it with enough conviction that he actually hesitated. Denver was awesome and they'd had a hell of a good time together there. But there was no way the majority of the appeal was the mountains and food.

"You've loved *hanging out* with me?" he said. "That's what the last three and a half years have been about?"

"In *Denver*," she emphasized. "And, yes."

For an instant, he had a flicker of doubt. *He'd* had a good time, but maybe she loved the mountains more than he'd known. But she lifted her chin slightly after she said it. That was her tell that she wasn't feeling quite as sassy as she seemed but that she was going to fight anyway.

He grinned. This woman had been making his ego sting for years. It was part of her appeal. He could never get too full of himself with her around. The smiles he got, the spontaneous hugs, the way he could get her out of her clothes in five minutes or less, was all about him and had nothing to do with his medals or commercials.

Anyone could take her zip lining. He didn't know anyone else who could make her giggle and blush.

She was still standing outside of her front door and Ty realized he'd never been inside her house.

Interesting.

She had laid out ground rules when they'd first started sleeping together—no one in Sapphire Falls could know and they couldn't act like a couple when he came to Nebraska to visit.

It had been fine with him at first. He'd been focused on having her. Yes, he'd wanted the world to know, but it had been enough that *he* knew.

It was pathetic, but he had been willing to take what she would give him—and not tell the world that he'd won her over, gotten her into his bed, into his *life*—over losing her completely.

Until now.

He was done with all of that.

He'd wanted two things since he was fifteen years old—a gold medal and Hailey Conner.

He'd *almost* gotten both.

Now the gold was no longer a possibility and all of his focus and energy and hopes were on this woman.

She was going to have to get used to it.

"It's going to take a lot more than that to get rid of me," he said, moving in close and backing her up against the door. "In high school, you cut me down a lot further and a lot more often and I still stuck around."

Hailey pressed back against the door, fumbling for the knob behind her. "I was hoping you'd matured since then and would take no for an answer. You and I both know that I can be bitchier if needed."

"I can't take no for an answer when I know you want to say yes. And now I'm even more confident I can change your mind," he said, bracing one hand on the door next to her ear, the other still holding the plate of smashed brownies.

"Oh, really?"

"Yeah, because now I know how to really get to you."

He dipped his head, intent on kissing her, when she finally got the knob turned on the door. Their weight caused it to swing inward and they both tripped across the threshold.

Ty didn't give her a chance to catch her balance— figuratively or literally. He let the plate drop to the floor as he cupped her face between his hands, kicked the door shut behind him and turned her to press her against the inside of it.

He leaned in until their mouths were a millimeter apart. "Say yes," he told her gruffly.

She started to shake her head, but he held her firmly, willing her to look him in the eye.

"Hailey Ann, look at me."

Finally, she lifted her gaze.

"Ask me to kiss you."

He loved making her ask for what she wanted. Many a time, he'd made her *beg*. Was it because he had a deeply ingrained competitive streak and huge ego? Maybe. Was it because he was naturally dominant in the bedroom? Probably. Did it go back to high school, when hoity-toity Hailey had walked the halls like a queen? Oh yeah.

But this wasn't a time for begging.

All he needed was a nice please.

Hailey wet her bottom lip. The one he was sure had *not* trembled earlier. Her gaze moved to his mouth and Ty felt his body tighten and heat.

"Okay, you can kiss me," she said softly.

Yes. She would never be *easy* for him, and that was exactly what he wanted.

He shook his head slowly. "I'm not asking permission. This isn't your mayoral office. You're already getting ready for the orgasm you know I can give you. But only if you ask nice."

"All you have to do is speak and I'm on the verge of orgasm, huh?" she scoffed. But the breathlessness in her voice took some of the sarcasm away.

He grinned and stroked his thumb along her jaw. "You're so conditioned to coming apart for me that you hear my voice, you smell me, you feel my hands on you and you're about halfway there."

She rolled her eyes, but her breath caught too.

He knew he was right, and he felt a jolt of adrenaline akin to the feeling he got pulling ahead of the pack on his bike. Excitement and anticipation and arrogance all combined to give him a heady pleasure he would continue to seek out, against all odds.

It was better than any high he could get from any other source.

"Come on, Hailey," he encouraged huskily. "Ask me to kiss you."

He bent his knees and put his nose against her neck, breathing deep and relishing the way she seemed to *stop* breathing. He ran his nose up and down, skimming the soft skin of her throat with a barely there touch of his lips.

And finally, he felt her lift her hands and slide her fingers into his hair.

"Ty," she said, panting softly.

"Say it." His lips were against the pulse point at the base of her throat that was fluttering fast and hard.

Her head fell back against the door and she arched into him. "Kiss me, Ty, please."

God, those words...a primal sense of triumph streaked through him and he dropped his hands to her ass, brought her up against him fully, and took her mouth with his.

She dug her fingers into his scalp as he slicked his tongue over her lower lip. She opened to him and he took the kiss to hot and wet and deep in an instant.

The scent of her shampoo and her skin and chocolate

combined around him, ratcheting his hunger higher and higher, until he needed so much more than her mouth. He needed all of her. Right now.

He leaned back and stared down at her.

Her eyes were unfocused, her lips pink and glistening.

His cock tightened behind his zipper and he pressed against her instinctively, seeking relief.

She moaned and he couldn't have stopped if someone had tried to hand him a million dollars.

He reached for the hem of her dress and gathered the skirt in his hands.

She knew exactly what he intended. She lifted her arms over her head to aid him in stripping it off. He tossed the dress over his shoulder and took in the sight before him. It was not new. He'd seen her in various stages of undress many times over the years. Bra, panties and heels were a favorite of his.

But every time, he paused for a moment, stunned. Not by her beauty, though that was undeniable, but by the simple fact that she was here with him, letting him look at her, touch her, know her, understand her and give her pleasure.

He was grateful—*grateful*—every damned time. And it didn't feel pitiful to admit that. It felt right. He hoped any man making love to the woman of his dreams would feel the same.

He traced a finger along the upper edge of her bra, making goose bumps spring up in his wake. He was also grateful for that—that he could make some of her dreams come true too. He knew he was good at what he did. He was driven by an inner force to be the best at *everything* he did. Word searches, races, seductions. It was all the same for him. And that meant relationships too. Hailey might not know it yet, but he was going to be the best boyfriend ever.

She had no chance of ultimately resisting him.

But he didn't mind if she tried. Wearing her down

would be a pleasure. Again.

In high school, she hadn't given him the time of day. Now she was in his bed—and his bed alone.

Damn, that felt good.

Silver-medal good.

Now all he needed was to get to that top tier on the podium. So to speak.

"Even two weeks is too long now," he told her. They usually went even longer in between visits but the two weeks between her last visit to Denver and his trip to Sapphire Falls had been hell. "We're not doing that anymore."

"Ty—" she started.

But he leaned in and flicked his tongue along the streak of chocolate frosting he'd left on her cheek after holding the brownies. "I love brownies," he told her. "But you're sweeter."

"Ty," she said again. But this time it was a breathless near-plea.

"I'm hungry for both," he said, running his hand through the chocolate frosting and bits of brownie still stuck to his shirt. "And I think I can take care of both cravings at once."

Before she could protest his obvious intention, he wiped his hand over her stomach.

She gasped. "Ty!"

Then he went to his knees and took a long lick of the frosting smeared above her belly button.

She groaned this time.

"Take your bra off," he told her, scooping up some of the brownie mess from the plate on floor beside him.

She took a deep breath but reached behind her for the clasp on her bra. A moment later, it gave and the bra slid down her arms. She tossed it to the side.

Her breasts were easily the most perfect he'd ever seen. And he was not ashamed to say he'd seen a few. Hailey's were full and firm. The tips were the same color her cheeks were when she got really turned-on and they were very sensitive. They were already hard, and Ty knew from experience that just playing with her breasts could get her to the point where one good, firm lick to her clit would send her over the edge.

He lifted a handful of chocolate and wiped it over both breasts, covering the nipples.

She gasped and then groaned again at the contact. Ty brought her forward with his palm on her back and she put her hands on his shoulders, leaning into him. He licked the chocolate from her skin, leaving her nipples until last. He flicked over one, then the other, back and forth until she was squirming and whispering his name. Then he took one in his mouth and sucked slowly, steadily increasing the pressure.

She arched closer, one hand cupping his head, his name growing louder from her lips.

He switched sides, replacing his mouth with his fingers on the now clean side, playing and rolling the tip as he sucked on its twin.

"Yes. God, Ty. Please."

That's what he needed to hear. He stood swiftly, slid a hand into her panties and found her hot, wet core. He swirled two fingers over her clit and then into her pussy, pumping deep as he kissed her again.

He teased her for only a minute before circling his thumb over her clit and sending her flying.

She dug her fingers into his neck and cried out his name as her inner muscles clamped on to his fingers and pulsed through her climax.

Still enjoying the fading ripples, he said, "Unzip me, babe."

Without hesitation, she reached between them, unzipped his jeans, and pulled him free from the cotton and denim confines.

Her hand wrapped around his achingly hard cock was heaven and hell at once.

"Damn, Hailey. I've missed your hot little hand."

She stroked up and down his length, her pressure perfected over three and a half years of the best sex of his life.

"And mouth," he added.

She gripped him tighter and added a stroke of her thumb over the head as she passed it.

"And pussy," he said through gritted teeth.

They were both vocal about what they liked and wanted. Hailey let him take the lead, loved it in fact, but that didn't mean she was shy about what she needed and wanted.

There had always been heat between them. Ty had known early on that their chemistry was off the charts, and that when they came together it would be explosive. What had surprised them both was how well their preferences fit. Ty loved to take charge and make her beg. Hailey loved to be bossed around. In bed, anyway.

For Ty, he knew it came from the part of his personality that had sought out a sport where he could excel and be rewarded as an individual. He'd never been into team sports as much. He loved having the victory all to himself. He liked to be the one on top. And that spilled over into everything else. He liked to be fully in control of what was happening. All praise and glory then went to him. When he was with Hailey—whether they were naked in bed or having lunch at El Ranchero or white-water rafting—he wanted to take up all of her attention and energy, and he wanted to make whatever they were doing the best she'd ever had.

Which was why, stupid as it may be, thinking that she loved visiting because of enchiladas and someone else's massages bugged the shit out of him.

Sex for Hailey was the opposite, and it fit so perfectly

with Ty that it sometimes seemed too good to be true.

She was in charge every day, all day in her normal Sapphire Falls life. So when she came to Denver to be with Ty, she let him take over everything. He decided what they would do and when. He was dominant in the bedroom as well as during their non-bedroom time. And she loved it. She loved not making decisions, not worrying about schedules and reservations. She kicked back and followed his lead.

In everything.

He lifted her against the door and she automatically wrapped her legs around his waist.

He pulled her panties to the side and thrust, burying himself deep with a long, simultaneous groan from each of them.

He rested his forehead against hers, pausing for a breath to appreciate everything about the moment.

They didn't need to use condoms. Hailey was on the pill and they had been monogamous for three and a half years, and he loved having nothing between them.

"You feel so fucking good." He pulled back and thrust again. "Every." He pulled out and then slid back in deep. "Fucking." He thrust again. "Time."

Hailey's thighs tightened, as did her inner muscles around his length. "Damn you for messing all of this up," she panted.

He paused and shook his head. She could think that. For now. He'd prove her wrong.

"I'm *never* going to be done fucking you, Hailey," he told her brusquely. "Don't even think this pussy is anything but *mine*."

"Not—" she gasped as he thrust hard, "—in—" she took another deep breath as he picked up the pace of his strokes, "—Sapphire Falls," she finally finished.

"Oh yes," he told her firmly, pressing her hard against the door and lengthening his strokes. "In Sapphire Falls. In

Denver. In Paris. On the fucking moon."

He continued to pump into her as he spoke and he felt her climax building again, her muscles tensing around him, milking his cock.

"You're mine, Hailey," he said, looking directly into her eyes. "Always. Everywhere. Forever."

She held his gaze for only a moment. Then she shook her head and closed her eyes, tipping her head back as he continued to move her closer to her orgasm.

But she didn't close them fast enough. He saw the flicker of distress before her lids slid shut.

Distress? What the fuck was that?

Then she gasped his name and clamped down on him hard, her second orgasm rolling over her. The pleasure of being buried deep in her as she came overrode everything else, and all he could do was follow his body's urgings to move faster and harder. He thrust again and again, feeling his release building until it finally broke loose and he came with a shout.

The waves of satisfaction washed over him and he relished the long moments it took for them to weaken to mere ripples. He kept Hailey pinned between him and the door, her legs around him, her body open and possessed by his.

Even when his climax finally faded away, he took his time pulling out and letting her go.

He sensed that once he let her go physically, she would close off to him emotionally as well.

But he'd expected a fight.

If Hailey gave in easily, he'd be concerned. Or suspicious.

Hell, half the time he was convinced she made things difficult for him because she loved having him work for it all too. In high school, she'd barely acknowledged his existence, but when he'd taken Melissa Stover to the Christmas dance, Hailey had somehow managed to get him under the mistletoe. It was as if she wanted him adoring her and would only give him enough to keep him hanging on.

And he'd hung on.

And now he was the best she'd ever had.

And she'd never walk through her front door or eat a brownie again without thinking of him.

Oh yeah, he loved that. If he could arrange it so every damned thing she did every damned day reminded her of him, he'd do it.

"Those brownies were amazing," he said, letting her go.

She ran her hand through her hair and pulled in a deep breath. "Adrianne made them." She reached for her bra.

"I'll be sure to tell her thanks."

Hailey's head came up quickly. "No. You can't."

"Why not?" He grinned.

Her eyes narrowed. "Because of that," she said, pointing a finger at his lips.

"What?" But he felt his grin grow.

"That I-just-had-sex-with-your-brownies smile," she said. "Adrianne will think it's weird that you're smiling like that about her brownies."

"We didn't really have sex *with* the brownies," he told her, zipping up. "We had foreplay with the brownies."

Hailey rolled her eyes and pulled on her dress. "Just don't say anything to her." She crossed the foyer to the steps leading upstairs.

He started after her.

She stopped on the bottom step and turned. "What are you doing?"

"Coming upstairs with you."

"No, you're not."

He tipped his head. "We're going to bed."

Her eyes widened. "We're *not* going to bed. I'm going to clean up because I have to go to work."

"It's Saturday."

"I'm the mayor. That's a twenty-four-seven job, Ty."

Yeah, yeah. Whatever. He knew she took her job seriously. She was involved with *everything* in Sapphire Falls. He loved his hometown too, but Hailey was obsessed.

He knew a bit about that though. Racing had been his life for the past eleven years. It had determined where he lived, how he spent his time, even what he ate. It had taken over everything.

Until Hailey had come to Denver to pitch an investment idea to him and he'd ended up spreading her out on his desk.

Then his life had been about racing and a woman who tied him up in knots.

His buddies in Denver knew about him and Hailey. They were the only ones he could talk to about her since she didn't want anyone here to know about them. And his friends all thought he'd be better off with a woman who was more laid-back and more about *him*.

He was surrounded by women of all types. Finding a girlfriend who put him on a pedestal instead of the other way around would be easy enough.

But he didn't want that. He wanted Hailey. With Hailey, he was in competition with her great love—her position as queen bee of her beloved hometown, the position she'd made a goal when she was fourteen years old. But, while he might only get a couple of days at a time, during those days, he won. He possessed her. He took over everything. She *needed* and wanted him and didn't even remember where she was from in the midst of it all. And that was a sweet victory indeed.

Finally, he nodded. He wanted her to keep that dress on. He wanted her to keep on the panties that were wet from wanting him. He wanted her skin sticky and smelling like chocolate so that all day she'd be thinking of him.

But that was over the top.

If she was going to the office or had other mayoral

duties to attend to, he couldn't expect her to go rumpled and sticky.

He was going to have to come up with other ways to be sure she was thinking of him.

He stepped up beside her, cupped her head and kissed her. A last long, hot, wet kiss that would make her tingle for a while.

"I'll see you later," he said when he finally released her. "Neighbor."

He let himself out the front door and headed for home, whistling. Partly because he was actually happy. Home was right next door to Hailey. This was going to be great. And partly because he knew she could hear him and it would drive her crazy.

CHAPTER TWO

Three hours later, Hailey was in her office attempting to work.

And already proving what she'd known would happen.

She couldn't get a damned thing done now that she knew Ty was back. To stay.

She was distracted. Not because she was daydreaming about him and his sun-hot skin or the way his mouth obliterated every thought in her head or the way he knew exactly where to touch her and what to say…

Okay, not *just* because she was daydreaming about him.

She was distracted because she was already feeling his effect on her. She felt softer and happier simply thinking about his smile this morning. His *smile*, for fuck's sake. How could she be tough and demanding and bossy when she was feeling all goo-goo remembering her boyfriend's smile?

It was Saturday, so she didn't have any meetings or appointments, but it was her report-reading day. She constantly had a stack of boring reports and letters she had to read and the weekends were the perfect time since she didn't have a thousand other things competing for her attention. When she could read out loud if needed to keep her mind on her work. When she could read out loud in different voices and accents to keep her mind on her work. When she could read out loud in different voices and pace her office.

All of these were techniques Lena had taught her. Hailey had to find ways of keeping her focus on her work and managing her quirks. Lena called it Adult Attention Deficit Hyperactive Disorder with a comorbid anxiety disorder.

Hailey *definitely* preferred "quirks".

She was addicted to sticky notes, highlighters,

notecards and binders, but they kept her organized. They kept her on track. They helped her maintain her façade of being a totally in charge, intelligent, handle-anything mayor. A mayor who helped make Sapphire Falls a wonderful place to live. There was no harm being done here.

But the sticky notes and planners were only part of her management program. Lena had suggested several things in lieu of the medications that helped Hailey focus but gave her incapacitating headaches, including pacing and jumping jacks and even putting on some loud dance music and dancing for a song or two every thirty to sixty minutes to expel some of her pent-up energy.

Hailey didn't sit still very well.

That was another reason she and Ty worked. *In Denver.* He didn't sit still either, so they were often on the go when she visited. Ty's favorite activities were physical ones, which worked well for Hailey. Hiking, rafting, skiing—it all kept her busy and calmed her overactive mind and didn't take the concentration required by, say, reading reports. They would sometimes do a movie night or get wrapped up in a whole season of a TV show on Netflix, but it required a long day of exertion and at least three orgasms before either of them could be quiet for that long.

Of course, long days of exertion and three orgasms were common occurrences...

She *had to* stop thinking about Ty.

Hailey kicked her shoes off and did some calf raises and lunges as she tried to focus on the report in her hand.

Expansion along Nebraska highway 81 is necessary at this time due to a number of issues. 1. Traffic volume has increased 17% over the past ten years, due in part to truck traffic between Omaha and several larger farming operations in the area.

Hailey rolled her neck. This wasn't working. She started pacing again.

She'd tried to read the reports at home, but there were way too many other things to pull at her focus. She'd look up and notice a cobweb and that would launch her into three hours of cleaning. Or she would go to get a pen and end up rearranging her living room.

The office wasn't perfect either—she'd rearranged her office a number of times—but it was better than home. Lena said it was because in Hailey's mind, her office was *for* work, so it made it easier to stay on track.

Hailey thought it was because she purposefully kept her office un-fun.

There were no cute prints on the walls, no Newton's balls allowed, no quote-of-the-day calendars. It was plain and functional. White walls, gray carpet, black leather chair, desk calendar without so much as a brightly colored flower in the corner.

It also functioned to make the people who came to see her view their meetings as business and view *her* as un-fun. When meeting with someone un-fun, people tended to get to the point more quickly. That made it easier for Hailey to pay attention and care about what they were saying.

She turned at her window and paced back across her office, staring at the paragraph she'd highlighted in blue. This highway expansion proposal was serious stuff. She needed to get all of these details.

Towns along the affected route include Dawson City, Justice, Sapphire Falls and Chance. The areas of each town affected are outlined in section four, paragraphs three through six.

She knew which part of town was affected in Sapphire Falls. The area along the highway where her pet project, Sapphire Hills, the collection of locally owned shops, was located.

Which made her think about the most successful of the shops, Scott's Sweets, her friend Adrianne's candy shop and bakery. Which made her think about brownies. Which made her think about Ty. And get a little hot and wet under her second sundress of the day.

Damn him.

This was exactly why he couldn't move back here. Never mind live *next door* to her.

She did a few jumping jacks and some of the deep breathing her new friend Hope had taught her.

Then she forced herself to read the first page of the report without stopping. Without thinking about ways to get Ty to move back to Denver.

But at the top of page two, it all went to hell. Had he already sold his house? God, *that* would be tragic. That house was beautiful. It was one of her favorite places in the world. Okay, mostly because of Ty and the great memories they'd made there. But the view was amazing and—

Dammit.

She moved behind her desk, sat, spread the report out on her desktop and read out loud, "Detouring traffic around construction areas will take travelers away from the towns in question, which brings up the issue of diverting potential business from these communities for an extended period of time."

No kidding. And that was only one issue with the highway expansion proposal. The biggest for Sapphire Falls was that it would take out land on both sides of the highway. Land that had the shopping mall on one side and a walking trail that led to the park on the other.

It was a mess. A huge mess that most of the people in town didn't even know about yet. Hailey didn't think she could solve all the town's problems completely by herself, but she did try to take care of the things she could without getting everyone all worked up.

Her job wasn't as demanding as many mayoral positions, of course. For instance, she didn't have to worry about traffic patterns. There wasn't anything anyone would call *traffic* in Sapphire Falls. She didn't have to worry about city workers' pension plans. They had less than a dozen city workers who all also farmed part-time. The pension plan was healthy and the demands were few.

Besides, a lot of the general cleanup and maintenance was done by the people. The flowerbeds around the gazebo were replanted every spring and maintained by a citizen group. Everyone loved to help with festival decorating activities. And last winter, after nine inches of snow were dumped on the town overnight, everyone had showed up downtown with their shovels and snowblowers and the snow removal had turned into a big party with a snowball fight and hot chocolate for everyone afterward.

Hailey smiled at the memory. It was one example of many.

She loved her hometown.

So did Ty. She shouldn't be surprised that he wanted to move back. His entire family was here and most of his friends. And her.

She knew his crush was serious, and that sleeping with him three and a half years ago had been a sign to him that she was willing to be more than a crush. And she was. Kind of. From a distance.

No one made her feel like Ty did. Ty thought she walked on water. In spite of her leading him on for two years in high school, in spite of her leaving him without a word the morning after they'd first slept together, in spite of her being a snotty bitch to him over the years, Ty Bennett thought she was amazing.

No one had ever thought she was amazing like he did. That was pretty hard to *not* be addicted to.

And then they'd started an actual relationship. Long distance, yes, but they'd still spent a lot of time together over the past three plus years. She'd been vulnerable with him. She let him dominate her in the bedroom—and even out of the bedroom to some extent. She'd let him do things to her she couldn't imagine trusting anyone else to do.

She'd said things to him, expressed needs and fantasies that *no one* else would ever hear.

So the distance was truly a necessity for her.

He took over everything when they were together, and it was a needed break, a wonderful mini-vacation for her every time. But in Sapphire Falls, she had to be on. She had to be in charge. She had to be confident and bossy and thoroughly engaged.

She already had trouble managing her life *with* a plethora of sticky notes, digital reminders, three planners and a great assistant covering her ass. One more daily distraction would be the straw that broke the camel's back. Her house of cards would come tumbling down.

And Ty was so much more than a distraction. He not only took over her body and thoughts and emotions—he made her *want* him to. She didn't care about anything else when she was with him. And he loved that. She knew conquering her, convincing her to have a relationship with him, had pumped his ego up to mammoth proportions. She also knew that every single time he made her want him and beg him and then surrender to him physically, it met a need in *him* as well.

It was a win-win situation—he needed her to give in to him and she needed him to want her that much.

In *Denver*.

But in her own backyard—almost literally? No. She could not be completely wrapped up in Ty every day for the rest of her life. She'd never get anything else done.

She realized she had her chin propped on her hand and was staring into space. She shook her head, sat up straight and frowned.

Dammit.

She was tingly and distracted and dreamy and she'd known he was back for three hours.

She might love her hometown, but to be a leader, even in a place full of honest, kind people, you had to be tough.

She had to make hard decisions. She had to tell people when they'd screwed up.

She couldn't be sitting around in her office writing *Hailey + Ty* on her notebooks and drawing big hearts around their initials.

"*Ty* bought the house next door to you?"

Hailey looked up to find Adrianne Riley standing in her office doorway. Hailey smiled at her friend. Then frowned when she processed the question. "Yes."

"Wow, are you okay?" Adrianne came into the office, set a lavender bakery bag in front of Hailey and took a chair in front of Hailey's desk without invitation.

She didn't need an invitation. Adrianne was someone special to Hailey. Because Hailey hadn't been able to scare Adrianne off. Adrianne listened to Hailey's wild ideas and tolerated her moodiness. Those were cherished traits in Hailey's world.

Besides, at one time, she and Adrianne had run their sorority with a firm but glamorous hand, and Adrianne had been Hailey's first assistant when she'd become mayor. Adrianne understood her. They'd both grown up, of course. Adrianne had mellowed. She was laid-back and accepting and didn't mind being behind the scenes. Hailey was…none of those things. She'd matured, but she still liked to be in charge.

Regardless of their differences, Hailey sincerely liked Adrianne. And that was saying something. She hadn't sincerely liked a lot of women in her life. She typically saw them as competition. She knew she could thank Angela, her stepmother, for that. But Hailey knew that many of the women she interacted with were more than beautiful and bossy—which were the two things Hailey brought to the table. So she worked to be *more* of both of those things than any of the other women.

"I'm ticked off no one told me," Hailey said. "But I'm mostly pissed that he thinks he can do whatever he wants."

Adrianne crossed her legs and gave Hailey a smile. "Well, I guess he *can* buy a house if he wants to."

"But he's—"

Crap. She couldn't tell Adrianne that he'd bought the house because of *her*. How would she explain that? She couldn't admit that they'd had a three-and-a-half-year-long affair going. That was the longest—by about three years— Hailey had ever dated anyone. Adrianne would know that meant something.

Like that she was in love with Ty.

But she was in love with Denver Ty. Not the in-her-business, take-over-everything, mess-up-her-job Ty.

"He's doing it to drive me nuts."

If she didn't drive him nuts first. Ty didn't know about her quirks. He believed she was perfect, and when she was with him, she could forget she was an eccentric, scattered mess for a while.

But now, Ty had decided to insert himself into her life, and he was doing it in his big, showy, take-no-prisoners way. Like he did everything.

It amazed her sometimes how similar they really were. Yet opposite at the same time.

Hailey's public persona was the bossy I'm-always-right, do-what-I-say person. Ty's was the as-long-as-I'm-having-a-good-time-I-don't-care-about-anything-else guy. But behind the scenes, they reversed roles.

After Ty had lost the gold medal in the Olympics, his agent had spun the whole thing in Ty's favor. He'd convinced Ty that at silver, he could pretend to take the whole thing less seriously. Instead of news stories about his training regimen, they could do stories about him living it up. Instead of him becoming a spokesperson for bikes and helmets and swimwear, he could endorse beer and fast cars. Instead of his day-in-the-life feature on ESPN being about training and inspirational speeches to elementary schools, his could include gorgeous brunettes, crazy clubs and an entourage of adrenaline junkies.

His agent had painted Ty as a world-class triathlete because he lived and played hard and did it for the rush rather than the serious, disciplined, highly trained competitor that he was. And sure enough—he'd missed the top of the podium, but no one remembered the gold medalist's name, while Ty had become the cocky, charming playboy darling to the media.

But behind closed doors—he was in-charge, dominant, determined to be number one.

That realization niggled in the back of Hailey's mind. Ty was a competitor through and through. She knew that arguing with her turned him on, and he loved informing other men in bars and clubs that she was with him when they tried to talk to her or get her number.

He wasn't jealous. It was more than that. He liked having something other people wanted.

But before she could mull that over further, Adrianne laughed.

"Well, he definitely knows how to push your buttons."

Sexually and otherwise, Hailey thought. He not only knew how, but he delighted in it.

"I'll have to figure out ways to avoid him or ignore him," Hailey said. Which was never going to happen. "Hey, how did you hear about it?" she asked, realizing that the news hadn't been public knowledge as of a few hours ago.

"Ty told everyone himself this morning at the bakery," Adrianne said.

Saturday morning at Adrianne's bakery. Hailey looked at the clock on the wall over her bookcase. It was eleven thirty. By now, everyone in town would know.

"And of course, everyone fussed over him and welcomed him back and told him how thrilled they are that he's come home," Hailey said.

She knew Ty. He'd made it a mystery on purpose partly

so that the big reveal would be even bigger. She sighed.

Adrianne grinned. "Pretty much. I think he ate almost a dozen muffins and had about a gallon of coffee on other people's tabs."

"Was Kathy there?" Hailey asked of Ty's mother.

"She was," Adrianne said. "She came in with Hope."

Hope, another new addition to the town, was Ty's oldest brother's girlfriend.

"I'll bet she was happy," Hailey said softly. She could imagine Kathy's face when she found out her baby boy was coming home. Ty was the only one of the Bennett boys to ever leave Sapphire Falls for an extended period. Eleven years was definitely an extended period.

"She really was," Adrianne agreed with an affectionate smile.

Kathy Bennett had a way of inspiring affection in everyone who knew her.

Hailey's heart twinged thinking about Kathy hugging Ty, likely with tears in her eyes. She loved Ty's mom. From afar.

For a girl who had grown up with an evil stepmother, Kathy Bennett was the quintessential mother figure in Hailey's opinion. She cooked huge dinners from scratch, relished big family gatherings, was outwardly, lovingly demonstrative toward her family, and was so clearly accepting and proud of all of them it made Hailey ache sometimes.

Hailey was plain jealous of Lauren, Delaney and Hope—the three women who had fallen in love with Kathy's other sons and were now a part of the Bennett family. They had been welcomed into a family that was known for love and laughter and a warmth that touched everyone around them.

Hailey had never had a chance to get close to Kathy. Why would she? No one knew that she and Ty had any kind of relationship. Kathy knew Hailey as everyone else in town knew her—the bossy, spoiled little girl who had grown into a bossy, spoiled woman who, somehow, made a pretty good mayor. Mostly because she *was* bossy, and being spoiled meant she was used to the best of everything, and that carried over to her wanting the best of everything for her town.

She did park cleanups and participated in the festivals and served hot chocolate in the square at Christmastime, but she knew everyone assumed she had to as mayor. Truth was, she was happy doing those things, and if her position gave her more reason to take two shifts or attend *every* single event during the festivals, things got done and she got to be in a little bit of her heaven.

People didn't know that about her though, and people like Kathy Bennett made Hailey wish she could show that side. Kathy would like that about her. She would maybe even be proud of Hailey.

Hailey wondered how that would feel. To have a woman you looked up to and admired, admire you back.

"*No one* else is upset that he kept it a secret?" Hailey asked. She already knew the answer. Of course not. This was Ty. Everyone loved Ty and expected crazy stuff from him.

Kathy wasn't thrilled with his public persona, but Hailey knew Ty had clued his mom in that it was an act. At least mostly. He *did* hang out in clubs with beautiful women. He had had a short-term affair with a fellow Olympian. He did stay out late and did have a posse of hell-raisers he hung out with on a regular basis. But most of it was for show.

"No," Adrianne confirmed. "Everyone is really happy to have him home. I take it you've talked to him?"

Hailey was pulled from her thoughts by Adrianne's question. She nodded. "This morning, when he was mowing the yard at six a.m."

Adrianne grimaced. She knew Hailey wasn't an early

bird. "What did you say to him?"

That she was going to miss the enchiladas.

But she couldn't be honest with him and tell him that she was going to miss being the woman she was in Denver. Because then she'd have to explain how that woman—the one who could turn over all decisions and schedules and worries to him—was different from the woman she had to be in Sapphire Falls.

But she *would* miss that Hailey. She loved that woman. So much that she wanted to cry thinking about not taking that drive to Denver again.

"I told him to go back to Denver."

Adrianne laughed and Hailey smiled.

"Really? He told everyone that you made him feel very welcome to the neighborhood. Obviously, I had to come over and find out what *that* meant, exactly."

Hailey felt her cheeks flush again and she gritted her teeth. Of course, everyone would be wondering about that. Most would likely think he was being sarcastic, but her nosy friends would—

"*Ty* is the one that moved in next door to you?"

Phoebe Spencer came through the door, followed by Kate Leggot, Delaney Callan and Lauren Bennett.

Phoebe took the chair next to Adrianne but scooted it closer to the desk. Delaney stood behind Phoebe's chair and Kate leaned on the wide window sill. With a sigh, Hailey pivoted in her chair to face the inquisition.

It did not escape Hailey's notice that most of her closest friends were women who weren't from Sapphire Falls and who didn't know her very well. Or at least who hadn't known her back in high school.

Phoebe was the exception. She'd grown up in Sapphire Falls too, and had been witness to many of Hailey's mean-girl moments. It had taken her some time to come around. Without Adrianne, Hailey doubted she'd be able to call Phoebe a friend.

But Phoebe was a true Sapphire Falls girl—once she was your friend, it was for life.

"Yes, Ty is the one who moved in next door to me," Hailey confirmed, shooting a glare at Delaney. "Really not cool, new girl. Keeping secrets from me isn't a good habit to start."

Delaney shrugged. "He paid me an extra ten grand to not tell you."

Hailey narrowed her eyes. "You mean not to tell *anyone*."

"No, he specifically said you. But I couldn't really tell anyone else, or they would have told you."

Hailey shook her head. Ty was in so much trouble. "Like I said, not a good habit."

Delaney nodded. "Duly noted."

"This should be interesting," Phoebe said, focusing on Hailey. "Ty Bennett right next door, driving you crazy until the day you die. Or kill him."

"Considering I plan to live a very long time, and every time I see him, he makes me crazier, I'd say you should all put your money on option B," Hailey said. She looked around. "What are the specifics of the pool, anyway?"

"The pool?" Delaney asked.

"The pool everyone has set up about me and Ty. Is it that one of us toilet papers the other's trees or booby traps the front porch, or is it really big—mouse or roach infestation?" She'd thought of all of those since seeing Ty that morning.

Delaney's eyes were wide. "You really don't like each other that much?"

It was well known in Sapphire Falls, carefully cultivated by Ty and Hailey personally, that they rubbed each other the wrong way and couldn't be in close proximity without tossing insults back and forth.

"Let's put it this way," Hailey said. "I would love to come up with a plan to get him out of the house next door."

True enough.

"Well, we don't need all that hoopla. You want me in *your* house instead, all you have to do is ask nice."

The deep voice from her doorway made tingles go dancing up and down her spine, and Hailey wanted to close her eyes and ask him to say dirty things to her in that voice.

Which he knew.

Bastard.

She swiveled her chair slowly to face Ty.

She hadn't had more than ten consecutive minutes without him on her mind today. Why did she get the impression that was exactly what he wanted? Dammit, what was he up to?

He pushed away from the doorjamb and sauntered into her office, giving everyone a charming grin that worked on women, married or not. Married to his *brothers* or not. All of the women grinned back and she could have sworn Kate batted her eyes.

Kate's boyfriend, Levi Spencer, was a notorious flirt, however. Looked as though he was rubbing off on his pretty blonde love.

"What do you want, Ty?" Hailey asked.

She immediately regretted the question.

Ty had publicly announced he had moved back to Sapphire Falls. Who knew what else he was ready to publicly announce?

For a moment, she panicked. Ty had said he wanted them to be together. He knew that she liked their arrangement as it had been for the past three-plus years, but he didn't know all of the reasons for that. He knew she wanted to keep her cool outward façade in place. He didn't really know why she *needed* to keep it in place.

"I tried to make an appointment to see you Monday, but Tess told me to come on over here now. Said you would be happy to see me."

Tessa Sheridan, Hailey's assistant, had been in Ty's

class. She, like all other women who knew Tyler Bennett, probably couldn't think of one reason why Hailey would *not* want to see Ty.

He braced a hand on her desk and leaned in on his extended arm. "Guess you need to update your blacklist for her."

Hailey looked up into those blue eyes that she'd seen full of happiness, passion and even affection. She loved his eyes.

God.

She glanced around. The women were all watching with rapt attention. She'd been careful not to let on how she felt about him, but now that he was here full time, hiding her feelings about him would be a full-time job. She didn't need one more thing to worry about hiding from her constituents. Once in a while, here and there, she could play her part, but it was going to be hard to keep up the pretense of not liking him every single day.

"I don't really have time right now, Ty," she said. "Sorry. I can check my calendar for Monday though."

"That's fine. There were some people I wanted to talk to first anyway. I'll see most of them tonight at the dance. Then I can bring that information on Monday when we talk."

There was a wedding dance tonight in the town square. Reena Bosch and Eddie Stevens were getting married that afternoon in the gazebo and throwing a huge party afterward. As was common in Sapphire Falls, not everyone in town would be invited to the ceremony, but everyone was encouraged to come celebrate with them afterward.

"You're going to the wedding dance?" she asked.

"Of course. Great chance to see everyone," he said.

"And talk with them about what, exactly?"

"Oh, no," he said, pushing off the desk. "You're busy. I don't want to take up too much of your time." He started for the door.

"Well, I could maybe make some time," she said quickly.

Dammit, she didn't want to give him his way and she *really* didn't want to seem available to him at the drop of a hat. But she also wanted to know what he had up his sleeve. Preferably before he talked to everyone else in town about it.

She loved being in the know. Definitely a perk of her job.

She *needed* to be in the know where Ty was concerned.

Ty stopped at the door and glanced back. "Or you could come over for dinner tonight before the dance and talk about it. That will give us something to talk about rather than, you know, throwing cutlery at each other."

She stared at him. Had he seriously just asked her to dinner? In Sapphire Falls? With witnesses?

They were her friends, but he knew they didn't know about her travels to Denver to see him. And they weren't exactly gossipmongers. They wouldn't go tell the town. But they would likely tell their husbands, fiancés and boyfriends. Who *would* tell the town.

Seriously, the men here were like a bunch of overgrown kids when they got together.

"Um, I…no…that's…"

She was *stammering*. Hailey Conner did *not* stammer.

"We can have dessert in my hot tub."

He had a *hot tub*? Had Delaney put that in? Or had he brought the one from Denver? Because *that* baby was nice. It was big enough to—

She pulled in a long breath, calming herself.

"I'm in the mood for brownies, how about you?" he asked.

"Did you take my brownies over to him?" Adrianne asked. "I thought those were for your neighbor."

Hailey gritted her teeth.

"She did," Ty said. "Absolutely delicious." He kept his

eyes on Hailey as he said it.

She knew that he had her exactly where he wanted her—ruffled and hot and bothered and unsure of herself.

Well, screw that.

She wasn't going to lose her cool, even for Ty.

"On second thought," she said. "Monday is fine." She glanced down, pretending to be looking at her desk calendar. In truth, all she could focus on was her heart racing. "How about eleven?"

She had no idea if she was free at eleven. But she'd make it work.

"You bet. Eleven is perfect," Ty said happily. "Thanks, Madam Mayor."

She looked up and he gave her a wink.

"Hot-tub-dessert offer stands, though."

And then he was gone.

Hailey *so* wanted to slump down in her chair and just breathe, but she couldn't. She couldn't show her friends that Ty had shaken her up.

She jotted a note on her calendar about Ty on Monday morning. She also resisted drawing a heart around his name. She also had no intention of having that meeting. She was going to find out what he was up to long before Monday rolled around.

"What was *that*?" Lauren demanded as soon as Ty had shut the door.

"What do you mean?" Hailey asked.

Seriously, what *did* she mean? Could Lauren read how shaken up Hailey was now?

She needed to get it together. God knew what Ty was talking about. He could be planning to talk to everyone about holding some kind of charity 5K race or something. Or he could have been making the whole thing up. She knew he planned to make his mark, to be sure everyone was aware he was home and that they all had the chance to ooh and ahh over him. But he wouldn't go person-to-person at a wedding dance and casually mention that he and Hailey had been sleeping together for three and a half years and that he was home because he wanted a more serious relationship.

No, he'd do something public, something in front of a bunch of people at once.

Like ask her out in front of a crowd of her friends.

Hailey really wanted to thump her head on her desk, but she put on a smile that said no big deal. At least that's what it was supposed to say.

"Ty just asked you out."

"Ty just asked to have a business meeting with me," she corrected.

"In his *hot tub*," Kate said.

Hailey made herself roll her eyes. "He was messing around. He knew I'd say no."

"And I still don't get it," Kate said. "Why would you say no to that? He's gorgeous, charming, sexy and you're both single."

Because he filled her body with restless energy and her mind with fun and fantasies—and obliterated every thought of anything serious or meaningful. Because he was the antithesis of all of her calming and organizational strategies. Because he could ruin everything she worked so hard at and that she was proud of. And because if he found out who she really was, she'd never get to play her favorite role—Ty Bennett's dream girl—again.

And she swore every time she thought about it, she could hear her stepmother saying to Hailey's father, "See Stan, she's a flake. You can't depend on her."

"Because," she said carefully in answer to Kate's question, "Ty and I could never make something work long-term. We don't want the same things."

And that was the most honest answer she'd ever given in regards to her and Ty. Usually, she said things like, "He drives me nuts," or, "He's not my type."

But the truth was they had different visions of life in Sapphire Falls.

It hit her suddenly. That was exactly the problem. If they were together in Sapphire Falls, Ty would want her all wrapped up in him. He *loved* that he could take over her every thought and become her sole focus. That helped satisfy the part of him that needed to be number one. In short weekend bursts, it worked. He was happy and she was able to relax and let him run the show.

But day after day in Sapphire Falls? She had to multitask twenty-four-seven. She had to be able to give her full attention to this town that had elected her twice to take care of them. Taking care of Sapphire Falls was *her* crowning achievement, the thing that made her feel the way winning races made Ty feel.

Adrianne seemed to notice that Hailey had answered more seriously than usual. "You both love this town, and now that he's living here again, maybe—"

"Not going to happen," Hailey cut her off.

"TJ is concerned." This came from Delaney.

"He is?" Hailey asked, trying to seem casual. "Why is that?"

"He thinks it's strange that Ty is suddenly leaving his training and everything to move back here. Something must have happened."

Hailey looked at her, her mind spinning. Delaney was right. Or rather, TJ was right. "Does TJ know something?" she asked, trying to keep the depth of her interest out of her voice.

Delaney shook her head. "Ty's only said that some things changed and he was ready to come home."

Things had changed? Like what? Had he lost some of his sponsors? Had he lost some big race? She racked her brain. He was planning on competing in the Olympics for the second time next year. He'd not competed at the most recent games three years ago, but she hadn't delved too deeply into that with him. He'd told her that he was having a hard enough time fitting all of his medals into his display case. A typical Ty answer. But she knew that he was ready to go for the gold again. There had been a big race in early August that counted for Olympic qualification. But he'd raced in it. She was pretty sure. She also knew the qualification period went until next May.

No, he definitely should not be in Sapphire Falls. He needed to be training and racing in the big races if he was going to compete in Rio de Janeiro next summer.

Monday was suddenly way too far away for them to talk.

"Well, maybe TJ can figure it out," Hailey said nonchalantly. As Ty's oldest brother, TJ might be able to get it out of him. But a better bet would be Tucker, the closest in age to Ty. Of course, all the Bennett boys were close to one another. "I, on the other hand, have work to do." As if she had any prayer of getting anything done now. Thoughts of Ty had been distracting her before. Now that she was curious and concerned, her day in the office would be a waste.

Another perfect example of why Ty could not live in Sapphire Falls and be a part of her daily life.

What if he got the sniffles? She wouldn't be able to get anything done that day. Heaven forbid he get the flu. She'd be worthless for a week. And what if they had a fight? Or worse, broke up? She'd have to step down as mayor.

She knew that sounded dramatic, but she had a hard enough time keeping focused on her job and not letting her anxiety about *not* doing a good job get the better of her on a typical day.

"Don't walk on my grass when you take your casseroles and desserts over to welcome Tyler to town, okay?" she said casually as the women gathered their things to leave.

She wasn't so worried about these women. It was all of

the pretty single girls in town. And it was hardly her grass that she cared about.

She couldn't be with him, but having him right next door meant she was going to get to see the parade of panties up and down his front steps.

She might need to pull up the real estate listings before she left the office.

CHAPTER THREE

Hailey Conner looked completely fuckable.

That was nothing new.

Hailey had looked fuckable to him since he was fifteen. And that was before he knew what that really meant.

Since then, he'd done a lot of fucking. And none had ever come close to being as amazing as it was with Hailey.

Some might say it was because he'd had the fantasy of her built up big before she'd even let him hold her hand. But he would argue that if anyone knew the fantasies he'd had, it would have been difficult for her to ever live up.

But she had.

Ty was never going to be able to walk away from her. And she needed to start understanding that.

He was currently dancing with another woman though. In fact, he was dancing with a woman who looked so much like Hailey it was pretty incredible. He should be completely attracted to Kate Leggot. She was beautiful and funny and a good dancer. But he didn't want her. And it had nothing to do with the fact that she was very spoken for. Ty didn't really know Levi Spencer. There was no bro code at work here, no history between the men that would automatically make Kate off-limits.

It was all Hailey.

"I certainly hope you're going to go ask her to dance after this," Kate said, looking up at him.

Ty smiled as he two-stepped her around the dance floor. "Who?"

"The woman you've been watching ever since you got here."

"Shouldn't you have eyes only for Levi?" Ty asked. "What are you doing watching me so closely?"

"That is definitely not a denial that you've had your eyes on Hailey all night," Kate said with a grin.

Ty gave her a single nod. "Fine. No denial."

Kate smirked.

"But the question remains about you and Levi. If you're a free agent after all…" He trailed off suggestively, not actually meaning any of it at all.

Kate laughed. "Levi and I are good. Better than good. Madly in love."

"Yet here you are dancing with the most eligible bachelor in town."

She shook her head, still laughing. "I see the Bennett self-confidence wasn't all used up before it got to you."

Ty grinned. "Hard to believe there was any left over though, huh?"

She nodded. "Definitely."

Ty laughed, spun her away and then pulled her back in. "Levi has no problem with you dancing with other charming, sexy men?"

Kate and Ty both glanced to where Levi was leaning with one elbow on the bar, talking with his brother Joe. His eyes were firmly on Kate, however. He saluted them with his glass of scotch. He didn't quite smile, but he didn't look concerned either.

Kate shook her head. "Levi might have more ego than all of you Bennett boys put together."

"Jesus," Ty muttered, only half kidding.

"Well, the millions of dollars help."

Ty chuckled. "Yeah, I suppose. It's hard to remember he's a millionaire sometimes."

"He looks good in denim, huh?"

"No comment." Ty spun her again as the song ended.

"Go get her," Kate said as they let go of one another.

Ty sighed. "It's not that easy with Hailey."

"Well, who ever said it was supposed to be easy?" Kate gave him a wink and then turned and headed for Levi.

Ty watched as Levi held out an arm to her. She snuggled under it and he pulled her up against his side.

Levi kissed the top of her head and then leaned to whisper something in her ear. She laughed and turned her head to catch his lips. Levi dropped his hand from her shoulder to her ass and deepened the kiss.

Uh, yeah. Ty cleared his throat. They had nothing to worry about as far as chemistry and attraction.

But that wasn't always enough.

He pivoted to find Hailey again. She'd moved on from the previous conversation with Dottie, the owner of the diner downtown, and was now talking with the father of the groom.

Ty headed in her direction.

As he approached without her seeing him so he could study her unnoticed for a moment, he flashed back to the first time he'd been brave enough to approach her in high school.

Hailey had been a senior when he'd been a sophomore. At fifteen, he'd been attracted to her silky blonde hair, long legs and gorgeous breasts. Okay, at fifteen, he'd been attracted to all breasts. But even then he'd known there was something different about Hailey. It was in how she carried herself, how she seemed so sure of herself and got everyone to do whatever she wanted. He saw her as a challenge. He could admit that. Hailey was the type of girl who brought out his dominant side. He wasn't drawn to girls he could protect. He wasn't drawn to women he could provide for. His primitive instincts were riled by a woman who could hold her own, meet him head-on and make him work for it.

She'd stirred something in him that had been determined to possess her because she would fight him.

He'd taken it slow though. He'd been patient. And he'd let her think that he was a naïve kid with a crush. He'd flirted and doted, showered her with compliments and attention and gifts. She'd *said* that he was wasting his time. Her eyes and body language had told a different story.

Hailey had absorbed his attention and affection like a flower did a summer rain.

But it had taken until the night after *he* had graduated for him to finally get his victory. And it had knocked him on his ass.

"Hailey." He stood back a couple of feet, not wanting to intrude on the conversation she was having with Ken Stevens. But he knew she recognized his voice instantly. It was in the way she lifted her chin slightly.

She glanced at him. "Yes, Tyler?"

She tried to call him Tyler as much as possible in Sapphire Falls. It was part of their charade. She thought it seemed more formal than calling him Ty like all his friends and family did.

If only everyone knew how she sounded breathing his name when he kissed her neck, or the way she cried his name out when she came.

"Dance with me." He wasn't smiling, and he threaded some of the commanding tone into the request that he knew turned her on.

He never talked to her like this in Sapphire Falls. Again, part of their agreement. In the past three and a half years, he'd never gotten her naked in Sapphire Falls. Unless, of course, he counted her foyer that morning. Which he did.

She was difficult.

Except when she wasn't.

He loved both sides of her, but *damn*, he loved when she was sweet and relaxed and putty in his hands.

Hailey looked at his hand, as if confused. "Excuse me?"

She wasn't confused.

"Dance with me," he repeated. "If it's okay that I steal her?" he asked Ken.

Ken nodded quickly. "It's a dance. Everyone should be dancing."

Ty hid his grin. Either Ken was feeling jovial because it

was his son's wedding and he truly felt everyone should be celebrating, or Hailey had been talking business. Ken owned a taxidermy shop in town called Stuff It. Not only did he stuff dead animals for a living, but he rarely donated to community projects or helped out in any other way. Hailey was on his ass a lot.

Hailey turned to face Ty and Ken took the opportunity to move quickly in the other direction.

"You know that I can't turn you down," she said.

"Glad to hear it." He wiggled his fingers that were still extended toward her, and that she still hadn't taken hold of.

She took his hand and let him tug her closer.

"That's not what I meant. You're the beloved prodigal son returned home. You're happy to be here and you're being friendly with *everyone*. If I turn you down for a simple dance, then *I* look like the big bad bitch."

"Thought you liked being the big bad bitch."

She nodded. "I do."

He smiled in spite of himself.

"But that's an overreaction even for me."

"Why the temptation to say no then?" he asked.

"Because it's not going to be a simple dance, is it?" she asked. "You've had this very *not* simple air about you since you got here."

He was glad she'd made note of that. He pulled her onto the dance floor and then up against his body. "Well, you can relax. I'm not going to fuck you right here in the middle of the town square."

He saw her reaction in her eyes. She was surprised at his words, but he also saw the heat those words evoked. It wasn't the words, but the place. She loved when he talked dirty. No doubt hearing the word fuck in the middle of the picturesque town square was a bit of a shock though.

"But say the word and I'll take you behind the post office and make you beg for it," he added.

Her eyes widened and then narrowed. "Stop it."

"Or we could head over to city hall. You know I've always had a fantasy about sitting in your big fancy leather office chair while you're on your knees, sucking me off."

She stiffened in his arms, and he knew she was thinking about slapping him. But she was also thinking about sucking him off while he sat in her big fancy leather office chair.

She had a few fantasies about him and her desk as well. He'd made her tell him all about them one night when he'd had her hands tied to his headboard.

"You're not going to slap me here in the middle of a wedding in the town square," he said. "So relax and act like we're just dancing."

"Why can't we just *be* dancing?" she asked.

"Because I can't have *you* thinking that this visit to Sapphire Falls is like all the others."

"It's not just a visit," she said softly.

He nodded. "Exactly."

She sighed.

"Do you remember when we went skiing the first time?" he asked her as they moved together on the dance floor.

She pulled back, confused at first. She studied his eyes. Slowly, she nodded. "Of course." She almost looked sad.

"That was the first time we spent more of our time outside of my house rather than in." They had a hard time getting out of the bedroom typically, but he'd taken her skiing that trip. It had been her first time, and they'd had so much fun that sex had become secondary to the laughing and skiing.

"I'll miss skiing."

He frowned. "We can go skiing, Hails."

She shook her head. "Not together."

"Why the hell not?"

She shrugged. "I guess we could each go and meet up there. But if we do that kind of stuff a lot, people are going to notice that we're always gone at the same time."

"And who the fuck cares if they notice?"

But he knew—she cared.

She frowned up at him. "Are we really going to have this conversation *every* day for the next hundred years?"

Ty ground his teeth for a moment and then forced himself to relax. Like he forced Hailey to stay in his arms when the song ended. "We're not done."

She sighed and they began dancing to the next song.

She wasn't going to make a big scene here, and Ty was grateful it was a wedding dance. If they'd been at the river hanging out around a bonfire with their friends, she wouldn't have hesitated to shove him back and maybe even throw a beer at him in her irritation. But she wouldn't do that here at a wedding reception, with most of the town present and the postcard-perfect gazebo in the background.

"I want to date you. Publicly. We don't have to tell anyone that we've been having a relationship. It will seem like it's just started," he said. She opened her mouth to reply and he growled, "And if you fucking say it hasn't been a relationship, I will make the biggest, most romantic public declaration of love anyone in this town has ever seen right here and now."

She snapped her teeth together and swallowed hard.

He knew she hated how well he knew her.

That was too fucking bad. It was going to be right in her face all the time now.

"No," she finally said.

"No, what?" he asked with a scowl.

"No, I don't want to date you."

"You want to get engaged?" he asked. Hell, he could pick out the perfect diamond in ten minutes.

"Don't be stupid," she told him. "We can't do this."

"Why not? I'm living here now. In *our* hometown. I want to get married and have kids and be with you every day instead of two days every ten weeks."

Her mouth dropped open and she stared at him.

"What?" he asked crossly. Was that *really* a shock? They'd been together for three and a half years. He'd been in love with her for more than a decade.

"You want to get *married*? Live together? In the same house? Have *kids*?"

The pitch of her voice rose a bit on the last word, and Ty couldn't help but grin. He loved making her forget herself, forget where she was, and have her just react to him.

But this probably wasn't the place.

"Of course I do. You thought we were going to have weekend flings six or seven times a year forever?"

She nodded. Quite emphatically. "Yes. That's exactly what I thought. What I *hoped* for, Ty. That was perfect."

But it wasn't. Not for him. Not anymore.

"How could you think that?" he asked. "You really thought nothing would ever change?"

"I *thought*—" she started, then glanced around, lowered her voice and moved in closer to keep their conversation between the two of them. "I *thought* that you were pretty into your own thing, all caught up in your life and your training and everything, and that our arrangement was perfect for you too."

He frowned. Okay, she had a point. When she hadn't been with him in Colorado, he'd certainly had enough to fill his time and take up his energy. Until it had all come apart and his training had been axed, his goals had been shattered and everything ahead of him had seemed depressing.

But it wasn't fair that she thought he'd *never* want more from her.

"Things were perfect, for a long time," he said honestly. "But things change, Hailey. Life moves on. And do you really want to grow old *next door* to each other? Do you really think *that* will be enough?"

"No, I really *don't* want to grow old next door to each other," she said, sounding partly exasperated and partly sad. "But *you* put us in that situation without a word to me."

"So date me."

"You keep talking about change," she said, instead of answering him. She studied his face. "What's changed, Ty? Why Sapphire Falls? Why now, all of a sudden?"

He hadn't told her about the accident. It was one of those things that fell into the weird gray area they had in their relationship. They lived separate lives. They were having an affair. More personal details would have meant a deeper relationship and, frankly, he'd been afraid she'd break it off entirely if he tried to go there.

It had taken him years to get her the first time and it had been over in one night. It had taken years after that to get her back into his bed.

Over the past three and a half years, pathetic as it seemed sometimes, he had taken what he could get. And that meant in Denver, he called the shots. In Sapphire Falls, she did.

When the accident had happened, he'd thought about calling her and then...hadn't.

"Do you really want to know?" he finally asked.

She paused to actually think about that and he felt like laughing. Sort of. But that was Hailey. She would carefully weigh how involved in someone else she wanted to get.

"Yes," she finally said.

"Bryan's in a wheelchair."

She stopped dancing and stared at him. "What?"

Ty glanced around and then took her hand and pulled her off the dance floor and over to a more private space near the wooden structure they used for everything from a kissing booth to a hot chocolate stand. Tonight, it held the punch bowl and other non-alcoholic drinks.

"Bryan..." He *almost* added, "And I," but hesitated.

He'd trashed his knee and he'd known within forty-eight hours that his days of competing were over. But he'd had months to deal with that. He had a new plan now. "Bryan was in a biking accident. A truck crossed the center line on a highway he was riding. He swerved and hit the shoulder and was thrown over the edge. He hit a rock and partially damaged his spinal cord."

Hailey covered her mouth with her hand. She knew Bryan. He'd grown up in Sapphire Falls. He'd been two years behind her in school with Ty, so she didn't know him well, but she knew what the injury would mean. Bryan was an adrenaline junkie, always on the go. He loved extreme sports, and if he'd been more disciplined, he could have potentially been a pro biker. But that would have curtailed his party activities and his tendency to say, "Ah, fuck it." Still, professional biking or not, being wheelchair ridden was obviously a tough blow and a huge adjustment.

"Oh my God," she murmured.

Ty nodded. Every time he thought about it, and how much *worse* it could have been, his blood went icy.

"It's an incomplete spinal cord injury," he said. "That means he's not totally paralyzed, and they think a lot of his function will come back. He's already seen some return. But he's still in rehab as an outpatient and uses a wheelchair some of the time." Okay, so the, *"Bryan's in a wheelchair,"* had been a little dramatic. But he was. Seeing one of his best friends in a wheelchair even some of the time was a lot to deal with.

Ty would have been in Sapphire Falls the day after he realized that his competitive life was over, but he'd stayed in Denver to be with and help Bryan. His friend was now out of the rehab hospital and back home with the modifications and help he needed.

"Wow, I didn't...you didn't..." Hailey pressed her lips together and Ty was shocked to see tears in her eyes.

Fuck. She would hate it—hate *him*—if he made her cry

in public in Sapphire Falls.

He looked around. There were several people watching them. Some were trying to pretend they weren't, but most looked as if they were waiting for the show to start.

He was going to have to give them a show. Just not one that involved Hailey's tears. He raised his voice. "I want that fence between our houses down. You can do it or I'll do it."

She frowned. "What are you talking about?"

"That huge-assed fence," he said. He did hate it. He didn't want a damned thing between them. Though demanding she take it down was over the top, he knew. It was for the sake of the fake argument. Or so he told himself. "I don't like it and I want it down."

She stared at him for a millisecond. Then it all seemed to sink in. Or she actually got pissed. She pulled herself up tall. "You touch one splinter on my fence and I'll have you arrested."

"Will you be the one putting me in handcuffs?" he asked. And the answer would be no. When they played with restraints, it was him restraining her.

Her eyes narrowed. "You wish."

"I'm not so sure," he said thoughtfully. "Silk ties are more my style, and I like to be the one tying the knots."

As she well knew.

Her cheeks were flushed and he again had to wonder which emotion was dominant—anger or desire.

"That fence stays exactly where it is. And your fantasies are going to have to stay in your head."

He read between those lines easily enough. The fantasies were going to have to stay in his head *in Sapphire Falls*.

"We'll see about that." He knew the crowd would assume he was talking about the fence. He also knew Hailey would know he wasn't.

He tried not to smile. Even when it was fake, he loved

when she was fired up.

"You might be used to having women do whatever you want them to in Denver," she said. "But you're in *my* town now."

Then she turned on her sexy black heel and left the square, haughty and snotty.

In other words, the Hailey Conner he knew and loved.

പ്രൂ

Hailey hated herself for it a little, but she kept looking out her window to see when Ty's lights went on next door. She knew he wouldn't be far behind her.

He'd been at the dance to see her. He might have talked to a few people about whatever this mystery project was, but when she'd walked into the square, she'd felt his eyes immediately, and his attention hadn't wavered in spite of her making her way through the crowd, chatting with other people, and him dancing three dances with Kate. Not that Hailey had been counting.

The problem was, she'd *felt* him the entire time she was in the square, even before he'd approached her, and she'd had an incredibly hard time keeping her mind even on small talk.

She'd felt itchy and restless and keyed up.

And that was *before* he'd told her he wanted to get married and have kids.

Kids. Hailey could barely keep *herself* together, how was she going to be able to handle kids? And marriage? Even having him next door was preferable to having him living in her house with her. At least there were some barriers between them. Walls and windows and *space* and…her huge fence.

She'd finally picked up on the fact that he was faking a fight with her for the onlookers, but she'd seen the truth in his eyes—he didn't like having anything between them.

This was getting out of hand quickly.

She had to put a stop to all of this. Even if it meant she quit speaking to him and turned up her bitch setting to high.

She saw Ty's truck pull into the drive and her heart kicked against her ribs.

She could put her bitch back on tomorrow. For tonight, she needed Ty. She needed to know more about Bryan's accident and how Ty was handling it and if Ty was okay and…

Yeah, she was in trouble.

Talking and sharing wasn't part of their…thing. She sensed sometimes Ty wanted to push it and go deeper, but she also knew he was waiting for a signal from her that *she* wanted more, and the truth was she didn't.

She'd liked things exactly as they were. She liked having a life in Sapphire Falls and an escape in Denver. She didn't want the two to mix. The times when Ty was home to visit were bad enough. She lost her edge when he was around. She let go with Ty. She unwound. She didn't worry about things. She didn't push herself. She left behind her sticky notes and highlighters and meditation exercises and the feeling of constantly being *on*. And it felt great.

But it was like eating the Everything Pizza from the Stop, the convenience store/gas station/pizza place/ice cream shop. It was okay once in a while, as long as she was back to working out and watching her carbs immediately afterward.

She saw Ty's living room light go on and started for her back door. She was going over.

She needed to know more about Bryan and she… *Dammit*, she wanted to hug Ty.

Hailey wasn't a hugger by nature. Keeping people at arm's length made hugging difficult. But she wasn't going to be able to help it.

She was so torn. She wanted to keep her distance from him but couldn't now that she knew he was going through something. He and Bryan were close. Seeing his friend so badly hurt doing something they both loved had to be hard on Ty too.

The realization that Ty had been driven home to Sapphire Falls by seeing Bryan's life-changing injury was really bugging her. Ty had clearly been spooked by it all. But Ty had to understand that it was Bryan's challenge, that continuing to compete didn't make him a bad person, and that he couldn't hide out in Sapphire Falls.

And he couldn't use her as an excuse.

She stepped through her gate and into Ty's backyard. As Ty was coming out of his back door.

She hesitated and then frowned. Ty called the shots when they were together in Denver. But, as she'd told him at the dance, this was *her* town.

There was a streetlight on the front sidewalk between their houses and the light made its way dimly into his backyard, giving it a glow.

"You're gonna have grass clippings all over your backside if you don't keep coming," he said gruffly.

She knew that voice. She *loved* that voice. It meant she was going to be getting an orgasm that was going to make her head spin, her toes curl and her eyes cross.

The Tyler Bennett special.

"Ty, I—" But God, she actually wanted to *talk*. To see if he was okay.

She never wanted to talk. Talking led to revelations and revelations led to telling secrets and exposing insecurities and weaknesses.

It wasn't just her flakiness or her inability to set goals and see them through without a crutch—or twenty—that held her back from diving into this relationship. Yes, he distracted her. Yes, he made her natural disorganization worse. But more than that, Ty thought she was someone she wasn't. His crush was on the woman she wanted to be, the one she put on for the world. Which meant his crush wasn't *real*. She'd never been able to tell him that. She hadn't been able to handle the idea of losing him and the attention that made her feel as though she was someone special.

Ty was one of the strongest people she knew—in body and in spirit. He was confident and driven. He'd had to be to accomplish what he'd accomplished.

He thought they had that in common. Most people believed that her confidence and ability to tell others what to do meant she was strong. How would he react if he knew it was all one big mirage? How could a guy like Ty, who pushed himself and the people around him to be better and stronger every day, respect someone like her, who was driven by desperation rather than strength?

"Keep moving, Hailey."

She took a deep breath and acknowledged that she was selfish enough to take one more night. One more chance to be with the man that made her feel like a strong, sure, amazing woman who he could love forever.

She crossed the yard and climbed the back steps. Ty welcomed her into his arms, pulling her body up against his and burying his nose in her hair. She could feel his erection and almost laughed—fighting really did turn him on. Even when the argument was all for show.

Of course, their disagreement about the tiny details of marriage and kids hadn't been made up.

She could not marry this man. But she also couldn't deny that she wished it was different, that *she* was different, and that she could have Ty in her life every day.

She wrapped her arms around his neck and put her lips against his skin, breathing in the scent of him with a hint of blue-raspberry punch. She resisted saying she was sorry about Bryan. At least for right now.

Ty's hands went to her hips and he pressed against her, taking a deep breath, and she felt some of the tension in his shoulders leave him. As if she was comforting him.

Then a thought hit her—had Ty been with Bryan when the accident happened?

The two rarely rode the mountain highways alone. It was the harassing each other that kept them going up and around those torturous climbs and curves.

God, had he seen it happen? Was he somehow blaming himself?

She pulled back to look up into his eyes. "Were you there?" she asked, her voice hoarse. She had to know. She didn't really want to know, but she had to.

He stiffened, and she was sure he knew what she was asking about.

He hesitated just long enough that she was certain of the answer.

"Yes," he admitted softly.

Oh, God. Her heart missed a beat and she pressed her lips together. He'd seen it happen. But even more, it could have been *him.*

She held back the sob that threatened though. If she started crying and wanting to simply hold him, especially when he was clearly planning on sex, he'd fall over dead from shock.

But she did pull out of his arms as he stepped back into the house. She had to see his face fully when she asked the next question and his kitchen was dark.

She pushed him back, her hands on his hard chest. He walked backward and she followed into the dining room off the kitchen.

The light from the foyer and the light from the streetlight outside lit the room dimly. But enough. She pushed him into a chair, slid her hands underneath his shirt and pulled the cotton up and over his head.

Then she went to her knees in front of him.

Ty loved her on her knees. But she rarely got there without his command. For some reason tonight, having her willingly kneeling made him catch his breath. He lifted a hand and tangled it in her hair.

She went to work on the button and zipper of his jeans. When the fly was open, he lifted his hips without her request and she pulled his jeans and underwear down his legs and over his feet. She tossed them to the side, her full attention on his erection.

She wrapped a hand around his shaft, working him from base to tip, breathing on the head.

"Were you hurt?" she asked softly.

She felt his surprise in the sudden tension in his body. He tightened his fingers in her hair. "Suck my cock, Hailey."

She wasn't using this to get answers out of him. She didn't want to manipulate him. And his words sent heat coursing through her body, need gathering deep in her belly.

But she needed to *talk*. To know more and get closer. As much as she might regret it later.

"I need to know," she said, lifting her eyes to his. "You were there. Were *you* hurt?"

He met her eyes, his filled with a strange combination of emotions. She was used to seeing the desire and the intensity. Part of her loved knowing that powerful, serious side that he rarely showed those close to him and never showed the world who loved the laid-back playboy persona he wore so well. But she wasn't used to seeing the warmth. Different from the heat of passion, this warmth seemed as if he was touched by her concern.

"Yes. But I'm okay."

Worry shot through her anyway. Maybe it didn't make sense. He was here, seemed fine, was saying he was fine. But the idea that he'd been in the accident, that he could have been seriously injured…even killed…made her chest and throat tighten, and she was frozen for a moment.

"Hailey," he said, tugging gently on her hair.

"Where were you hurt?"

She saw him battling with the urge to deflect or deny what had happened. But finally he said, "My left knee."

She moved her hands to his knee.

He made a frustrated noise, but she ran her hand over the joint anyway. She knew this man's body as well as her own. She'd had her hands and lips and tongue all over him. There were no wounds on his knee, no scars. It didn't seem swollen or deformed. He hadn't been limping. In fact, he'd lifted her up and fucked her hard against her front door without so much as a grimace. He was fine.

"Where?" she asked anyway.

He sighed. "I partially tore my ACL," he said. "A major ligament. Along with part of another one and some cartilage."

She frowned, feeling her heart rate accelerate. That didn't sound *fine*.

"I thought you said you were okay."

"I am okay. I've...dealt with it. It could have been a lot worse."

She ran her hand up and down over his knee again. The muscles in his legs were hard and thick. He biked and ran and swam for a living. He had an incredible body. The idea that anything in him could tear or give way was hard to comprehend.

"It doesn't hurt?" she asked.

"Not really. Not most of the time."

She studied his face. He was telling the truth about that, she knew, but it seemed as though there was something he *wasn't* saying.

"You did race at the beginning of the month?" she asked. "In Rio? Right?"

He looked surprised.

"Yes, I know about the Olympic qualifying race in Rio," she said.

"You do?" he asked, obviously amazed.

"Yes. And I looked up who won. You weren't in the

top eight, but the US team didn't fill all their spots with that race, so I know you still have to race in Chicago in September."

He stared at her.

She'd wanted to call him after the race in Rio. It was unusual for Ty to not be in the top three, not to mention top eight. But she hadn't. They didn't do that.

And he was talking about getting married. They didn't talk about the biggest things in their lives, but he wanted to get married. Sure, great idea.

"Ty?" she asked, when he still hadn't even blinked. "Did you race in Rio?"

He took a deep breath and shook his head. "No. And I won't be racing in Chicago."

She frowned. "You have to. Someone else might get the Olympic team spot."

He nodded. "Someone else will."

She stood swiftly. "You're not trying for a spot?"

"I can't. I'm done."

Hailey looked down at him, processing his words. He was done? If he didn't go to the Olympics next year, he was giving up his chance to finally claim the gold.

"You can't?" she asked. "Because of your knee?"

"Yes." He wasn't meeting her gaze now.

"So get it fixed. They repair ACLs all the time." A kid on the Sapphire Falls football team had undergone the same surgery last fall.

"I couldn't get it fixed and rehabbed in time for the races," he said. "So I gambled on training even with the partial tear."

"You've been training on it anyway?"

He shifted, leaning forward to rest his arms on his thighs. Hailey knew he was fully comfortable naked, and it was something she appreciated about him. Very much. But she marveled that he could be naked and still have this serious conversation.

"I've tried. I have great strength," he said. "That's what the physical therapist told me. That helps reduce the instability caused by the tear. And a partial tear isn't as serious as a full tear, and the only time a full tear *has* to be repaired is in high-impact sports. Mine are...borderline."

"Running six miles at full speed on paved mountain roads is borderline?" she asked, propping her hands on her hips.

"Yes," he said, lifting his head. "High-impact sports are where there's a lot of sudden stopping and twisting and contact. Football, basketball, that stuff."

"But it didn't work?" she asked, dropping back to her knees. He shifted back and she ran her hand over his knee again. It was hard to believe that underneath the hot skin and hard muscle was damage that had changed everything so quickly.

He shook his head. "No. It didn't work. I couldn't get back to the level I needed to in time for the race."

"Okay, but you have time before Chicago."

He cupped her head again and looked directly into her eyes. "No. I don't. I'm done, Hails. And I've come to terms with it. I'm moving on."

What he was doing was moving to Sapphire Falls.

Suddenly, she understood. Being a triathlete was Ty's life. It was who he was. It was everything he cared about. Competing at the level he'd been at, putting his physical and mental strength up side by side with other men filled a need in him that nothing else could.

And now it was gone. The accident had upended his life, changed everything, and instead of fighting his way back up, he was letting himself roll *down* the mountain.

He was giving up.

And coming home.

To her.

She and Sapphire Falls were the consolation prizes.

That realization bothered her, even as she truly

understood it. Her first priority was her job. Her *only* priority was her job. It was more than what she did. It was who she was. She and Ty had that in common. Still, knowing that he was here with her only because his other options were now gone hurt.

Even more, that Sapphire Falls, *her* town, the place she loved more than anything, was his plan B *really* bugged her.

And she cared about him enough to *not* be that fallback plan.

She knew what he was thinking. If he was home again, with friends and family, planning for marriage and kids, then he would be able to convince himself that leaving competition was okay. Good even.

If he didn't have another option, if there was nothing to fill in those gaps for him, nothing else that made him feel accomplished and important, then he'd fight back, rehab his knee and get back on his bike.

Hailey pushed to her feet. "I can't believe you're giving up. This was your chance for the gold, Ty."

He stood swiftly, taking her hips and turning her so her butt pressed against the dining room table. "You're my gold, Hailey. You and a life here in Sapphire Falls. That's my new gold medal."

A little piece of her melted at that. She'd never been anyone's ultimate prize before.

But she swallowed hard on the heels of that thought. She wasn't really his ultimate prize. The prize he wanted was the Hailey he thought she was—confident, strong, take-charge Mayor Hailey, a woman who was as much a fighter as he was.

"I don't like quitters," she said, lifting her chin. "That isn't the guy I thought I was having a relationship with."

His eyes narrowed. "You are not with me because I'm an Olympian."

"You're so sure of that?" She put the chill in her voice

that made most people back down immediately.

Of course, Ty was not most people.

He pressed closer and lifted her onto the table. "I *am* so sure of that. My medals don't mean anything to you."

"Nothing at all?" she asked. "Wow, and I thought you knew me."

He slipped his hands under her skirt, grasped the sides of her panties and pulled them down and off.

Her breath caught and her whole body heated.

"You're not fucking me because of that silver medal," he said.

"It wasn't about the silver," she said. "It was about the gold."

He reached for the straps of her dress and pulled the bodice away from her braless breasts. "I didn't have a gold any of the times I made you come so hard you couldn't remember your own name."

He cupped one of her breasts, running his thumb over the sensitive tip. She bit back the moan and tried to close her legs, to press against the spot that was throbbing with need for him. But he was there, between her knees, keeping her spread open.

"That gold was everything to you. It's what you've been working for as long as we've been sleeping together."

"My medals don't matter to you," he repeated, rolling one of her nipples between his thumb and finger and then tugging. "When you think about me, it's not about the races and where I finish."

She was already on the verge of begging him to take her—something he *loved*. But that would be giving in. And if he thought that *he* was all that mattered to her, getting him back to Denver would never happen.

"You're happy being number two?" she asked, working hard not to sound breathless as he continued to tease her breasts. "You're satisfied knowing there will now be *three* other gold medalists in front of you?"

He hadn't competed in the last games, and she'd believed he hadn't cared, but now she wondered. She followed the sport. She couldn't help it. And she knew the man who had won the gold in the last games had also beat Ty in three other races leading up to those games. Ty had never beaten him. Had he been scared? Worried that he'd be number two again?

That man wasn't competing this time around. He'd retired, leaving Ty as the one to beat.

Until now.

"I'm the best at a lot of things, Hailey," he said, moving a hand between her legs and running a finger over her mound. "You have been a far greater challenge than any race course. And look where I've got you now."

Like the clichéd light bulb, it was all suddenly clear. Ty had chased two things over the past eleven years that had both stayed just out of reach. The Olympic gold medal. And her.

Oh…*crap.*

Even as she was amazed and warmed by that—no one had ever wanted her like Ty did—alarm shot through her. She could *not* be that important to him. She hadn't been hard to get because *he* wasn't good enough to win her over. It was because *she* wasn't good enough. She wasn't gold-medal material. He couldn't put her on the same level as that…and believe that all he needed was to marry her and he'd be completely satisfied with his life.

She'd known he'd put her on a pedestal. She'd known in high school that he'd thought of her as this older, more sophisticated, out-of-reach, too-good-for-him woman. And she'd basked in that. Thought it was cute and sweet. But he'd grown out of it. The playing field had evened out after he'd rocked her world at the river that first summer night. And then, when she'd gone to Denver needing something from him, the playing field had definitely tipped in his favor.

He gave her the ability to unwind away from her responsibilities, to give everything over to someone else, to enjoy and be enjoyed without worrying about messing everything up.

She knew he wanted her, but she needed what he gave her more than anything she gave him.

She was *not* everything he'd ever dreamed of.

She pushed against his chest, squirming to get off the table. She could not let this go any further.

He grabbed her by the hips, held her still and dipped his knees so he could look into her eyes. "Hey, I'm not done with you." His voice was still husky and his touch was firm, but the way he looked at her was soft, almost tender.

And it nearly undid her.

She took a deep breath. "I can't be the answer to all your problems, Ty."

"Yes, you can."

Dammit. He was stubborn, that she knew well.

"I have a life already. A life I love, that I've worked hard to create. You can't just move back here and expect me to make everything about *you* and fixing the things that have gone wrong for you."

"You have a life already," he agreed. "And I'm not asking you to change it. But I want you to let me in so I can make it even better."

If winning a gold medal would have made him *more* cocky, he wouldn't have been able to get his head through standard doorways.

She huffed out a frustrated breath. She could never live up to the fantasy he'd built of them together over the years. Not the sexual fantasies—those she did all right with—but the other fantasies. The ones she was only now fully understanding. Winning over the woman no one else could get, thawing the Ice Queen's heart, turning the bossy bitch into a loving wife and mother. Oh God.

"You need to stop thinking so hard." He leaned in and

captured her lips with his.

The kiss was slow and sweet to start. But it quickly heated when she squirmed against him again, hoping that if his guard was down, she could get her feet to the floor. And then run.

But how could she forget that Ty *liked* the fight? He loved thinking she was tough, that she only gave in after he'd made her want to submit.

She shoved him back. "Not everything can be fighting and fucking, Ty."

He let her stand but kept her up against his hard chest, rippled abs and thick, hot cock with his hands around her upper arms.

She pulled in a shaky breath.

"You don't want to fight with me? Great. Get on your knees."

She shivered as the command went through her. The guy knew her and knew how to make her want what he wanted. And he was completely naked and she was mostly naked and the chances of her walking out of the room without him touching her any further were pretty small.

They had more to talk about. She shouldn't get distracted. She was *right* about the fighting and fucking.

But he was using that voice. And he had that look in his eyes. And he was wounded.

Physically and emotionally. Part of her needed to feel his strength, *feel* that he was physically fine. And part of her wanted to make him feel better. Even though she knew it was a bad idea and he had things built up in his head that weren't true and weren't real.

Sex made them both feel better, of course. But right now, he didn't know that she *wasn't* everything he wanted and needed her to be. So maybe, for tonight, she could still be the Hailey Conner he had conquered and seduced— mind, heart and body. And if that made him feel better, she was fine with waiting one more day to ruin his perception of her.

And those thoughts meant the chances of her leaving the room without him touching her further were zero.

One more night of pretending wouldn't hurt.

CHAPTER FOUR

She looked him directly in the eye for a long moment. Then she slid to the floor, dragging her body against his. She took his cock in both hands and stroked up and down the length, her eyes still on his.

His hand went to her hair again and he brought her forward. She opened her mouth and let him glide the head of his cock past her lips. She swirled her tongue around the head and then sucked lightly, watching his eyes darken and relishing how he tightened his grip on her hair.

"Take me," he said gruffly, moving his hips, pressing his cock deeper.

She opened wider, cupping his balls at the same time.

"Yes, damn, Hailey." He moved in and out of her mouth in short, gentle thrusts.

She tried to focus on the fact that this man was a finely honed athlete, that his gorgeous body was a machine he used to make a living, that he had stood on the Olympic podium representing his country, that he pushed himself and strove for greatness every day.

Those were all things she should admire and that should turn her on.

But that wasn't what did it. He was just Ty. He could have flipped burgers or worked the register at the gas station or bartended or been the President of the United States. She would have wanted, and—yes, dammit—*liked* him as much. She knew it.

And he knew it.

Did she admire him? Yes. Did his drive and ambition intimidate the hell out of her? Yes. Was his body worthy of every ounce of worship she could muster? Absolutely.

But in that moment, she was just Hailey and he was just Ty. And she wanted him with an intensity that never diminished, no matter how many times they were together.

She increased her rhythm, working her hand along his length and soaking in the sounds of his groans and the way he gripped her head.

Finally, he pulled her to her feet and took her with him as he sat back on the chair. She straddled his lap and Ty lifted her over him. She sank down, taking him in as they groaned together.

There was no pause, no deep breath. Ty curled his fingers into her hips as he immediately moved her up and down. Hailey followed his direction, only the balls of her feet touching the floor and barely giving her enough leverage to lift and lower herself.

Their pace was frantic. He was as deep as he could be and yet she felt as if she wanted to pull him in and absorb him. She wrapped her arms around his neck, pressing every inch of her body against his. Ribbons of heat and need spiraled through her, coming from everywhere—her breasts against his chest, his hands holding and moving her, their ragged breathing, the way he stretched and filled her. Then, all at once, her climax swept over her. It was so sudden, she cried out from the surprise as much as the intense pleasure and was still reeling when Ty shouted her name with his release.

She slumped against him a moment later, spent.

She felt as though the heat they'd generated had melted all of her bones and muscles. Even her brain felt mushy. She was completely content to stay draped over him like a blanket for the next several days.

"You're amazing," he whispered against her hair.

And she wanted to be. For him. She really did.

"Stay," he whispered a few minutes later.

"Yes."

Because she really did like being the woman he'd always dreamed of.

And hell, he lived next door now. It wasn't like she wouldn't see him. They could talk about gold medals and races and fighting and marriage anytime.

But she definitely noted when he carried her upstairs to his bed that his knee seemed to be doing fine.

Sunday morning, Hailey woke to the sound of the shower running. Which, considering she lived alone, was strange. Until she remembered she was at Ty's. In Sapphire Falls.

Oh boy.

She rolled to look at the clock. Eight a.m. She had an hour to get to church.

In Denver, she never had to worry about what time it was or about getting anywhere.

She threw the covers back and sat up.

Ty had awakened her twice more in the night and she was sore and exhausted.

And happy.

Until she remembered that she was waking up at Ty's *with* a schedule.

That definitely tarnished the happiness of being with Ty.

She sighed.

Okay. Well, she didn't have time to deal with any of that, and Ty was in the shower, so this was her chance to escape.

Her clothes were downstairs, so she grabbed one of Ty's T-shirts and pulled it on as she headed for the steps. She gathered her dress from the dining room but couldn't find her panties. She supposed she should be grateful this one time that she only lived next door.

Clutching her dress to her chest, her sandals dangling from her fingers, she let herself out the backdoor. But as she pulled the kitchen door shut and turned to descend the steps, she found herself face-to-face with a Bennett after all.

And this one was much worse.

She pasted on what she hoped looked like a sincere smile. "Good morning, Mrs. Bennett."

Kathy Bennett's eyes were wide. Understandably.

"Good…morning." She took in Hailey's attire and then tried to pretend that she hadn't. "Ty invited us all for brunch later. I was dropping the cinnamon rolls off before church."

Yep, sneaking out Ty's backdoor on her way to get ready for church after a night of hot sex and running into his mother definitely won for most humiliating moment of her life.

Hailey lifted a hand to smooth her hair and clunked herself in the cheek with one of her shoes. She also felt the morning air on her butt cheek and realized she didn't have enough shirt length to reach too high. She winced and lowered her hand. She probably didn't want to know how bad her hair looked, and she definitely did *not* want to flash Kathy Bennett.

"He's…" Her cheeks flamed. She also could not tell his mother that he was in the shower. Because she shouldn't know that he was in the shower. Because she shouldn't be in his house this early in the morning—or maybe ever—and certainly not *while* he was in the shower.

"I'll let myself in," Kathy said as she came up the steps. "I'll get the coffee started."

Hailey tried to move out of her way, but the top step was small and they ended up performing an awkward dance shuffle that made the moment even worse somehow as Kathy took Hailey's spot on the step and Hailey ended up a step down.

Kathy opened the back door and then turned to Hailey. "You're not staying?"

She shook her head. "I need to go…get ready for church." The last word came out softer than the first and

Hailey felt her cheeks burning.

"Oh, wonderful, I'll be looking forward to seeing Ty in church. It's been a long time since he worshipped in Sapphire Falls."

Hailey swallowed hard. She wasn't taking Ty to church. Or she hadn't been. But somehow she felt her head start nodding. "That will be nice. But maybe he can go with *you* now that you're here." She didn't even have a full hour to get ready. And now she couldn't skip. And she could *not* take Ty with her.

"Oh, you didn't make plans?" Kathy asked, pulling the door open.

Hailey had started down the steps, but she swung back quickly, almost sliding off the step she was on. "For church? No...not..." Hailey cleared her throat. "Not this morning."

Kathy nodded. "I'll let him know you headed home. And I'll make sure he wears a tie."

And because she was a terrible person, Hailey immediately thought of a particular red tie that he'd wrapped around her wrists a number of times. "Okay, great," she managed, her voice weak.

Kathy was in the doorway now, but she hesitated, her gaze dropping to the front of the shirt Hailey wore. She smiled. "I can't believe he still has that shirt."

Hailey glanced down and couldn't help her smile in return. It was the shirt from the 5K run in Sapphire Falls five years ago. Ty had barely broken a sweat and everyone knew he'd held back, finishing only a couple of minutes ahead of the second-place winner. But having him there had brought a lot of local and even state-wide attention to their race, and they'd raised well over their goal amount for the new track at the high school.

"That was the first time I saw him run," Hailey said. Then she realized that she'd said it out loud. She looked up at Kathy. And looking at the other woman who loved Ty most in the world, she said, "I love seeing his face right after a race. He's so happy at that moment."

Kathy looked surprised for a millisecond and then she smiled. "I used to think that he was never happier than when he crossed a finish line."

Hailey debated for a moment about what she wanted to say next. She hated the idea that Kathy thought she and Ty had just had a one-night stand. But admitting that it wasn't, that it was more, was dangerous. Especially with Ty's mother. Surely Kathy would want details, and lots of them, if she had even an inkling that Hailey and Ty had something going on.

But the risk of that bothered Hailey less than the idea that Kathy might think Hailey was only having sex with her son. It *was* more than that. She hadn't even truly admitted it was more than that to Ty, but for some reason, she wanted Kathy to know.

She took a deep breath. "Bryan is always at the finish line of all his races. He videotapes the finish on his phone and sends it to me."

Kathy seemed to take that in with much less surprise. Slowly, she nodded. "I would love to see those sometime, if you'd send them to me. I assume you've kept them?"

And what would *that* admission say to Ty's mother? But Hailey nodded. "I'd be happy to."

Kathy hesitated for a moment, as if having second thoughts about what she wanted to say. Finally, she said, "I *used* to think crossing the finish line was what made him the happiest. But since he's moved back, he's been happier than I've ever seen him."

Hailey gave a surprised laugh. "It's only been a couple of days."

Kathy nodded, as if that was a puzzle to her as well. "I know."

Hailey had no idea what else to say to that, so she said, "I'll see you at church," and quickly ran down the rest of the steps and across the dewy grass, praying that Ty would *not* wear the red tie to church.

⚜

Ty smelled the fresh coffee and grinned. Hailey had stayed. When he'd first stepped out of the bathroom to find his bed empty, he'd been annoyed. She'd snuck out? Really? But as he pulled on a pair of workout shorts and a T-shirt, he'd smelled the coffee and knew that everything was right with the world after all.

Hailey knew about his injury, knew about the Olympics, knew he was serious about staying and she was in his bed, in Sapphire Falls.

Everything was good.

And then he walked into the kitchen.

"Mom?"

His mother was standing at his coffeepot, pouring a cup. She turned with a smile. "Good morning, darling."

Ty looked around the room. "What are you doing here?"

"I brought the cinnamon rolls over for brunch on my way to church."

He moved farther into the room. "Okay. And you made coffee." He glanced toward the living room and then at his pantry door. Was Hailey hiding? If she'd seen his mother coming, he wouldn't put it past her.

"She went home to get ready for church." Kathy sipped from her cup and leaned back against the counter.

Ty sighed. "You ran into her."

"And if you're looking for your blue and white 5K race shirt, I know where it is." Kathy sipped again.

Stupidly, for a moment, Ty was disappointed he hadn't seen Hailey in his blue and white 5K race shirt.

He crossed to the pot and pulled a cup from the cupboard, filled it and turned to lean against the counter perpendicular to where his mother stood.

He sipped. And waited.

"How long has it been?" Kathy asked.

Ty took a breath. "Three and a half years."

His mom looked truly surprised at that.

"What?" he asked.

"I…" Kathy shook her head. "It was nice running into her on your back steps."

Ty chuckled. "Really? It was *nice* seeing her coming out of my house early in the morning dressed only in my shirt?"

Kathy shrugged. "What I should say is that it was nice seeing her disheveled and rattled and blushing. And I might have seen the first truly sincere smile from her."

Ty watched his mother's face, fascinated by this.

Kathy glanced at him. "She's so put together and composed and cool all the time," she went on. "But I've long suspected there was a softer side. It was nice seeing her less than pulled together."

Ty was pleasantly surprised by this. "You've suspected a softer side?"

Kathy nodded. "I assume when she's not in public, not in Sapphire Falls, that she's a completely different person."

Ty thought about that. He shrugged. "Not really. She's more relaxed, she laughs more, but she always looks amazing and she's constantly on the go. She's still strong and bossy," he said with a smile. "She's kick-ass, all the time."

Kathy didn't smile in return. She looked thoughtful.

"What?" Ty asked. "What are you thinking?"

"That three and a half years is a long time to be together without it changing you."

Ty frowned. "What do you mean?"

"You're both the same people you've always been. Being in love changes you. In small ways, sometimes, but in important ways."

Ty was surprised by how easily his mom was using the word love in regard to him and Hailey. But then he thought more about what she'd said. "Trav and Tuck and TJ haven't changed."

Kathy laughed. "Of course they have."

"Well, Travis travels more now and Tucker has *kids* and TJ smiles more, but they're all still doing what they were doing right where they were doing it before they met the girls. *I'm* moving back here. My whole life is different."

Kathy raised an eyebrow.

"*What?*"

"First of all, your brothers are all different. Not completely, no, of course not. But Travis is more open to new things now. He's more adventurous, more open to change. And Tucker is more patient and accepting of things that don't go according to his plans. He realizes that his ideas aren't always the right or only ones. And TJ is happier and...softer. He's willing to let people close and let them help *him* once in a while." Her smile grew with that. "Hope was only here for a few *days* and he was opening up and softening. Now they're on a trip together to Arizona. So, yes, being in love changes you. It should. It should make you a better person."

Ty thought about her summation of the changes in his brothers and realized she was right.

Huh.

"Well, I'm *here*," Ty said again. "I've realized that I want to be home again, with my family and friends."

Kathy narrowed her eyes. "You're here because of Hailey?"

"Yes." But there was a niggle in the back of his mind that said *not as romantic as it sounds, Champ.* He focused on the rim of her cup instead of meeting her eyes.

"I haven't asked you about this big move," Kathy said. "I assumed you had a good reason and a plan. I didn't realize it was a woman. Especially that it was Hailey."

He shifted his weight, suddenly uncomfortable. "I do have a plan."

"And does it include competing in the next Olympics?" she asked.

He sighed. "No."

She nodded, clearly not surprised. "Because of what happened with Bryan?"

He'd had to tell his family about Bryan. It had been too much to deal with without his family's support and advice. But he hadn't told them about himself.

"Partly," he said, shifting again, knowing she was studying him.

"What else?"

He didn't answer at first.

"Tyler Daniel Bennett," Kathy said firmly.

He lifted his eyes.

"What else?"

"My knee."

She let out a breath. "I knew there was something."

"I tore my ACL." He told her the story, including his surgery options that would have put him out of the upcoming races for sure, and how he'd gambled on being able to perform anyway…and lost.

Kathy moved close and put her hand against his cheek. "I'm so sorry, honey."

He nodded, his throat tight at her concern. "I'm okay."

She took a deep breath and nodded. "Thank God." She stepped back and leaned on the counter again. "And now you're here."

"To stay."

Kathy didn't say anything for a moment. Finally, though, she turned to him. "Does Hailey know about your knee?"

He nodded. "I told her everything."

"She knows you're not competing anymore?"

"Yes."

His mom looked…concerned.

Ty frowned. "What's wrong?"

"I…" Kathy sighed. "Poor Hailey."

Ty straightened. "Poor Hailey? Because she has to put up with me full time now?"

Kathy laughed lightly. "Of course not. And if you say you have feelings for her, I believe you. But it's too bad…"

"What's too bad, Mom?"

"That you hurt your knee. That you didn't come back here for her. Or not *just* for her."

"But I…did come back here for her. I could have gone anywhere in the world. But I chose to come here. Because she's here."

Kathy nodded. "You need to be sure you tell her that. Because you know how it feels to be the silver medalist."

Ty frowned. "What?"

"You know how it feels to be second place."

"But she's not. I told her last night that she's my new gold medal."

Kathy sighed again. "Yes, now that the other gold medal isn't an option."

Ty set his coffee cup down and turned to face his mother fully, planting his hands on his hips. "What are you saying?" he asked firmly.

"Hailey… I think she's always been second place. And that's what's been driving her all this time, like it drives you. But you feel some control over where you finish in the pack. I'm not so sure she does. And I feel bad for her that the man she loves has made her feel like she's second place again."

His mom really thought Hailey loved him? Ty shook his head. No, that wasn't the important part here. Well, it was. Of course. But it was not the most important thing at this very second. His mother knew something about Hailey that he needed to know. He could sense it.

"She's not second place at all. She's the mayor. That's number one. She's always been number one—head of every committee, class president, homecoming queen, the girl every guy wanted to date and every girl wanted to be."

Kathy looked a little sad. "She ran unopposed for mayor. Both times."

Ty thought about that. "That's not really the same thing as being number one," he finally said.

Kathy shook her head. "No. It's not. And…"

Ty felt everything in him tightening. Hailey *was* number one. She was the girl who no other man had ever won over, the unattainable one. "And what?" He really tried not to growl at his mother. But it was tough.

"Her father, Stan…he was only ever involved with her if she was running for something, only ever showed up if she was accepting an award."

Hailey's father was a state senator and he had moved to the state capitol years ago. Ty knew Hailey didn't see him much but that was another thing they didn't talk about a lot.

"And her stepmother was a piece of work. She was so jealous of Hailey. It was as though she was always in competition with Hailey for Stan's attention, worried about being prettier and more popular."

"How do you know all of this?" Ty asked, his heart hammering in his chest.

He had an urge to confront Hailey's father and he wasn't even sure he understood all the reasons why. Just the idea that someone had hurt her made him feel a crazy mix of emotions. He wanted to defend and comfort her, even while he wanted to protest that it was even possible. Hailey was tough. She didn't let people get to her. She knew not everyone in town liked her, and she was okay with that as long as they respected her decisions and let her do her job. Fathers and even stepmothers were different than constituents, of course, but it was hard to imagine anyone shaking Hailey's self-confidence.

"Her stepmom, Angela, was involved with every committee and every volunteer organization in this town. I worked with her a lot and was her co-chair and vice president several times. I witnessed a lot of it when she didn't think I was paying attention. She would put Hailey down all the time and, I'm sad to say, was usually Stan's first choice over his daughter."

"So Hailey's felt like second place with her dad and that's what made her run for things and want to be in charge," Ty said.

Kathy nodded. "I think so. And I've watched her grow up and become cool and aloof and…it's made me sad. I was so happy to think that my sweet, amazing, loving son had seen beneath all of that." She narrowed her eyes, studying him. "But now I wonder."

"Hey."

She shrugged. "Seriously, Ty. I think you care about her, I believe that you like her, but you've still put her in second place behind the things that are important to you."

Several long, uncomfortable, painful moments passed.

"Wow," Ty finally said. "And I'm your baby. I can't imagine how you talk to TJ when he's messed-up."

Kathy cocked an eyebrow. "You don't even want to know."

Ty sighed and slumped back against the counter again. "Crap."

"Well, it's not too late."

"Too late for what?"

"To make sure she knows that she's the most important thing. To make her number one in your heart and life."

Ty felt his stomach knot. How? It would take something big. And meaningful. Something she would really believe. They weren't talking a bouquet of flowers here. It had to be something that would help her see that he thought she was amazing.

"I, um…"

"What is it?" his mother asked.

"I...I don't have a lot of experience here. I'm usually working pretty hard to make sure the people around me are *not* number one."

He wasn't so great at making *other* people feel important. He was usually too concerned with ensuring *he* was the best.

Kathy smiled. "See what I mean? Being in love makes you a better person."

Ah, so he had some work to do.

And it was nice of his mother to not come right out and say that he was a selfish prick.

❧

They barely made it to church in time. And they still beat Hailey.

He looked for her the instant he stepped inside the building but didn't see her until she slid into the back pew during the second verse of the first hymn.

Ty was glad that his mom was pleased simply to have him beside her in church, because he didn't get anything out of the service. His mind was too full of thoughts of Hailey and her feeling second best all her life. His mom assumed they were in love and he really thought he was too, until he also thought about his mom's words about him coming home for Hailey only after all of his other options were gone.

But this seemed simple enough. They needed to date.

They needed to see if they had real feelings between them and if they could actually make something work.

No matter *why* he was here, he was here to stay. He didn't actually believe that she had been attracted to him because of his medals. He also didn't believe that the enchiladas in Denver were what she missed most when she wasn't there.

The service ended before he'd solved any of his problems and questions. But he made a beeline for Hailey anyway. He'd figure something out.

She was heading for the door when he caught up with her. He grasped her elbow.

"Hailey."

She turned and gave him a tight, totally fake smile. "Hi, Tyler."

Tyler. He gritted his teeth. She never called him Tyler in private and it rubbed him wrong now.

"I'm having brunch at my house with my family. I'd like you to come." Hell, she knew his sister-in-law Lauren better than he did. And she'd had a moment with his mom that morning. It would be great.

She was clearly shocked by the invitation though. "Thanks. That's nice. But I can't."

"Please."

Her eyes widened. Ty very rarely said please.

Still, she shook her head. "I'm sorry."

He moved in closer, fully aware that they were attracting attention. He didn't care.

"Because it's with my family?"

"I already have other plans."

But he knew it was because it was with his family. Brunch with family was something a girlfriend would do. She was supposedly not his girlfriend. "What plans?"

Her eyes narrowed slightly. "None of your business," she said quietly.

Everything in him rebelled at that.

Until his conversation with his mom that morning, he'd truly believed that he and Hailey were going to dive into this relationship. He knew she had hesitations and that he'd surprised her by moving in next door. But he'd really trusted that they'd get past those. He knew he'd have to work at it—he *wanted* to have to work at it, that's how he knew what mattered. But he hadn't doubted the outcome.

This was one challenge where he'd known he'd come out on top.

Now he wasn't as sure.

His mom loved him, and because of that, she'd always been totally honest with him. With all of them. And she'd just called him on his cockiness.

On his bike, on the road or in the water, he could be himself. He'd been biking, running and swimming all his life. In those, he had to push, had to want it, but he could rely on instinct and fall back on experience when things got tough.

With Hailey...he couldn't. He didn't have instinct or experience in convincing a woman he was in love with her.

Women had always been pretty easy for him. He knew that was one of the reasons he was drawn to Hailey. She wasn't easily impressed and the field of competition for her attention had been a lot bigger.

But she'd been right last night. It had to be about more than fighting and fucking now.

He didn't know exactly what that meant, but he did know that he wanted her.

And he definitely wanted her business to be his.

He was proud of himself for taking a deep breath and *not* demanding that she tell him what she was doing today instead of spending it with him. Instead, he said, "I can reschedule brunch. I'll go with you."

She arched a brow. "You're not invited."

He had to grit is teeth again. Not because of the haughty tone and look she gave him, but because not being invited was not okay with him.

"Hailey, I think we need to talk."

She lifted a shoulder. "Okay. But not today."

He'd been with her last night. Naked. Inside of her. Made her come apart three times.

And now she was brushing him off. For the whole day.

"Do I need to—"

"Ty, I told you before. This is Sapphire Falls. My rules."

Frustration coursed through him as he watched her turn and walk away.

Looking beautiful as she did it.

Even more than watching for Ty's lights to go on after the dance, Hailey hated herself for hiding out from him on Sunday. All day. And night.

She was the first to admit that she needed down time sometimes and had no guilt about claiming it. And she was pretty sure she could have shut and locked the door in his face if needed. But she was only *pretty sure*, not absolutely sure. So she'd hid out in her house, watching Netflix behind closed curtains and dealing with the fact that she was out of lemonade mix and drinking iced tea instead when she got thirsty.

But not turning her lights on after dark felt a little pathetic. As did ignoring his calls and texts. She was *not* going to do this every weekend.

Ty had moved in next door without talking with her about it, without even caring what she would think or feel. Fine. But that did not give him permission to be in her life twenty-four-seven if she didn't want him there. If she didn't want to spend Sundays with him, he was going to have to deal with that.

Of course, she *did* want to spend Sundays with him. And every other day.

The idea of brunch had been intimidating, but what intimidated her more was how much she would love to be included in his family. She loved them. Even the four boys Tucker had become a surrogate father to. They cracked her up.

Kathy and Thomas were the type of parents she'd

dreamed of having. TJ, Travis and Tucker were good guys that she'd known her whole life. They were charming, hardworking, big-hearted men. She had no trouble spending time with them. And then there were the women.

Hailey and Lauren actually had a lot in common. Lauren was a powerhouse. She was intelligent and polished and had an amazing shoe collection. Before Lauren had gotten together with Travis, she had stayed in Hailey's guest room on her visits to Sapphire Falls for work. Hailey had cleaned the house up when Lauren was coming, so the other woman hadn't seen *all* of the sticky notes in Hailey's life. But she'd witnessed more of Hailey being scattered than most people usually saw. And Lauren had never judged her. If anything, it had brought them closer. They'd never had a big, deep, meaningful talk about any of it. Hailey had never said the words, "I have ADHD and am not really confident all the time. In fact, most of the time I have no idea what I'm doing." But she knew Lauren knew. And Hailey liked that she didn't have to talk about it to be understood.

Delaney, Tucker's fiancé, was more of a newcomer, but Hailey admired the woman. She wasn't perfect but she was tough and interesting. She had lost both her sister and her brother-in-law within months of each other, so she'd been through a lot. She did home renovations and if she had a sledgehammer in her hand, she was completely confident. However, when it came to the four boys who she was now the legal guardian for, or even fitting into small-town life, Delaney had definite moments of weakness. But she owned them. She put them out there and asked for help. Hailey admired that. And envied it.

Then there was Hope. Hope had TJ Bennett, the oldest and hardest of the Bennett boys, soft and smiling. She was really new. She hadn't even been around for a month. But Hailey wasn't sure she'd ever met someone like Hope. She was...peaceful. She was a free spirit who openly and easily gave of herself and took care of those around her. Hailey would love if some of Hope's serenity would rub off on her.

Hailey's closest friends, Adrianne and Phoebe, were kind, loving women as well. Hailey loved Adrianne for her softness and patience and acceptance, and Phoebe for her perky bubbliness and enthusiastic sincerity in all things. And they knew her. She *had* said the words to them that explained her rigid outer shell and bitchy persona. She'd compared herself to the Wizard in the *Wizard of Oz*, presiding over the Emerald City from behind a lot of flash and intimidation. They'd understood and hadn't judged her.

Hailey appreciated every one of the women in her life and wanted to be a little like each of them.

So hanging out with Ty's family, including the new additions, was tempting.

But it was Ty she was worried about.

It wasn't exactly him finding out that she wasn't the woman he thought she was. He'd likely be understanding about it. It was that she wouldn't be his type anymore after that.

And though she was trying to keep him at arm's length now, she didn't want to *not* be the woman he wanted.

God, she was so confused.

Monday morning, she went through her normal routine and arrived at her office just after eight. She even managed to get some work done before Tess knocked on her door.

"Yes?"

"Your eleven o'clock is here."

Hailey took a deep breath. Ty. She hadn't been sure he would show for the meeting they'd scheduled on Friday. Before...everything.

She was equally pleased that he was respecting the appointment and nervous that he was here.

"That's great," she told Tess. "I'm ready."

Tess ducked out, and a moment later, Ty strode in

through the door.

"Morning, Madam Mayor," he said with a grin.

Madam Mayor. He'd called her that a million times over the years, but this time it sounded more intimate. Strange.

She cleared her throat. "Good morning."

He dropped into the chair in front of her desk. "Thank you for agreeing to see me."

"You didn't give me much choice."

His grin grew and she wondered what he was thinking.

"I'm excited about my proposal," he said.

The word proposal sent a shiver through her. And not a bad one. A very good one. A warm one. And when he put a typed report in a sapphire-blue plastic report cover on her desk, she felt like an idiot.

He actually had a proposal for something. Not that they get married, but something related to her being mayor.

Which was completely appropriate for a scheduled meeting in her office on a Monday morning.

Great.

"Thank you," she said. She flipped the report open to the first page.

The Tyler Bennett Triathlete Training Center.

She looked up.

He grinned.

Her heart skipped.

God, that grin. It was as if he was a kid waiting for her to open a homemade Christmas gift he'd made in class or something. His excitement and pride were almost palpable.

She closed the report and folded her hands on top of it.

Okay, she was intrigued.

"I'm assuming all of the tiny details are in here for me to refer back to," she said. "But I'd like to hear you explain this to me in your own words." She hated reading reports.

Ty leaned in with his forearms on his thighs and met her gaze. He was excited, but she could see he was also completely serious.

"I've been developing a training program for athletes wanting to get into triathlons, or those who want to simply up their performance in one of the included sports. I've been outlining all of the things I've done in my training over the years, analyzing what I've done right, things I should have done differently, and I think I have a unique and effective program written."

Hailey knew Ty was serious about his training. He didn't even take time off when she was in town visiting. He continued to run and bike when he was visiting Sapphire Falls. She'd witnessed his eating habits up close. His smoothies were to die for. And she certainly knew the shape his body was in personally. But she knew what he did was effective because he won races. Not because they ever really talked about it.

"Okay," she said. It sounded like a good plan, but she didn't know why it warranted a meeting with her.

"I'm bringing the program here. And I'm building a state-of-the-art training facility."

Hailey listened with growing trepidation as Ty outlined his plans for the facility, including use by the town as a fitness club, as well as using his new house as a boardinghouse for athletes coming in and hiring locally for everything from construction to maintenance.

He was bringing this program to Sapphire Falls. He was going to build a training center *here*. A training center. A huge building with his name on it and he was going to spread the word nationally.

"I'm contacted all the time by athletes who want advice or mentorship. I've had coaches bring me in for workshops and such. But I want to do more. Reach more people and bring something back here to Sapphire Falls. It will bring people to town," he said. "Along with some sports media attention, at least at first. Then as our trainees go out and start winning and talking about the program here, we'll have even more attention and more interest."

Hailey studied Ty. He hadn't paused for more than a couple of seconds throughout his presentation and she marveled at how much thought and enthusiasm he put into this.

He'd been planning this for a while.

This was even bigger than she'd realized last night. He'd said he was done competing, but this…if he put money into this, if he announced publicly to the national sports media and his sponsors that he was doing this, he'd have to announce that he was done racing. He couldn't take that back. He would really be done.

She couldn't let him do this on a whim during a period of emotional crisis.

He needed to get his body healthy first. Then he needed to look at his options. Carefully and rationally.

She wouldn't accept a marriage proposal brought about by this accident and physical injury, and she wouldn't accept a business proposal for the same reasons.

"Well, I can tell you that the city doesn't have enough money or land available for something like this," she said, putting finality in her tone.

Ty shook his head. "I met with Levi Spencer this morning. He has agreed to financially back part of the project. I'm also going to allow locals to be investors. It will not only up their engagement in the project and facility, but it will pay them back as things get up and running."

Hailey wasn't surprised Levi had agreed. He was a smart businessman, but he also loved quirky ideas that would result in mass entertainment. His family's business was entertainment. Specifically casinos, but an interesting collection of shows and touring companies as well. A fitness facility may not seem entertaining, but it would have big public appeal and benefit, and bringing world-class athletes to town could be fun.

"What about the land?" she asked. "You're going to need space."

Ty nodded. "We'll make a very generous offer to a couple of the local landowners and see what they say."

"You seem to have thought this through." *Dammit.*

"It's a reality that professional athletes can't be professional athletes forever," he said reasonably. "And you never know when something might happen that can change it. You have to be ready for it. And I was."

Nope. She didn't believe that. She bought that he'd put a plan in place, had been thinking about this as a go-to idea down the road. What she didn't buy was that he was ready for it now.

Ty liked to be the best and he had enough ego to believe that he was *always* the best. But he got a rush from proving it. He loved having people underestimate him.

She'd just never seen him underestimate himself.

Studying his face and listening to him so calmly tell her that his whole life was now different and he was fine, Hailey realized that she might be exactly the person he needed right now. She could stir him up, fire his competitive nature. There was no way he was ready to be done. He might be talking himself into being ready, telling himself it was fine, throwing himself into this new project so he could *be* fine. But he wasn't. Not really.

"You're giving up." She made sure to put a touch of disappointment in her tone.

"Not giving up. Changing my focus."

"Because you can't win anymore," she said. "Easier to stop doing it and blame it on your newfound goals for happiness and fulfillment than to lose, I suppose."

He frowned and Hailey felt a thrill of *I know you.*

"If there isn't even a chance that I can be on top, I'm not sure what the point is."

She nodded. "You're probably right."

"Not competing isn't the end of my world."

"Okay."

His frown deepened. "I mean that."

She knew he *wanted* to mean it. "It sounds like you have all of these plans firmly in place."

"I do."

"Then good luck with it." She slid the report back across her desk to him.

"You don't even want to look at it?" he asked, still frowning.

"I don't need to. You have several steps to complete before you're to the point where you need permits."

"That's the only reason you're interested?" he asked. "Because I'll need to come to the town for permits?"

"Is there another reason you *want* me to be interested?" she asked.

He looks good.

The thought hit her all at once and seemingly randomly.

Ty always looked good. He was a very good-looking guy. He oozed charm and sexiness. And of course, she could hardly look at his mouth or hands or ass or…any of him without recalling how those parts felt under her hands and mouth and against her body.

But there was a confidence about him she hadn't seen before. It was hard to imagine Ty being *more* confident than usual. But his trademark cockiness was different than this assured air.

And now he also looked ticked off that she wasn't responding with enough enthusiasm.

She would be enthusiastic about it, if she could look at it objectively and only as the mayor of Sapphire Falls. But of course, she was all discombobulated when it came to Ty and she was being anything *but* objective.

She didn't want it to be easy for him to leave competition, the thing he loved and had dedicated so many years to, the thing that brought him so much reward.

"There *is* another reason I want you interested," he said.

"What's that?"

"You're my girlfriend."

He was just going to lay that out there. Hailey took a deep breath. "What you mean is, you expect special treatment because we've slept together."

"What I *mean*," he said, his voice dropping to a near growl, "is that I expect you to give a shit about something that matters this much to me."

Hailey was a pro at keeping her cool no matter what, at not letting people see when they were getting to her. But this was Ty. And he not only got to her, he would keep it up until he got a reaction. Fine, she'd give him a reaction.

She put her hands on her desk and stood. She leaned in. "I care, Ty. Okay? I care. Too much. I can't approve your plans or tell you to go ahead because I care about you."

He stood as well, leaning onto her desk and meeting her eyes. "You don't have to *worry* about me. I'm fine."

But he *wasn't*. And she could not shake the need to make sure that he was.

Dammit.

How had this happened?

They'd spent years with things the other way around. He'd had a crush first and had slowly won her over. He'd taken over at the river that summer they'd first slept together. He'd turned their business meeting in Denver into more. He'd been the one that had said he wanted to keep seeing her.

It had always been about him pursuing her, him caring more about her, him wanting her more.

And somewhere in the midst of him making her feel like a goddess who deserved romance and seduction, he'd become important to her.

It was sad maybe, but Tyler had given her more genuine attention over the years than anyone else had. His unwillingness to give up even in the face of her repeated refusals to get involved had made her feel wanted. Other than election nights, Hailey hadn't felt wanted a lot. It was her own doing, of course, but there were times when she'd regretted choosing to be the intimidating bitch over the years.

She knew it was her father's fault in large part. She'd done everything she could to get his attention, to make him proud, hoping that he would want to spend time with her. And he had. In short bursts. Until something else had come along that was more interesting or important. Then she'd have to start all over again doing something he'd notice.

Ty's unconditional affection, his desire to have *her* attention, the way he seemed to just want to be with her, had filled her up in a way nothing else had. And had made her determined to at least *seem* like the woman he was crazy about.

And, yes, he'd become important.

Moments when she felt insecure about a decision or nervous about a speech or when she had to deliver an unpopular opinion, she would recall Ty telling her she was amazing and strong and any of the other thousands of compliments he'd paid her over the years.

"What are you thinking?" Ty asked. His voice was still low but the angry edge was gone. Now *he* seemed worried.

She shook her head and straightened. "Nothing. I'm fine."

"The wheels inside that pretty head are spinning so fast I can hear the whirring out here, Hails," he said.

"I was reeling from relief," she said, tossing her hair back and giving him a smile.

"Relief?"

"That this move home was not a big romantic gesture that you're going to spill to the whole town." She said the words that she *should* mean. "It's a business venture. That makes so much more sense."

Ty straightened and crossed his arms, watching her carefully. "Why can't this be both?"

She wasn't going to answer that directly. "I mean, if this injury hadn't happened, you would still be in Denver and everything would be the way it's always been. I know you've been happy with our arrangement."

She did know that. It had been perfect for both of them.

Ty nodded. "It's been really good."

"So I was thinking about how all of this makes more sense now. That's all."

A few seconds passed, then Ty turned and headed for the door.

Hailey stared at his back. Okay. Was he upset? Had he said his piece and that was it for now? Was he—

He stopped at the door.

The sound of the lock turning was so loud in the quiet that Hailey jumped.

Ty turned to face her. "Mute your phone."

"Wha—"

"Do it, Hailey." He came back toward her desk.

She reached out, her hand trembling with a sudden surge of adrenaline, and pressed the button that would forward her calls to her voice mail.

"Now take your clothes off."

Ty crossed to her window and twisted the rod that would close the blinds.

"What are you—"

"There are several advantages to my move home where you're concerned," he said, coming back to the desk. "One of them is being able to make love to you in the middle of a workday on your big mahogany desk."

She swallowed hard. She should *not* let him do this. But they'd been arguing and that was like Viagra for Ty.

Still, he'd said *make love*. Not fuck. Not *make you scream.* Make love.

"Cherry."

He stopped with the desk between them. He cocked an eyebrow. "What?"

"The desk is cherry."

Butterflies were swooping through her whole body, not just her stomach, and her clothes felt tight and rough against her skin.

"One of them is being able to make love to you in the middle of a workday on your big *cherry* desk."

It wasn't just the words—though she couldn't remember him ever saying *make love* before. It was the way he was looking at her and the warmth in his voice. Affection. Tenderness. Caring. It was all there.

How was she supposed to resist *that*?

Okay, so she could use a little adoring from him right now. Dammit. She hated that at the same time she embraced it. He was here for a dozen reasons *other* than her and she didn't want him to be here because of her anyway, but knowing that at least she was a fringe benefit of him being here made her heart trip.

It was pathetic. If she was only a fringe benefit, she should slap him and shove him out the door.

But she wanted this. In high school, his notes and the occasional chocolate kiss in her locker and the constant compliments made her like him even though she had a hundred reasons why she shouldn't. Him spreading her out and making her feel like the most beautiful woman in the world was something she couldn't say no to. Just like she'd never turned down chocolate.

Hailey unbuttoned her shirt as Ty watched every flex of her fingers.

She shrugged out of the silky blouse and let it fall to the floor behind her. Her bra hooked in the front and as the clasp gave and opened, she saw Ty pull a long breath in through his nose.

The bra fell on top of the blouse and she reached for the zipper at the back of her skirt.

"I love when your nipples get hard from me just looking at you," Ty told her.

They tingled too, but she didn't mention that.

Her skirt pooled at her feet a moment later. She opted to keep her heels on.

"Make them harder for me," Ty said, his eyes still on her breasts.

She knew he loved when she played with herself. It wasn't uncommon for him to make her give herself an orgasm in front of him before he took her. It was a short few minutes though from undress to orgasm with him watching her, encouraging her with lovely dirty words.

Hailey lifted her hands to her breasts and fingered her nipples, rubbing her thumbs over the tips and then rolling and squeezing them.

"Fuck yes," Ty said huskily.

His voice and the sensations from her nipples shot straight to her pussy and she was hot and wet in a matter of seconds.

"Show me how you've imagined doing this with me here," he said, lifting his gaze to hers.

She had more than one fantasy actually. But she chose her favorite.

"Sit down," she told him, nodding to the chair behind him.

"Not the fancy leather one?" he asked, taking a seat.

"My fantasy involves you coming in here wanting something and me making you do something for *me* first," she told him. "You have to at least start off on that side of the desk."

He leaned forward again, arms on his thighs like he had before, his full attention on her. "Well, I definitely want something, Madam Mayor."

The way he was looking at her made goose bumps dance up and down her body, and she knew he took note.

Ty liked having power at all times. That was, at least in part, why he'd initiated this now. She'd been telling him that she wasn't going to do favors for him as mayor. That had reminded him that *she* had the power in that situation. So he had to remind them both that he had her in the palm of his hand.

He loved knowing he could affect her without even touching her. She knew that power, the control, was another thing that made him such a competitor. He took control in his races and made sure things went his way.

No wonder he didn't want to race anymore if he wasn't able to ensure the outcome.

Well, he definitely knew the outcome here.

She rounded her desk in only her heels and panties.

Ty sat back so she could move between him and her desk. She boosted herself up onto the edge right in front of him.

She was already feeling pretty worshipped. His gaze roamed over her hungrily, and she noticed the way he was gripping the armrests.

He should have forgotten about her a long time ago. He should have walked away. But he never did.

She returned to playing with her nipples, close enough now that he could touch her if he wanted to. She spread her knees and ran a hand over the front of her panties. The pale purple silk was already damp, and she knew he could see that as well.

"I love when you watch me," she said.

"I love watching."

She pulled her panties to one side, and he groaned. She smiled. That groan. That meant she was making him crazy, and she loved knowing she could do that to him so easily.

Of course, there wasn't a single other man in the world that she would do this in front of, so clearly he made her crazy as well.

She ran her finger over her clit and then dipped the tip inside. Ty's gaze on her was better than any touch of her own though. She circled and dipped a few more times until she couldn't wait.

"Come here," she said softly.

As if he'd been waiting for the word, Ty hit the floor on his knees. His hands gripped her ass and his tongue was on her before she could take a full deep breath.

He licked and sucked, holding her still for his mouth, and all she could do was hold her panties out of the way.

And try to remember to breathe.

She felt her orgasm coming and she relished how effortless it was for him to cause it.

Ty thrust two fingers deep as he sucked her clit hard and she went up and over the edge that easily.

"Lie back." His voice was rough, his jaw tight as he stood.

Hailey's shoulder blades had barely hit the cold wood when she felt him grab the front of her panties and yank.

The tiny strings over her hips gave way as if he'd torn a piece of paper. She squirmed on the desk. "Yes, Ty, please."

"Oh, Madam Mayor, you're about to agree to anything I ask for."

She heard his zipper and felt him step between her knees. He didn't even push his jeans to the floor. He put a big hand on each of her thighs and pushed her knees up, propping her heels on the edge of the desk.

"I think we should have a Ty Bennett Day here in Sapphire Falls," he said.

She grinned. "I don't know. That seems very…"

He thrust forward, sliding into her, filling her up.

She gasped.

"It seems very what?" he asked.

She'd forgotten what they were talking about. "Amazing."

He pulled out and thrust again. "I agree."

She tried to move to wrap her legs around his waist, but he held her in place with his hands on her thighs, spread open to him, in total control.

He thrust again and again in a steady rhythm that started a burn deep in her core. But it wasn't enough.

"More, Ty. Harder."

"I think there's going to need to be a statue too."

Oh, damn him. She knew he was kidding about the statue, but not about the begging he wanted.

"Please. *Harder*." She reached for her clit and circled it, pressing, feeling her climax building.

"So impatient," he chided, picking up the pace, his eyes on her fingers.

Hailey arched her neck and picked up her pace as well. "You know, if these nooners are going to be a regular thing now, you're going to have to learn to make this happen faster."

He paused and she lifted her head. "Hey—"

He reached for her, cupping the back of her neck and bringing her up off the desk. Her legs swung over the edge as he brought her mouth to his. The kiss was hungry, and all Hailey could do was cling to his shoulders and hang on as he pounded into her.

Her climax rose swiftly, washing over her, and Ty was only a few seconds behind, groaning loudly through his release.

Their bodies shook for several long seconds afterward, plastered against one another.

Finally, she collapsed back on the desk and Ty leaned over her, bracing his hands on the wood.

"Damn," he said appreciatively.

She smiled. "Agreed."

"And these nooners *are* going to be a regular thing now." He stepped back and readjusted his clothes.

She sat up. Ah, so that's what had gotten to him. He liked the idea they would keep doing this after all.

She was so weak.

But her body was still tingling and she was having a hard time being upset.

She slid off the desk and started to redress.

"There was actually something else I wanted to talk to you about," Ty said.

A knock sounded on her door. "Mayor Conner?" Tess called.

She zipped up her skirt and started rebuttoning her blouse. "Yes?"

"Mrs. Langston is here."

Hailey smiled at Ty. "That's fine. Mr. Bennett is on his way out."

"But I—" Ty started.

"It's Thelma," she said. Ty knew Thelma Langston, and knew she was one of the more demanding residents. "I can't make her wait. Call me later."

"This is probably not a conversation for the phone," he said.

Hailey suddenly wasn't sure she wanted to have this conversation. "Sorry. It will have to wait."

"Um, we have to talk about it before five, okay?"

What the hell? But there was something in his eyes that made her nervous for some reason.

"I'll try."

"It's *really* important."

"Okay." She started for the door, hoping he'd follow. "I'll call you if I have some time and we can get coffee or something."

A public place seemed like a good idea. She couldn't even pinpoint why. It was something about his tone. Or the way he wasn't meeting her eyes now.

They'd just had sex and he couldn't meet her eyes.

"I'm glad you stopped by," she said, her hand on the doorknob.

Ty had come to the door as well. He lifted a hand and ran it over her hair, smoothing it, then drew his thumb along her bottom lip. "You look like you've been fooling around," he said with a self-satisfied grin.

And now he was meeting her gaze again. Hailey ran her hand over her hair too and brushed the front of her skirt. "Too obvious?"

He shook his head, his grin softening into an affectionate smile. "You're beautiful."

She was also pantieless.

She wet her lips and said, "For the record, I think the training facility sounds like an amazing idea."

"You do?"

"But I'm still going to vote against it."

He frowned. "What?"

She nodded. "I'm not going to vote as mayor. I'm going to vote as your girlfriend."

His frown eased at that. Then deepened again. "What? Why would my girlfriend be *less* supportive than the mayor?"

She shook her head. "*More* supportive. I think the training center sounds great. But it will also make it easier for you to quit racing. You can't do that."

"Hailey." He was clearly exasperated. "I have a long way to go to get back to that level. If it's even possible."

"But what if it is? With this amazing training program you've developed? Think how great *that* would be for your marketability. You rehab, compete again, win...and *then* start the training center. That would be a huge endorsement for your program. Not to mention that *you* need to know that you can come back."

He was quiet for a few seconds. He sighed. "I don't think I could win even if I get back."

"Isn't the racing about more than winning?" she asked. "Really? Shouldn't it be? You didn't win in the beginning but you kept doing it. Because you loved it. Shouldn't that be the reason you do it, with the winning as icing on the cake?"

He studied her eyes. "You should get this. You like to win too."

111

She shrugged. "I do. But taking care of this town is about more than that. It's about being passionate about something to the point of having to *do* something with it. Like racing is for you."

"I never thought of it that way."

Hailey nodded, thinking about her words. It was true. Politics was about having and delivering a message, sharing ideas, focusing people on issues and bringing them together to make decisions that mattered to them and making lives better. Cheesy maybe, but it was true. For her anyway.

"But you're going to vote as my girlfriend, not mayor," he said, as if pondering it out loud.

She nodded again. It wasn't that the training center wouldn't be good for the town, but he could do that down the road. First, he had to know he could get back into race shape and then ride, run and swim because he loved it, not because of a trophy or medal.

"Wow," he said softly, once more running his thumb over her lower lip. "You'd better be careful or I might start to think you kind of like me."

Hailey rolled her eyes and pulled the door open, nudging him through it with a hand on his back. "I have another meeting. I'll call you later when I have a break."

His expression sobered at the mention of the *thing* he needed to talk to her about.

Dammit. What could it be?

"Before five," he reiterated as he left her office.

Thelma breezed into the room, saving Hailey from replying. Or thinking about it again.

CHAPTER FIVE

It was ten after five and Hailey hadn't had a chance to see Ty.

Okay, she *might* have had a ten-minute window where she could have called, but she couldn't shake the feeling that she didn't really want to talk about whatever this was.

She was halfway down the front steps of city hall when she noticed Mason Riley coming toward her.

"Hailey."

"Hi, Mason." He was out of breath, which was very unusual. Mason wasn't the type to rush anywhere or get overly excited. He was a genius scientist who preferred plants to people—other than his wife, Adrianne, and their two little boys—and he didn't get worked up about much besides soil, water and sunshine.

Mason had been a high school classmate of Hailey's and probably the one guy she should have dated but never did. As opposed to many that she had dated and probably shouldn't have.

"Adrianne would like you to come to the bakery," Mason said. "She sent me to extend the invitation."

Hailey was surprised. The bakery had closed ten minutes ago and Adrianne surely wanted to get home to make dinner and do mom stuff. "Really?"

"She and Phoebe need to talk to you."

"I saw that they both called," Hailey said, glancing at her phone. She hadn't a chance to call back and neither had left a message or texted, so she'd assumed whatever it was wasn't an emergency.

"Come on." Mason started in the direction of the bakery, across the town square from city hall.

"Mason, hang on," Hailey called, following. "What's going on? Is everyone all right?"

He glanced back but kept walking. "No one's hurt or

anything."

Okay, well, that was something. "What's with the vague answers?"

"Adrianne told me to come and get you but not to tell you what was going on."

Hailey frowned at that. "Why not?"

"Because I'm not very tactful a lot of the time," Mason said honestly.

He was right. "And whatever's going on needs to be handled with tact?" she asked.

"Yes."

"Why?"

"Because you're going to be upset."

They crossed the street that separated the square from the strip of shops they called Sapphire Hills.

It wasn't really much of a hill. Mason and Adrianne lived on the only even-close-to-a-hill hill in Sapphire Falls. But Mason hadn't wanted to sell his land for the shops and…well, that was another story.

"Mason, you can tell me. I promise not to be upset."

No wonder he'd been out of breath when he'd met her. He was practically race-walking to the shop.

"No. I really don't think that's a good idea," Mason replied.

"You're *that* bad at delivering bad news?" she asked. She ran three to five miles a day and she was still feeling a little winded from their walk.

"No, I'm that bad at dealing with people's reactions to bad news."

"Really might be because of the way you deliver it."

He stopped in front of the shop and pulled the door open for her. And gave her a big grin. "You might be on to something there."

And he'd completely gotten out of delivering said bad news, she noted as she stepped through the door into Adrianne's bakery.

She forgot everything about Mason and their walk the moment she looked around.

The place was decorated in sapphire-blue and candy-apple red. There were balloons, streamers, tablecloths, more streamers, and blue- and red-frosted cupcakes. Everywhere.

"What in the..." she started.

"Welcome to your campaign headquarters," Phoebe said, coming forward with a big smile.

A big fake smile.

Which was so uncommon that Hailey thought maybe Phoebe was ill. She never had to fake a smile. Bubbly and energetic were Phoebe's hallmark character traits. Along with scheming. She always had a plan cooking.

"My campaign headquarters?" Hailey asked. "What are you talking about?"

The elections for mayor were coming up in two weeks. The term for mayor and the way elections were run were unique to Sapphire Falls. As were many things. The term for mayor was three years and elections were held on the Friday before Labor Day, per the town charter from 1895.

The election ordinance also stipulated that anyone who had a Sapphire Falls address could run and there were no term limits. The town turned out all at once. Each citizen wrote their selection on a slip of paper and dropped it into a big wooden box. The box was also from 1895 and sat in a special case in the city hall until it was needed for that one day every three years. There was a special committee of six who counted the votes. They were selected by the oldest Sapphire Falls citizen—Robert Zimmerman had held that title for the past ten years—from a bin that held the names of every person in town over the age of eighteen. Being selected for the election committee was considered an honor and everyone took the job very seriously. The committee counted the votes three times over the weekend and then wrote the result on a huge chalkboard on an easel in front of city hall on Monday morning. The new mayor took office on Tuesday.

It was all a very well-respected and beloved tradition in town and no one had ever thought to challenge it.

"You haven't heard?" Phoebe asked.

"She looks way too calm to have heard," Adrianne commented.

Phoebe nodded. "True."

"*What* is going on?" Hailey asked.

"You have some competition," Adrianne said.

"Competition?" Hailey repeated. Her eyes widened as that sank in. "For *mayor*?"

Adrianne nodded, watching her carefully. "He announced his candidacy at the Come Again at five o'clock. We thought maybe you knew."

"I don't. This is the first I've heard..."

But then five o'clock sank in as well. She narrowed her eyes. Ty had insisted they needed to talk *before* five. That couldn't be a coincidence.

"Is it Ty?" she asked. She knew her tone sounded ominous. She was definitely feeling ominous.

Adrianne and Phoebe both nodded.

"And he already claimed blue and white as his campaign colors," Phoebe said, as if *that* was his greatest offense. "Which is crap, since you've been mayor all this time. But then we decided that blue and red was snappier and much more *you*."

Well, thank goodness, her campaign *colors* would be snappy. Without that, what did she have?

Hailey tamped down the wave of panic that threatened at the obvious answer—*nothing*. She had nothing for this campaign. Except snappy colors, apparently. And cupcakes.

She focused, instead, on her anger. At Ty.

The bastard.

Yes, he'd tried to tell her before she found out this way,

but did that really make anything better? He was running against her for mayor. Because she wouldn't approve the training center? Because he didn't like that her job was more important than he was? That was actually quite possible. No one had an ego bigger than Ty's.

Hailey tossed her hair over her shoulder. "If I kill him, there won't be any opposition though, will there?"

Phoebe came forward. "As your campaign manager—"

"Campaign manager?" Hailey asked.

"Well, with Adrianne. But Joe spends a lot of time in D.C.," Phoebe said of her husband. "He knows how politics work."

"*I* will be her campaign manager."

They all swung to the front door of the shop.

Lauren Bennett had just walked in.

"*You* want to be my campaign manager?" Hailey asked the other woman.

Lauren had an I'm-in-charge vibe about her that rivaled Hailey's. It had been weakened over the past couple of years since she'd married Travis Bennett, gotten settled on the farm and had a baby girl. Still, if anyone in Sapphire Falls could keep up with Hailey, it would be Lauren.

"I've been hanging out in Washington all of my adult life," Lauren said. She was the co-founder and owner of Innovative Agricultural Solutions with Mason, a world-renowned agricultural engineering company that had relocated to Sapphire Falls when Mason fell in love with Adrianne. Lauren was a businesswoman, a political lobbyist, a scientist and a genius.

"But Joe—" Phoebe started.

"I'm Joe's *boss*," Lauren reminded her. "And," she said to Hailey, "you're running against a man. No one knows how to get into a man's head better than me."

"Joe *is* a man," Phoebe protested.

But everyone knew that Phoebe just wanted to be in the thick of things. She loved being involved in whatever new drama was going on. As long as Hailey and Lauren made her part of the inner circle, she wouldn't really care who was in charge.

"A straight man," Lauren acknowledged. "Which means Joe doesn't have my experience getting men to do whatever I want them to."

"Well, when my hands are wrapped around Ty's neck and I'm squeezing as hard as I can, I'm guessing I can get him to do whatever I want," Hailey said. "If that doesn't work, there's the machete-to-the-balls thing."

"Oh, no," Lauren said. "What you need to do is head over to the Come Again, buy a round for the whole place, and toast Ty and his campaign."

Hailey frowned. "Pretend I'm *happy*?"

"And totally confident that it doesn't matter who's running against you," Lauren said with a nod. "Show them that you don't care, that you're not a bit intimidated."

"I'm *not* intimidated," Hailey said firmly. A total lie. "I'm pissed."

And shocked. And hurt. And confused. But definitely pissed too.

"But you can't show that," Lauren said. "He's probably trying to get you to react like a pissed-off, emotional woman. He's trying to show that you can't take a challenge."

Hailey sighed. He wasn't doing that. Ty wouldn't try to discredit her.

But what *was* he doing?

This was bizarre.

"He's hogging the spotlight," Hailey said. She often accused him of that when he was in Sapphire Falls. It was part of their cover-up. He'd flirt, because he couldn't help it and he didn't like hiding their relationship, so she'd turn it into him simply wanting attention.

It was easy enough to believe. The guy loved being in the public eye and everyone knew it.

"Well, it's working," Lauren said. "Not only are people surprised he's running, they can't wait to see your reaction, and they can't wait to see the two of you together."

It was like in the old days on the playground when someone would throw out a challenge and the crowd would start chanting, "Fight, fight, fight."

Fuck, fuck, fuck.

Hailey didn't want to take anyone on, least of all Ty.

"Hey, wait a second," Phoebe said, stepping in front of Lauren. "You're a Bennett. You're from the enemy camp. This is your brother-in-law."

Lauren nodded. "We're going to be a divided household."

"What do you mean?" Hailey asked.

"Ty's got a team around him," Lauren said. "I was over there for his big announcement. He's got TJ and Hope, Tucker and Delaney, and his mom and dad all campaigning for him."

Hailey groaned. Only the most beloved family in town. There was no way she could compete with that. They were not only loved, the Bennetts were fourth-generation pillars of the community.

"Yeah, Hope and Delaney are too new to not side with their guys, I guess," Lauren said. "But we were friends before Travis and I got together," she told Hailey with a smile. "And girl power and all that. Plus," she added. "You're a great mayor. Ty is an Olympic athlete with an addiction to being in the tabloids. You've got this."

Hailey felt a warmth spread through her and was startled by the intensity of it—and the source.

Lauren was a lot like her, which meant she wasn't often the warm, fuzzy type.

Maybe the motherhood thing could be blamed here too. But Hailey would take the encouragement wherever she could get it.

"Thanks, Lauren. You're hired." She looked around the

bakery. "I can only pay you in cupcakes though."

Lauren laughed. "Well, these are Scott's Sweets cupcakes, so they're like gold."

"Aw, thanks," Adrianne said with a pleased smile.

"And I can't really pay *you* for all these cupcakes either," Hailey told her.

Adrianne waved her hand. "On the house, Madam Mayor. I also think you're great at your job and completely deserve to win this election. As your past assistant, I can attest to how seriously you take the job and how much you love this town. These cupcakes are part of my contribution."

Hailey felt the distinct sting of tears behind her eyes and she started blinking rapidly.

"Okay, so we head to the Come Again," she said.

"And after you toast Ty, you invite everyone over *here* for *your* party," Lauren said. "We'll use it as a way to illustrate the fact that Ty might be a good time, but no one wants a frat boy in charge of their town. They want the serious woman."

Hailey knew Sapphire Falls. A lot of people in town would be fine with a frat boy who could throw a good party. "I don't know. Beer up against cupcakes?" she asked.

"I thought of that," Adrianne said. "Which is why we have orange-ale cupcakes, whiskey-chocolate cupcakes and tequila-lime cupcakes. Along with the usual chocolate and vanilla."

Hailey's eyes widened as Adrianne pointed out the specialty cupcakes she'd made.

Lauren was clearly impressed. "Orange-ale?"

Adrianne nodded. "Used a wheat ale beer in that one."

"Wow." Lauren nodded. "This is a really good start. In fact," she said slowly, her tone indicating she was brainstorming as she talked. "We can use that. Ty's an average guy. They shouldn't get star struck. He's just buying them a beer. Like anyone else in town could. But *Hailey*," she said, her voice growing excited. "She's taking it to the next level. Like she will in office. Ty can do the basics. But Hailey is creative, willing to think outside the box, go that extra step to making everything better."

Hailey kind of liked that. "But Adrianne was the one who thought up the cupcakes," she pointed out.

"We're a team," Lauren assured her. "That means her ideas are your ideas. This is a great plan."

Hailey appreciated Lauren's confidence.

Hailey felt her first true smile bloom. "Okay, let's go to the Come Again. Just let me change into my campaign color first."

જ્જ

Hailey walked into the Come Again just after six.

An hour past when he'd expected her to come storming through the doors.

But she wasn't storming. She was walking confidently. In sexy four-inch red heels that matched the red skirt that molded to her hips, thighs and ass, and a sapphire-blue blouse that hugged her high breasts and brought out the blue in her eyes. Her hair was piled up on her head in a twist.

She looked like sex on a stick.

Patriotic sex on a stick.

She also wore a smile.

He hadn't been expecting that.

Right behind her were Phoebe, Adrianne, Lauren, Joe and Mason.

That, he *had* been expecting.

He wanted to grin at the show of support, including the way they flanked her like bodyguards. But he couldn't give away that he was *too* happy to see her rising to this challenge.

He also couldn't act *too* nervous about the fact that she was here without having talked to him about all of this prior to five o'clock, as he'd asked. He'd really intended to warn her, tell her his plan, make sure she understood that this was actually a grand romantic gesture.

He completely believed that she was capable of anything. But running unopposed twice hadn't let her feel the full glory of winning, of being chosen. Hell, that was even better than the winning he did—no one picked him, no one weighed him against someone else and said, "You're the best. We want you." He just had to be stronger and faster than the others. When he crossed the finish line, there was no question where he stood. But Hailey was being *chosen*. She deserved that. She needed that.

He was sure it didn't seem that way from where she was standing at the moment though.

"Good evening, everyone," she greeted as a hush fell over the room. She focused on him.

He was seated across the room from her, lounging at one of the tables with his brothers.

The place was packed and he'd had to cut off the open bar about twenty minutes ago. But the crowd was happy, jovial even, and had been growing since five when he'd made his big announcement and news had gotten around town.

"I wanted to stop by and congratulate Tyler on this big decision," Hailey said to the room.

Ty sat up straighter in his chair, charming smile firmly in place as everyone looked at him. "Why thank you, Madam Mayor."

He saw the faint blush in her cheeks and grinned wider.

Hailey looked around the room and nodded. "And Ty really does bring a sense of fun wherever he goes. That's important. It's important to kick back once in a while, appreciate the good life we have here, enjoy the people who make us smile."

Ty waited for the *but* that he could tell was coming.

"And like all of you, I'm happy whenever someone feels like their roots are here, and that Sapphire Falls is the home they come back to when life changes and they have a new perspective on what's important. I'm sure Ty has shared with you what has prompted his move back to Sapphire Falls."

Ty sat up even straighter at that. He hadn't, actually, shared about his accident or Bryan's situation. Bryan was from Sapphire Falls too, and Ty knew every one of Bryan's friends and family members, but it was his story to share when he was ready.

Ty coughed and got to his feet. "Actually, Mayor Conner, I announced my candidacy and, um, bought a round or two. We haven't gotten past the celebration into the nitty-gritty yet."

Hell, it wasn't as if he was actually trying to make this a serious competition. He was fine with never getting into the nitty gritty.

"Oh, well, don't be shy," Hailey said. "After all, you were living in Denver up until a few days ago. And for the past *eleven years*. We know that you haven't contemplated and planned this for long, but sometimes big life changes can prompt rash decisions. I'm sure we would *all* love to hear why you're suddenly running for mayor."

Ty bit back a smile. She was good. She was pointing out reasons why his running for mayor was a complete joke while sounding friendly and almost concerned. She was also putting him on the spot. If he actually wanted to win this thing, he'd be feeling like an idiot right about now.

When she looked at him, he clearly read the *what the fuck?* in her eyes.

She thought he was messing with her. He knew a few people in the bar earlier had asked how much he'd had to drink. Another had asked if he'd been dared.

He was running. He just didn't want to win. And she'd

understand as soon as they had two minutes alone together. If she'd met him before five, she'd know all of it already and wouldn't be looking at him like he'd spit in her root beer float—confused, ticked off, disgusted and even a little hurt.

Well, he wasn't going to tell everyone about Bryan like this. He'd have to go with the truth about why he was running even before he told Hailey.

Ty got to his feet and tucked his hands into his front pockets. "I'm in love," he said.

There was a collective gasp from the audience, but Ty was only looking at Hailey. She looked torn between wanting to puke and punch him.

"I came back to be with her," he said, turning to the audience and hoping to pull their attention away from Hailey's face, where it was easy to see that she was reacting to his announcement strangely for a woman who supposedly disliked him.

"Who is it?" someone called out.

"A high school sweetheart?" someone else asked.

"He dated Maddie Temple for a while," someone suggested in the back.

"You're running for mayor to impress her?" someone closer asked.

Wanting to take the speculation off of Maddie, Ty said, "I want her to see I'm serious about all of the things we've talked about. About my life and how I feel about her and how I see the future."

He could feel Hailey's tension even across the few feet that separated them.

"Being in love with someone is a strange motivation for running for office," Hailey said coolly, crossing her arms.

Yep, especially when he was running *against* the woman he was in love with.

"Well." He turned to her with a big grin. He happened to think it was perfect. "No one appreciates where they're from as much as someone who's been away and longed to come back."

"And how does that qualify you to govern the town?" she asked. "Loving it and knowing how to take care of it are not the same thing."

He nodded. "That's true." She was right. Everyone in the room at the moment loved Sapphire Falls. But no one in the room could lead them like Hailey did.

That's what *she* needed to understand.

But he also couldn't nod and agree with her and still expect to run a decent race. He intended to run maybe even a slightly better-than-decent race. Just not a *winning* race. "But I have some big ideas for increasing revenue here. And I'm a nationally known name and face. When the media finds out I'm running for mayor of my small hometown where I got my start because I'm in love and wanting to settle down, they'll be all over it. Sapphire Falls will get some great attention."

"Attention because the notorious troublemaking playboy who is really good at riding bikes and swimming decided to run for mayor?" Hailey asked. "How does that help anyone but *you*, Ty?"

And this was what he'd known would happen if she *didn't* know about his plan ahead of time. She'd get bitchy and snarky toward him in public. It was also why so many people were looking at this mayoral race as a great source of entertainment over the next couple of weeks.

But that wouldn't help her in *her* race at all.

She really should have talked to him before five like he'd asked.

"Well, I do know a little something about *races*," Ty quipped. "Against *other people*," he added. Okay, that was a dickhead thing to say, but if he was an ass, then they would all forgive her for being snotty in return. They would both look bad, but at least they'd be even.

Hailey drew herself up tall. "I would love to know your

thoughts on the state-proposed highway expansion that would include the section that runs by Sapphire Falls," she said.

He blinked at her. "You would?"

"If you win, I'll be your constituent. I would really like to know what the man leading my hometown thinks about the major issues."

Fuck, there were major issues? That was one of the things people loved about living here—there were no major issues.

He studied her face.

Or maybe it felt like there were no major issues because Hailey took care of them before anyone had to be bothered or upset by them.

"Expanding that section of the highway sounds great," he said. He didn't know what the expansion actually included, but he did know that if you got stuck behind a tractor or a combine on that part of the highway, there was no getting around it for miles.

"They'll take out the sidewalk all the kids use to get down to the park and ball fields," someone said.

Oh. Okay, that was a problem. The main city park where the swimming pool, ball fields and picnic and play areas were located was across the highway and two blocks east of the town square.

"They'll also have to get rid of at least six camping sites at the park," he heard someone call out.

The camp sites were for tents or RVs and brought revenue into the park's budget and people into town for gas, food and amenities from Memorial Day to Labor Day. Losing six spots was a lot.

"And they'll knock out the town's entrance. That arch is historic," someone else mentioned.

There were several places people could come into town, of course, but the main entrance was at the southwest corner of the square and was marked by a wrought-iron arch that curved over the street and read *Sapphire Falls, 1892*.

It was, indeed, historic. And the people in Sapphire Falls were very sentimental about it.

"We'll have to reconfigure and rebuild some things," Ty said, trying to sound confident.

There was some general grumbling and Hailey looked pleased with his answer. Which made him positive he'd answered incorrectly.

"And do you think the funds for the reconfiguring and rebuilding should come out of the park's budget or the city-maintenance budget or the discretionary fund?" Hailey asked.

She was setting him up. It was completely obvious. But she was showing the town her opponent's weakness. Namely that he didn't have a clue about town government.

But he was a smart guy. He could figure this out. Maybe.

The park's budget surely had been set prior to all of this and probably included things like maintaining the pool and so on. Shutting down the pool was not a good option. Probably. The city-maintenance budget might work, but again, like in any budget, if you used money for something new, it took money away from something you'd planned for. Discretionary funds, however, were for things like this. He was pretty sure.

"The discretionary fund," he finally said. "After careful review and consultation of course."

Hailey gave him a small smile. But said nothing.

She didn't need to.

The room immediately erupted into conversation. Loud, argumentative conversation.

"That fund is supposed to provide grants for home owners to do energy-efficient improvements!"

"I thought the city was considering a memorial to our veterans!"

"The school needs supplies. Our teachers shouldn't be paying out of pocket for crayons!"

Hailey looked at Ty with a smug smile. "Probably not the discretionary fund," she said.

Ty ran a hand through his hair and observed the roomful of people.

So maybe his quiet, happy hometown wasn't always quiet and happy.

"Clearly I have some things to learn," he finally said over the din. "I would love to hear how our current mayor plans to fund the reconstruction after the highway expansion."

Hailey dropped her arms to her side and faced the room with confidence. "The best way to deal with the reconstruction costs is to avoid them. I'm fighting the highway expansion."

There were murmurings of conversation but also lots of head-nodding.

"The highway past Sapphire Falls is not heavily trafficked. The expansion conversation started with truckers complaining about the narrow lanes and slow-moving farm equipment."

Just as he'd thought—tractors caused slowdowns.

"I've come up with a counter proposal that will suggest widening the existing lanes, without adding any additional full lanes. We *will* lose the sidewalk," she said to the woman who had brought up the issue. "But we will raise the funds to put in a new one. In fact, we'll put in a wider, smoother one that will allow for bike and foot traffic at the same time. I'm also going to suggest the addition of a passing lane on the area two miles outside of town to allow trucks to get around any slow-moving traffic safely. That will not affect anything here in the city limits. However, part of my argument is that the speed limit past Sapphire Falls is supposed to be forty-five miles per hour and that the semi-truck traffic often exceeds that. The slowing down behind farm equipment through Sapphire Falls is actually a benefit to the town in that regard."

Ty knew he was staring but…damn.

He'd never seen her in mayor mode. He'd seen her dressed up and attending events as the mayor, of course. But he'd never actually witnessed her addressing the town about an issue as their mayor.

It was strangely hot.

"If anyone has any further questions or concerns, I'd be happy to answer them," she said. She started for the door and the crowd parted as if it was choreographed. "Over at my new campaign headquarters at Scott's Sweets. There's food and drink for everyone."

"Food and drink" were the three magic words to get the crowd moving out the door.

The words "Scott's Sweets" didn't hurt either.

He had regular old beer. Adrianne had the world's best cupcakes.

Yeah, he was probably heading over there too.

Of course, that had more to do with the star of the party. He really needed to talk to Hailey.

She solved that for him a minute later.

Ty stepped out the door at the back of the crowd and felt someone grab his arm. Hard.

He caught a whiff of her body spray as she pulled him around the corner of the building, out of view of the crowd.

"What the *fuck*, Ty?" were her first words to him.

"That was *amazing*," he told her with a huge grin.

She blinked at him, obviously taken back by his reaction. "What are you talking about?"

"The way you were all mayorly in there," he said. "Impressive. And hot." He moved in closer and took her hips in his hands.

She shoved him back. "Are you insane?"

"What? You know I love that powerful, confident, kick-ass side of you. I've never seen you address the town about serious issues. All I could think was *I'm fucking her*."

Hailey stared at him for a good ten seconds without saying anything. Then she nodded. "Right. You love me being powerful, because it makes you feel even *more* powerful when you think about how we behave in the bedroom."

He lifted a shoulder. "Well, yeah." Then he saw the look on her face and added, "Kind of."

She scowled.

"Um, you need to get to your party. Don't you think they'll be expecting you?" he asked. He was pissing her off and he wasn't even meaning to. He needed to regroup. He knew on the outside this looked bad. Like he was running against her and wanting to steal her crown. But Hailey knew him. She knew that he didn't really want to be mayor. Didn't she?

"Lauren's got it for a while," she said. "I have at least five more minutes."

"Five minutes will be enough time for you to yell at me?" he asked with a smile.

"Don't smile at me." She scowled again. "And, no, that's not nearly enough time. But I'm not going to be yelling. *You're* going to be talking," she said. "What the hell are you doing?"

"Making you do exactly what you did in there."

"Lose my cool in front of everyone? Thanks."

"Show off that you're the best person for this job."

She crossed her arms. "I was the *only* person for this job, until you got this wild hair to run. *What* is going on?"

"Making sure you're number one."

"Number one?"

"Mayor. That you are the top dog, the top pick, the woman of the hour, the—"

"Oh my God, stop." She put up a hand to stop his rambling and then used it to rub the center of her forehead. "You're making sure I'm elected mayor?"

"Yes."

"By running *against* me?"

"But not just elected. Elected against a strong opponent." He stepped forward and ran his hands up and down her arms. "You've been elected twice running unopposed. That doesn't feel as good as winning a *real* election. I want you to know that you're the best, and that the town knows that and trusts it, that they'll elect you no matter what."

"You *are* insane," she said.

"No." He grinned. "*Brilliant*. I'm making a grand romantic gesture *and* proving to you that you are absolutely capable of winning this election. I believe in you. Enough to run against you and show you that you are loved and trusted by this town."

Hailey pressed her lips together and took a deep breath. "Okay, you're not insane. You're stupid."

"Hey." He frowned.

"Or if not stupid, so wrapped up in yourself that you don't really see anything except the way you want to see it."

"What are you talking about?"

He hadn't expected her to be excited about running against him. But he'd expected her to see the gesture for what it was—and be touched by it.

"I can't win against you," she said, as if it should have been obvious.

"Of course you can. They *like* me, Hailey, but what do I know about running a town? They all realize that. We'll have some fun with the campaign, give you a stage for really showing them what you know and what you already do for this town, and you'll walk away with it."

"I don't want to really show them anything, Ty. I like it how it's been. I *like* running unopposed!"

He frowned. "But if there's no opponent, does it really feel as good winning?" He didn't understand that.

"*Yes*," she said adamantly. "If there's no opponent there's no debate, no Q&A, no get-to-know-your-candidates crap. If there's no opponent, no one is trying to find my flaws or figure out any dirt on me."

"This is Sapphire Falls," Ty argued. "They wouldn't try to dig up dirt. And they already know you." But he supposed that debates and Q&A probably were a good idea when putting people up against one another.

"They know what I want them to know about me," Hailey countered.

"And that's not the same thing?"

That made her pause and swallow before saying softly, "No."

He didn't really know what that meant. Sapphire Falls saw the tough, cool and confident side of her. His mother had said she'd suspected a softer side, but Hailey didn't show that side to everyone. That didn't mean the side she *did* show wasn't real. "Then we'll do the Q&A and show them how great you are," he said. "We'll spend time together and the contrast between us for the position will be obvious."

"It's all a game to you," she exclaimed. "This back and forth with us, this constant tug-of-war we have going on. And now you're making the election just another of our bickery fights. You think it's fun, that it's *foreplay*. But it *matters* to me, Ty. I haven't been insisting on keeping our relationship a secret because it makes for great sex. I've been doing it because I don't *want* them to see that side of me."

"Why not?" He stepped closer. "Show them your softer side. Show them that you can relax and laugh and can be romantic and in love. Show them—"

"They don't want to see that side," she said stubbornly. "They want the take-charge, coolheaded woman they elected."

"Of course, but if you spend time with me and we get

up in front of them, like we did in there," he said, gesturing at the Come Again, "they'll see that you're the best one for this town."

He thought back to what his mother had said Sunday morning about how nice it had been to see Hailey rumpled and rattled. Maybe more people needed to see that.

"And then," he said, thinking out loud, "they'll see our chemistry and see you softening and not only will that show them your nice side, but then we can naturally transition into a more public relationship. They'll all think we got together during the campaign and fell in love and—"

"I can't spend *more* time with you publicly, Ty," she said. "That will ruin everything."

He frowned. "How so?"

"Because I don't really have a tough, kick-ass side!" she said, clearly exasperated. "Because that's all a mirage. And when I'm with you, I get soft and lose my edge and I'll never be able to keep up with who they think I am. Who they *want* me to be as mayor."

"I make you soft?" he asked, feeling something shift in his chest. It was a warmth and tenderness he wasn't used to feeling. Mixed with worry.

"You make me *me*." She stopped, as if stunned she'd admitted that, and pressed her lips together.

Ty studied her face. "What does that mean?"

"They elected the kick-ass, bitchy Ice Queen. Twice. They don't want *me*. They don't want the woman who takes two hours to get ready in the morning or who would *much* rather be reading Cassandra Clare novels than boring city reports. They don't want the woman who wants to cuddle in bed all day and hold hands and write love notes with her boyfriend!"

"But the kick-ass, bitchy Ice Queen *is* you too," he said. Then he held up a hand quickly. "In a good way. That's what I love about you—you're a fighter, you're in charge, you're amazing." Not that he didn't love her confession about wanting to hold hands, cuddle and write love notes. But that was a conversation for another time.

She shook her head. "I'm not, Ty. It's all an act. I started running for things because it was the way to get my dad to spend time with me and pay attention to me. But, as my stepmom constantly pointed out, I'm not really smart or creative enough or organized enough to be in charge of anything, certainly not to be mayor. So I put on this persona. This in-charge, smart, creative, organized persona. And as long as no one gets close, they don't know it's all fake."

And the worry intensified, though he couldn't fully explain why.

Hailey wasn't soft. Not really. He loved *making* her soft and needy and submissive to him. But in general, she was tough. *He* made her soft. Not...the world. Or her lack of confidence. Or her stepmother. Or anything else.

At least, that's what he liked to believe. *He* was the only one with that power. *He* knew that side of her that no one else got to see because he was special, because she'd let him close. And he used it for her good. Not to hurt her like her stepmom and dad had, but to help her relax, let go, to take a break from her demanding job.

"Hail—"

"Let me finish," she said.

Ty shut his mouth and motioned for her to go on. Even as he felt his gut knotting and his hands itching to grab her and shake her and insist that she was everything he'd always believed she was.

But maybe he needed to hear the rest of this.

"I'm good at two things, Ty." She held up two fingers. "Bossing people around and looking good. I figured out early on that what people really want is someone who will tell them what to do with confidence. That's all a leader really needs—confidence. If you act like your idea is the best one ever, people will believe you because *they* don't have the confidence. People want to be led. All I've had to do is be the one willing to stand at the front of the pack."

"You think that people like to be led around like dogs on leashes?" he asked with a scowl.

"No. But I do believe that me being bitchy and in control makes them feel secure. I won't take crap from them, but I also won't take crap from the people working for the city or companies coming into town or the state when it comes to things like the highway expansion or allocating funds and resources."

Ty opened his mouth, but she wasn't done.

"People want to live in a quiet, friendly, clean, safe town," she went on. "They want to raise their kids and earn enough money to cover what they need and be taken care of when they're sick or when bad things happen. But they don't want to worry about the budget or legal aspects of keeping things quiet and friendly and clean and safe and they don't want to have to deal with the issues when things *aren't* quiet and friendly and clean and safe. They want someone else to do it for them. And I've convinced them that I'm the one. I don't want to mess that up."

"And you live in constant fear that they're going to find out that you supposedly don't know what you're doing," Ty said. And he fell a little more in love with her even as she was telling him a bunch of stuff he did not want to hear.

She hugged herself, looking sad.

He hated that. Even if they were arguing, he wanted her adamant and pissed off rather than sad and unsure.

"People like it when someone takes the hard decisions on for them," she said. "And they like it when someone tells them everything will be okay, and they like it when they can relax and let go of the worry and trust that someone has their best interests at heart. They don't really want me to be friendly and approachable." She swallowed. "Like how I feel with you."

135

Those words rocked through him and he had to work to stay where he was and let her go on.

"I love the freedom that comes from trusting you and letting you be in charge of making things good for me." She took a deep breath. "That's what I try to do for Sapphire Falls. I want them to relax and know that I'll take care of them and make life good here."

"And you do that," he finally said gruffly. "You've taken care of the town for a long time."

"I have. I love this town. Being mayor is the only thing I've done that I'm truly proud of. But I've gotten everything in my life because I'm pretty and/or because I'm bitchy and no one wants to cross me. If I put the right people in the right positions around me, things get done and life is good and no one cares that I'm not friendly or warm. As long as things are good for them personally, people don't necessarily have to like their leaders." She shrugged. "It's worked all my life."

He didn't say anything. He didn't know *what* to say.

"I told you this because I trust you," she said quietly, her eyes begging him to understand. "I'm not good at anything but making people *believe* I'm good at things. I can't let everyone find out that I'm basically the Wizard of Oz behind my curtain. They're happy things are good here, so I don't feel guilty. But if they get too close, they'll see the emeralds in this Emerald City are just rocks painted green."

Another long moment stretched in complete silence.

Then Ty said, "Sapphires. Our city is made up of sapphires."

She shrugged. "Okay, the rocks are painted blue." She took a deep breath. "Being mayor is all I have, all that's important to me, and now you're going to take it all way," she said. "It's hard keeping the façade going. Up against someone else… I don't know if I can."

He gritted his teeth at the all-that's-important-to-me bit.

Then he gritted his teeth against her not knowing if she could keep fooling everyone.

Ty ran a hand through his hair. "So don't keep it up. It's not a façade anyway. I mean, maybe you don't... Shit." He sighed. "I don't know what I mean."

He stood looking at her, realizing that maybe, just maybe, he'd fucked this up.

"It is a façade, Ty," she said quietly. "I'm bitchy. But I'm not kick-ass."

He took in the long silky hair that he knew curled into gorgeous waves if she let it air dry. He catalogued the straight, fitted skirt that showed off legs he'd had propped on his lap under a warm, fuzzy blanket in front of the fireplace a dozen times. He noted the heels that gave her three extra inches and made her arches scream—and he knew the spot to dig his thumb to make her moan. He studied the flawless makeup that seemed like a mask over the face that he'd seen relaxed in sleep and lit up with amusement and open with passion and vulnerability.

And he realized that he didn't get to see the straight hair, makeup, skirts and heels in Denver.

He'd also never seen her barefoot or with nothing but lip gloss on, her hair pulled up into a messy bun—or her vulnerable—inside these city limits.

But maybe that wasn't about him. Maybe it wasn't that he'd magically chipped through the ice. Maybe...she really wasn't kick-ass.

Instantly, he rejected that idea. She was. She just didn't know it.

"So fight me," he finally said.

She frowned. "What?"

"Fight me for mayor," he said with more conviction as the realization of what he needed to do sank in. "You love this so much, you want it so bad, run a campaign that will beat me. Don't fool anyone. Don't put on a show. Be yourself and win this damned thing."

"Oh, sure, it's that simple."

Clearly, Hailey wanted to be mayor. Clearly, she was the best one to *be* the mayor. But she was also already convinced that she'd be number two. Again.

Well, the town needed to see her fight. They needed to see her passion.

And Hailey needed to fight.

She had to know that when it came to something important, she could, and would, fight for it. For real. Not intimidate people or fool people into it. She had to be herself. And win.

"If you want it, come and get it," he said.

For a second, he thought she might cry. Or laugh. Or slap him.

But after several long seconds, he finally saw what he'd been waiting for—she lifted her chin and looked him in the eye. "You want to fight with me, Ty Bennett? You got it."

He wanted to blow out a long, relieved breath, but instead, he nodded and said, "I'm not going to go easy on you."

Now he realized he couldn't. He'd been intending to joke his way through the campaign. He'd planned to make it one big party. But he did love Hailey and he knew she was a fighter.

He just had to prove it to her.

"Oh, you better bring it," she told him.

She was faking her bravado right now. He could tell. But at least she was saying it. Feeling it would come later.

He knew about competition. He knew that having a worthy opponent made him work harder. He liked racing the best guys in the world because it made *him* give more, try harder, push.

So he'd make her work for it. She needed that. And the town deserved it. They deserved to know how damned much their mayor loved them. Had always loved them.

All at once, this had come to be about a lot more than

making sure Hailey felt important and respected and like number one for a change. Now it was about making sure Hailey knew that she actually *was* the woman he'd been in love with all these years.

"I'm going to bring it. But, babe," he said, stepping forward and putting his hands on her upper arms again. "I do love making you *soft*."

She gave him a smile, then shrugged out of his hold and stepped back. "Glad you enjoyed it."

He sighed and dropped his hands. "Because it's over until the election is over, right?"

"You got it."

Yeah. Another thing he hadn't totally thought through.

She turned on her heel and started for the bakery and her campaign kick-off party. Ty fell into step beside her.

"I find it funny," she said conversationally when they were about halfway there. "That you really thought you were going to run against me and keep getting laid."

"Well, turns out I might be a little stupid after all," he said.

She didn't reply to that.

She didn't really need to.

CHAPTER SIX

Ty had been edgy the rest of the night after Hailey's party at the bakery.

He'd gone over for a while, in the spirit of friendly competition. But his mood had definitely been stifled compared to how he'd felt and acted at the Come Again.

If anyone noticed, they'd probably chalked it up to him being embarrassed about how Hailey had put him in his place.

Instead, he had been dealing with the reality that he was kind of a dumbass and that he was in love with a woman who wasn't really who he'd thought she was.

Or at least she didn't think she was.

Or something.

Ty tried to smile and make small talk with his family around his mother's dining room table. They were having a big family lunch since TJ and his new girlfriend, Hope, had just gotten back from a trip to Arizona to retrieve some of Hope's belongings for her move to Sapphire Falls.

Oh, and to celebrate Ty running for mayor.

Yeah, yippee.

Last night, the idea of taking Hailey on in the campaign and election had seemed like the right thing to do. Initially, he'd wanted to showcase what a great leader she was and give her some competition so when she won, she would feel like the gold medalist of Sapphire Falls.

Then, it had become a mission to help her see that she really was the tough, sharp fighter that he'd been crazy about since tenth grade.

And now, sitting at his mother's table for lunch, sleep deprived and confused and worried about Hailey and worried that he was truly fucking everything up for her and for their relationship, he didn't really know what he was doing.

That bugged the shit out of him.

He always knew what he was doing. He always had a plan, a goal, something he was working on and toward.

What was he working toward here?

Throwing an election. To win over a girl. Who would have won for sure if he'd just stayed out of it. And who he'd thought he already had.

Now he wasn't sure he had anything. Throwing a race, of any kind, went against everything he knew. The girl wasn't a fan of his training program idea. He didn't have a solid knee, which meant everything he'd done since the past Olympics, where he'd come in *second*, didn't matter. The girl was mad at him. And he was second place to her job and this election.

He really fucking hated coming in second.

Ty took a long drink of the iced tea his mother had refilled and told himself again that he was doing the right thing running against her. Hailey needed to see what she was made of.

But maybe *he* needed to see what she was made of too.

And he felt like a giant jackass thinking that.

He either loved her or he didn't, right? That's how it worked. You loved a person, no matter their flaws or their insecurities.

But surely he got some slack for having reservations considering he hadn't even known she had insecurities.

Fuck.

He looked across the Sunday dinner table at TJ leaning in to whisper in Hope's ear and then glanced over to see Tucker sharing a grin with his fiancé, Delaney, and Ty knew that, no, the truth was he was a jackass.

It was incredibly shallow of him, but he'd had no idea that Hailey had all of…*that*…hiding underneath all of her beautiful blonde bitchiness.

Dammit.

Maybe he should have known.

He'd been watching her for years. He'd been *sleeping with her* for three and a half. He'd known there was a reason she was a different person in Sapphire Falls than she was with him in Denver. But he'd thought he'd known that reason—she liked to be in charge in Sapphire Falls and she liked having him take over when they were in Denver. It really had seemed that simple to him, and he'd been okay with it. He liked simple. He'd liked thinking he knew her.

Now he realized he didn't. Or hadn't. And what did that say about their three and a half years together? What did that say about her ability to trust him? How about *his* ability to inspire her trust?

Ty smiled and nodded at something his mother had said without really hearing it and then went back to pondering. And watching his brothers.

Tucker sat at the end of the table, his arm draped over the back of Delaney's chair. To his right sat two boys, Charlie and David, to Delaney's left sat the other two, Henry and Jack. Tucker was a family man. As of only a few months ago. But it looked good on him. Tucker had a sense of contentment about him that Tyler had never seen.

Across from him, Hope and TJ were visiting with Ty's parents. But it wasn't the conversation Ty found interesting. It was that TJ also had an air of satisfaction about him. Like he'd finally taken a deep breath and relaxed. He was happy.

And then there was Travis.

The second Bennett brother came into the dining room carrying his baby daughter, Whitney. Whit was not quite two weeks old, but she had her daddy polishing her tiara already. Travis handed her over to her mother, Lauren, and as Travis looked down at them both, the love in his own was so obvious Ty felt his eyes widen.

Of the three of his brothers, Tucker was the only one Ty had ever really imagined in love. Tucker had wanted a wife and family since he was about six. But it had now happened for all of them and they made it seem so easy.

Ty had thought it would be easy for him too.

Hailey was a handful, but she'd been a predictable, fun handful. He knew how to make her spitting mad, how to make her laugh and how to make her moan.

What he didn't know was how to comfort her. How to empathize with her. How to encourage her.

He'd never imagined that she would need all of that.

He was seeing emotions from a female who didn't have many of those. Or didn't let on that she had many. And he was no expert in dealing with female emotions. Or any emotions.

He didn't deal with a lot of family emotion. They were all here together and had each other. He'd been raised in a loving family that was so *there* for each other it was sometimes overwhelming. And the rest of them were…better at it. His older brothers took care of things. They'd rarely depended on Ty, the baby, for anything. By the time he'd been old enough to take care of things or be supportive, he'd had three older brothers doing it all. He'd just been able to do his thing and not worry about anyone else's feelings or problems.

He didn't deal with a lot of friends' emotions either.

Some of what Bryan had felt and demonstrated after the accident and diagnosis and through rehab had been tough. Ty was used to pushing through, working harder, channeling his emotions into his sport. And he was used to two main emotions from the people around him—determination and pride.

The men he raced against were hardcore athletes like Ty. Yes, they got frustrated and happy and other things, but mostly they were determined and proud of what they did and accomplished.

But he wasn't friends with them. He respected them and didn't mind hanging out with some of them. But his friends were Bryan and Chris. And they were easy. They were fun-loving, laid-back guys who looked at life as a party and the world as their playground.

The worst either of them ever felt was hungover, and Ty knew that would pass.

Until the accident, he'd never seen Bryan sad or scared or angry. And he hadn't known how to help his friend through it. Which had made him question that relationship as well. If you couldn't encourage your friend through the worst time of his life, how good a friend were you?

Then there had been *his* emotions. He'd been scared for Bryan and had wanted to scream and yell and hit something when he'd heard the diagnosis and prognosis. And he'd hated every second of feeling things were out of control. The most out of control he ever liked to be was filled with elation after a win or overcome with pleasure when in bed with Hailey.

He'd taken a break from all of the worry and frustration and anger with Bryan. And now he was face-to-face with even more *emotion* with Hailey.

He wanted to fucking punch her mother—or rather her *stepmother*. And her father. He wanted to hug Hailey. And fuck her—but that one wasn't new.

Had he been attracted to her because she was strong and confident and hot? Because the emotions he saw from her were annoyance—caused by him on purpose—happiness and passion and nothing more?

Well…maybe…yeah.

And now she was more than all of that and he didn't know what to do.

But he did realize he was a jackass.

His mom offered him another piece of pie but he declined. He really did need to get back to training. His mother's cooking wasn't going to help. After eleven years of being gone and her not being able to feed him regularly, she was going to be feeding him a lot.

"You ride bikes too, right?" David asked Ty from two

seats down.

He looked over at his pseudo-nephew. "Yep. Sure do. Have lots of medals for it." But he grinned. He knew the boys were into dirt biking, not bicycle biking.

David's eyes rounded. "Medals? Really?"

"Uncle Ty doesn't ride real bikes," Tucker said. "He has to pedal his. There's no engine."

David wrinkled his nose. "You ride kids' bikes?"

From an eight-year-old that was pretty funny. "I ride a kick-ass Quintana Roo that's so cool it would make you cry."

David didn't look convinced. "Bikes like that don't go as fast as dirt bikes."

"I go faster than anybody else I race with," Ty said with a shrug. That was *mostly* true. There was usually only one other guy going faster than Ty. He worked on not scowling.

"Bikes like that aren't *loud* like dirt bikes," David said, clearly trying to one-up Ty.

Delaney laughed. "Loud is very important to David."

Ty grinned. "Well, I sure as hel—heck, whoop it up loud when I *win*." He probably needed to work on watching his language now that he was going to be around kids more.

"Dirt bikes can jump ramps and stuff," David said.

"I can jump ramps with my bike too," Ty said. "And I have a friend who can do flips and stuff with his bike."

David's eyes widened, as if he forgot to act unimpressed for a second.

Just like Ty had forgotten that his friend could no longer do flips with his bike.

Even getting back *on* a bike was a long time down the road for Bryan.

"Well, I never *cry* on my bike," David said, referring to Ty's comment about how cool his bike was.

"You do too," Jack said. "When you crash."

"Shut up." David glared at his brother.

"Well, I cry when I crash too," Ty said. He shook his

head. "I crashed on a mountainside a few months ago. That hurt like a bi—big...time...pain." He caught himself in time.

David still didn't seem impressed, but Charlie leaned in. "You crashed on a mountain?"

Ty glanced around the table. In his quest to be tough and cool with his new nephews, he'd opened his big mouth. His dad and brothers didn't know about the accident either.

His mother didn't say anything, but she was frowning.

It was his father, Thomas, who said, "You're strutting around here like usual, making as much sense as you ever did, so I assume you're okay. Tell us what happened."

Ty grimaced. Fine. It was time. "Bryan and I were up on a highway and a truck crossed the middle line. We swerved and went over the side."

"And?" Thomas prompted.

"Hit my head pretty hard and twisted up my knee."

"You can be more specific than that," Thomas said with a frown.

Ty sighed. "Knocked me out. I woke up in the hospital with a nasty headache and concussion. Tore my ACL."

TJ scowled at him. "You had surgery and didn't tell any of us?"

Ty shook his head. "I didn't have surgery."

"You don't have to repair that?" But he was asking Hope.

Hope was a nurse. Ty sat back and let her take it.

Hope shook her head, watching Ty. "You don't *have* to repair it. If the patient doesn't do high-intensity activities and doesn't have issues with instability."

TJ looked back to Ty. "And you're okay without surgery? You're a professional athlete."

Yeah, he was aware. "Should be okay. I have a brace I'll wear and I've had to work back into it slowly." Which had sucked. To go from running ten miles on a typical day to having to jog gently on a treadmill had been the most frustrating thing he'd been through in his athletic career. He wasn't quite back to ten but he was getting there. And he hadn't had any knee problems with it. So far. He also hadn't really pushed it yet.

TJ sat studying him for a long moment, making Ty shift on his chair. There were only two men who could make him do that and they were both at this table—TJ and their father.

"Taking it slowly means not competing for a while," TJ said.

Ty simply nodded.

"That's why you're back here," TJ said. "To recover."

At that, Ty shook his head. "I'm back here to stay," he said.

"How are you going to make a living?" TJ asked. "Will your endorsements still be intact if you're not competing?"

Ty took a deep breath. "That's in the air. Some of my sponsors feel like they can still use my name for a while. But, yeah, my marketability will decline with time."

"And then what? Have you been saving? Investing?"

Ty looked at Hope. She rolled her eyes. Sometimes TJ acted and sounded like a man twenty years older than he was. Since Hope had come into his life, he'd definitely mellowed some, but she'd only been here for a couple of weeks. And this was TJ. No one was going to make him fun-loving and fancy free all the time.

"I have been saving *and* investing," Ty confirmed. "And I have a new project I'm working on."

"Like what?" Tucker wanted to know.

"A training facility," Ty said. "Right here in Sapphire Falls."

"What kind of training?" David asked. "Tucker has a bike track that I train on."

He said the words so seriously, Ty didn't dare grin. He talked to his family enough that he knew David was the daredevil of the bunch. He lacked any fear of the ramps and curves and dips on the dirt bike track and loved to go fast and hard whenever given the chance.

"Kind of like your training," Ty said with a nod. "A place where people who are interested in triathlons can come and practice their sport and learn things from me."

"What's a triath—thing?" David asked.

"A triathlon is a race where you bike, run and swim."

David looked like he thought that sounded pretty dumb. "Why do you have to teach people to run and swim and ride a bike?"

Ty grinned at him. "I hope they already know how to do it all when they get here. I'm going to give them a place to practice and teach them how to build up to the point where they can be in races and stuff."

"Your name will be a big draw for that, I would think," Ty's father said.

He nodded. "I hope so. My agent thinks so."

"Your Uncle Ty has a silver medal from the Olympics," Delaney told the boys.

David tipped his head, looking *slightly* impressed at that. "Who got the gold medal?" he asked.

Ah, but not totally impressed. Ty smiled. "A guy from Great Britain."

David shrugged. Maybe Ty would show him his medal. Or his autograph from the gold medalist.

Or maybe he would quit caring what an eight-year-old thought of him.

But he'd probably start of by showing him the medal.

"What's the plan with the training facility?" TJ asked.

"Levi Spencer has agreed to financially back it with some local investors," Ty said.

"Like who?"

"Whoever wants in," Ty said.

"You don't have them lined up?"

"Uh, not yet." Ty frowned.

"You think people will be willing to come to Nebraska

to train?" Travis asked.

Ty nodded. "This is where I started. And I intend to incorporate the most important part of my training here."

"What's that?" Delaney asked.

"The community support and involvement," Ty said.

"How will you get the community involved?" Kathy asked.

"When we build, we'll hire locally. And after the facility is running, I'll have to hire people for maintenance and such. The community will also have a chance to use the facility as a fitness center. I'll make sure they get to know the athletes. They'll be able to see them training, get to know them personally. We're going to turn my new house into a boarding house for people who come to train here and we'll be hiring someone to run the place, cook, etc. We'll have to get the grocery store on board with ordering certain food items for us that they don't typically stock. That kind of thing."

No one said anything, and Ty looked around the table. "What?"

"You've put a lot of thought into this," TJ said.

"I have."

"Almost as if you'd been planning it even before you got hurt."

Ty met his brother's eyes. He shouldn't be surprised TJ had guessed that. TJ knew his brothers better than anyone. Mostly because he was always looking out for them to keep them from messing up, and he had a gift the other three Bennett boys hadn't mastered—keeping his mouth shut and simply listening a lot of the time.

"It had occurred to me as a retirement plan," Ty confirmed. "I just didn't know when that retirement was going to happen."

"I'm happy to help with any additional renovations you might need in the house," Delaney, their resident fix-it girl, said.

"Thanks. I'll take you up on that."

They talked for a bit about who in town would be good for some of the jobs and then cleared the dishes and helped Kathy clean up the kitchen. At least until she threw them all out because they were in her way and doing everything wrong.

Exactly as it had been growing up. Ty grinned. He knew his mother knew they all got in her way and did things the wrong way so that they would get out of helping, but it was a time-honored Bennett family tradition.

Ty made his way out onto the front porch as his brothers and their families gathered things up to leave an hour later.

"Trav, hey, can I talk to you for a minute?" Ty asked as Travis and Lauren stepped out of the house.

Watching his brothers with their girls, in love and happy, he'd finally decided that he needed some help. All of his brothers had figured out the relationship thing. Maybe they could actually be helpful. And Travis had been a high school classmate of Hailey's. Of all his brothers, Travis probably knew her best.

Travis glanced at Lauren. "I've got this," she said softly so as not to wake the sleeping baby. "Have one of them bring you home later. I'm going down for a nap too."

Travis smoothed her hair and kissed the top of her head, and Ty actually got choked up. Jesus. This emotion thing was going to kill him.

"What's up?" Travis asked, crossing to where Ty leaned against the porch railing. He settled his butt next to Ty's.

"I need some advice."

"Okay."

"About a woman."

Travis pivoted to look at him. "Seriously?"

Ty nodded.

"Hailey?" Travis asked.

Ty frowned but nodded. Travis knew?

"Yes!" Travis said. He swung around and called out, "Hey, City!"

Lauren looked back at him from where she'd strapped the baby in.

"Ty's asking *me* for advice on women."

Lauren raised both eyebrows and looked at Ty. She closed the car door quietly and then faced them. "Yeah?"

Ty shrugged. "Yeah."

"Hailey?"

Ty sighed. "Yeah."

"Okay, hang on." She turned back, retrieved Whitney from the car and came back up onto the porch.

"You don't have to stay," Ty said. In fact, he'd love it if she *didn't* stay. He was going to feel like enough of an idiot talking to Travis.

"It's no bother. I'm happy to help," Lauren said.

Yeah, that wasn't what he meant.

Delaney, Tucker and the boys came out of the house.

"Henry, will you take Whitney back in to grandma?" Lauren asked, handing the baby over.

"Sure. Why?" Henry asked, handling the little girl as if he'd been born to it. Impressive for a twelve-year-old.

"We need to talk to Uncle Ty," Lauren said.

Tucker looked at Ty and Travis, eyebrows up. "We do?"

Ty sighed. "No, *you* don't."

"About what?" Charlie, the ten-year-old, asked.

"His girlfriend," Travis said with a grin.

Charlie scoffed. "Girlfriends are easy."

"Are they?" Tucker asked.

"Yeah, just give them whatever they want," Charlie said.

Everyone laughed, but Ty couldn't help but think the kid was on to something. At least, he'd been giving Hailey what he'd *thought* she wanted.

"Are we really talking about a girlfriend?" Delaney asked.

"Well, he needs advice on a woman," Travis said. "And asked *me*." He seemed inordinately proud of that.

"Hailey?" Tucker asked.

Ty stared at him. *Dammit.*

"Yes," Lauren confirmed, settling into one of the white wicker chairs on Kathy's porch.

"Oh, great," Delaney said, taking the other chair. "We've all been dying to know what's going on with you two."

Lauren laughed. "You've only been here a couple of months. Think about those of us who've been around for years."

Delaney turned to her. "It's been going on for *years*?"

They know it's been going on for years? Ty thought. *Shit.*

"At least since they started building Sapphire Hills," Lauren said.

Ty said nothing. That had been what had prompted Hailey's trip to Denver. The trip that had resulted in them sleeping together for the first time as adults.

But it had all started long before that.

"Ty's had an unrequited crush on Hailey since he was fourteen," Tucker said.

Fifteen. But Ty didn't correct them.

"Well, apparently it's not unrequited anymore," Travis said.

Yeah, well, that wasn't completely true either.

"What's not unrequited?" TJ asked, stepping out onto the porch, Hope's hand in his.

Sure, why not bring in the whole family?

"Ty's crush on Hailey," Delaney supplied helpfully.

"It's *not* unrequited?" TJ asked.

"I wondered about the two of you that day she was at TJ's farm, all pissed off about someone moving next door to her," Hope said.

Ty sighed. And waited for them to finish.

"Something's been going on for a while," Lauren agreed.

"And now he wants advice, so I'd say it's getting more serious," Tucker said.

"He wants advice from *me*," Travis interjected.

"Well, that makes sense," TJ said. "Lauren is probably the most like Hailey of all our girls."

"What's that mean?" Delaney asked.

"You and Hope are sweet and patient," TJ said.

"I'm sitting right here," Lauren said.

TJ laughed. "Are you denying that you're less sweet and patient than Delaney and Hope?"

"Fine," Lauren said. "I'm not denying that Hailey and I both have the polished, bitchy thing going on when we need it. But you didn't say that we also share a quick wit, a talent for sarcasm and are highly intelligent."

"There," Ty said, pushing off the railing. "That. That's exactly right."

He became aware everyone was staring at him. He took his eyes off Lauren and looked around. "You all agree that Hailey is smart and witty, right?"

They all nodded, while looking at him like he was nuts.

"That's all I'm saying," he muttered, and leaned back against the railing.

"*What* is going on with you two?" Lauren asked, leaning forward in her chair. "I'm *dying* to know."

He looked around at the group gathered. Okay, unconditional love was up to bat.

"I think I screwed up."

"You mean by running against her for mayor?"

This came from his mother, who had stepped out onto the porch. The screen door slapped shut behind her. "When I told you to make her feel like number one, this isn't really what I meant."

Everyone swung their attention from Kathy to Ty.

"She knew about you and Hailey?" Tucker asked.

"Only since Sunday," Ty admitted.

"You knew about them on Sunday?" Travis asked his mom. "How?"

"I saw her leaving his house that morning half dressed." Kathy had a smug smile on her face.

"Half dressed?" Tucker repeated.

Everyone's attention turned back to Ty.

"You slept with her?" Tuck asked.

"We've been sleeping together for almost four years."

Five mouths dropped open at that. The exceptions were Kathy and, interestingly, Lauren.

"I can't believe you didn't tell us!" Delaney said to Kathy.

"This is between Ty and Hailey," Kathy said. Then she frowned at her youngest son. "At least, it was until he decided to run against her."

"I have a plan," Ty said weakly.

"I hope so. Because being mayor is the most important thing to Hailey. It's the thing she's most proud of, the thing that makes her feel important, and you're trying to take it away from her."

Holy shit, those were almost exactly the words Hailey had said to him. "No," he denied. "I'm trying to make it *really* mean something, to be real, for her to *actually* be number one."

"How?" Delaney asked.

"By giving her some competition. A win doesn't really feel like a win unless you beat somebody."

Delaney didn't look convinced.

"If you're the only one in the running, you come in first, but you also come in last," he said.

No one said anything to that either. And now Hope looked skeptical along with Delaney.

"It's not a victory if you're not victorious *over*

someone," Ty tried again.

"Not everyone needs the glory, Ty," Lauren finally said. "Some people are happy doing what they're doing because of what they're doing. Not because of the medals and trophies."

Fuck. Hailey had said that too.

"And what if you win?" Kathy said.

And up until Hailey had shared with him that she'd been faking the in-charge thing, he would have scoffed at that. But now... "Yeah, well, I didn't think it through entirely."

"So drop out," Travis said.

"I can't."

"He can't."

He and his mother spoke at the same time.

Ty sighed. She agreed. Dammit. Dropping out sounded great. He didn't want to be mayor. And he didn't want to hurt Hailey. And he wanted to keep sleeping with her.

And he really didn't want to be mayor.

"He can't drop out," Kathy said. "That would be worse. That would be like saying he knows that there's no way she'll be able to win and he's *giving* it to her. That's worse than winning an unopposed election."

She was right. Ty sighed again.

"So what were you thinking?" Travis asked. "How was this plan going to work?"

"Being opposed in a race—even a political one—makes people really try. They have to push. They have to stand up and show everyone what they've got," Ty said.

"And you think Hailey needs to do that?" Tucker asked.

"I do," Ty said firmly. "She's always been unopposed. Now she needs to show this town what she's got."

"She hasn't been doing that?" Travis asked. "Hell, she's been in charge of stuff as long as I can remember."

He took a deep breath. He couldn't out her. He couldn't tell everyone, even his family, that she'd been faking everything. Or thought she had been. Or whatever the fuck was going on.

"I want her to know I believe in her. But I think that maybe... I don't know her as well as I thought."

No one said anything to that initially and he scanned their faces. The guys looked as confused as he was. It was Lauren and his mother that seemed more thoughtful.

"What are you thinking?" he asked, pointing at Lauren.

"I'm thinking you might be right," she said.

"That I don't know her?"

"Yes. And that a lot of people don't really know her."

Ty watched Lauren carefully. Did *Lauren* know this other side of Hailey?

"And you're also thinking that I'm a jackass because I'm worried I might not be in love with her now that I'm not sure who she really is?"

Lauren shook her head. "Not that. That's not all on you."

He lifted an eyebrow. "That's not *all* on me?"

Lauren leaned back and crossed her legs and regarded him seriously. "She didn't let you in. So it's not *all* on you. But it's not like you dug deep, Ty. You were completely content with everything exactly as it was. You didn't want it to be different."

"No, but—" *Fuck.* "How do you know that?"

"Because you're Ty Bennett. You are wildly successful and popular. Because you've *made* yourself successful and popular. You've worked hard and made decisions and choices that have put you where you are," she said. "But you're not good with things not fully in your control. Like other people."

That was totally true. Like Bryan's situation and his own knee to an extent. But... "She totally gives up control when she's with me," he protested.

Then he realized he shouldn't have said that out loud to the majority of his family.

No one laughed. At least not that he could hear. But he saw Tucker's grin and Travis almost looked impressed.

TJ, of course, looked concerned.

"She gave up *enough* control to keep you happy," Lauren corrected, unfazed by what he'd blurted out. "Hailey's an expert at figuring out what other people want and then giving that to them. But only that. She doesn't give more than she has to."

Ty tipped his head back and looked up at the ceiling of the porch. This was complicated.

He breathed.

He hated complicated.

He liked control. He liked to be the one making decisions that would affect him. Hailey had given him control—in the bedroom, of their social calendar when they were together—but, yeah, he hadn't ever had control of her or their relationship otherwise.

Not in high school, not in what happened after that night at the river, not in how they conducted their relationship outside of Denver.

And he'd known it. Deep down. That was why the control in the bedroom was so important to him.

And maybe…

The next thought made his mouth dry and his stomach knot.

Maybe that was what had kept him from looking deeper and wanting more. Maybe he'd known she was holding something back. Maybe he'd known that there was more and that if he found it, he'd have to admit that he didn't have full control. And maybe he wouldn't have stuck around.

Lauren sat forward, looking at him with concern. "Uh, somebody better get him some water. And maybe some beer."

Tucker headed into the house.

"And how about everyone else clear out too?" Lauren

said.

Lauren was the first and oldest and most commanding of the Bennett daughters-in-law and she could get away with bossing everyone around.

The family, including Kathy, headed back into the house.

Lauren got up and approached him. "You okay?"

"I have no idea."

"She told you that she's been faking the tough-girl stuff, huh?"

He nodded. "And I'm a dick because...that tough-girl stuff was really attractive."

"And then you decided to help her figure out that she actually *is* a tough girl."

He shrugged. "It seemed like a good idea."

"Because that's what *you* wanted."

He nodded.

"And now?"

He hesitated. "Between us?"

"Of course. You're my favorite silver-medalist brother-in-law."

He smiled. But he didn't feel happy. At all. "It's just that..."

"You don't know if she really is a tough girl down deep and you don't know if she can win the election."

He nodded. "Exactly."

"I don't know either."

Fuck.

"But Hailey needs to stop being scared. I agree that the town needs to know her. As her campaign manager, I'm going to make sure that this all goes as much in her favor as possible."

"Campaign manager?"

"Yeah. Sorry." She didn't look sorry as she smiled at him.

That was the best thing he'd heard all day.

"Lauren, all I can say is, *please* kick my ass in this election."

❧

"Okay, so the debate is over," Lauren said, in a tone that was part relief and part worry.

Hailey dropped into one of the chairs in the front of Adrianne's bakery and kicked her heels off. She drew one leg up and massaged her foot.

"I kicked his butt," she said. "What's the problem?" But she knew what the problem was.

The debate had been her idea. It had been five days since Ty had announced his candidacy. That had equaled five days of him going around town and talking and laughing and buttering everyone up. He'd been at the Come Again every night—the perfect place to interact with the citizens their age. He'd been at Dottie's Diner every morning—the perfect place to interact with the citizens older than them. And he'd somehow thrown together an impromptu mini-triathlon for the kids in town ages six to sixteen. The perfect way to interact with the parents of the kids who were some of the voters younger than them.

Tucker's boys had been all about it. Hailey suspected that it was, in part anyway, Ty's way of trying to impress and bond with his new nephews. And it had been a huge hit. Of course. The kids had run around the square twice, biked to the pool and then jumped in to swim two laps. There had been multiple age groups with prizes and food and the party had gone all afternoon.

She really hated how good Ty was at making people like him.

So she'd marched into the Come Again last night and challenged him to a debate. An actual debate about the issues facing Sapphire Falls.

And she'd kicked his ass. He knew nothing about any

of the topics they'd debated.

"You did," Lauren agreed, taking another chair at the table. She gave Hailey a look. "It was almost too much."

Hailey started to protest but then slumped back in her chair and sighed. "Yeah, okay."

She was jealous of the ease with which Ty was winning everyone over and had wanted to prove to everyone— including herself—that she had *something* that he didn't.

All she had was knowledge about Sapphire Falls and the things the local government had been dealing with over the past few years. She'd decided to show that off.

"It's only a few more days until the election," Lauren said.

It was actually six days, four hours and thirty-two minutes until the polls closed. She had it on a sticky note.

"So I asked Tessa to do an informal opinion poll," Lauren added.

Hailey dropped her foot. "You what?"

"We need to have an idea of where you stand next to Ty."

But she didn't want to know. She couldn't drop out of the race. That would be humiliating. But she didn't really want to know how far behind she was. "How did she do the poll?" she asked.

"Went to some random places around town. She swung by the grocery store, the Stop, Dottie's—"

"Well, everyone at Dottie's loves him because he's been in there buying breakfast the last two mornings," Hailey protested. "He had that Pancakes-On-Me thing." If people came in between six and eight in the morning and bought something, they got a short stack of pancakes on Ty's bill.

Lauren lifted an eyebrow. "Do you want to buy waffles for the town? Dottie's waffles are better than the pancakes in my opinion."

"You're crazy," Hailey told her. "Her French toast is

better than both."

"You want to do a French-toast-breakfast meeting with the town?" Lauren asked.

"No. For one, it would look like I'm just doing what Ty's doing and for another...that's not really my style."

It was true. Hailey socialized. She loved attending various functions and festivals around town. Most of them were her idea. But they weren't about her meeting with the town. She had office hours for that.

"No, it's not, and it will look like you're only doing it for votes," Lauren agreed. "But you might think about starting something like that after you're reelected. It would be a nice, casual way for people to talk with you."

Yep, nice and casual were the opposite of what Hailey liked her meetings to be. She liked them to be businesslike and short and she really liked having her gigantic cherry-wood desk in between her and the other person.

And she cursed Ty for making her blush when she looked at that desk every morning now.

"You really think there's a chance I'll get reelected?" she asked Lauren.

"Of course you will." Phoebe came through the swinging door that separated the front of the bakery from the kitchen with a pitcher of tea in hand. "Ty's fun, but no one thinks he can actually lead the town."

"Actually—the poll shows you about neck and neck."

This came from Hailey's assistant, Tess, as she came through the front door, the happy, optimistic jingle of the bell over the door in complete contrast to Hailey's emotions.

"Really?" Lauren asked as Tess handed her a sheet of paper.

Tess nodded and took the chair next to Lauren. "A lot of people agree with Phoebe, but there are several who like what Ty's bringing to the race."

"Nothing?" Hailey asked. Then cringed. That wasn't

fair.

"They like that they're getting to spend time with him and talk with him. They feel like he's someone they can bring concerns and issues to," Tess said.

"They don't think they can bring concerns and issues to me?" Hailey asked. "I have meetings every single week with people who feel completely comfortable bringing concerns and issues. Even the tiniest, most inane concerns and issues."

Tess glanced at Lauren. Lauren looked at Hailey.

"Maybe you come off a little defensive about those concerns and issues," Lauren said dryly.

"I don't." But she totally did.

"Hailey, not every problem in town is your fault," Lauren said. "And you have to quit looking at people raising issues as them somehow insulting you personally."

"But I'm in charge here," Hailey said. "If there's something wrong it *is* my responsibility."

"It's your responsibility to try to *help* fix the problems," Lauren said. "But the problems aren't your *fault*. And no one expects you to fix all the problems yourself or have the answers all the time."

"I think the fact that you take everything so seriously is nice," Phoebe said, sitting down next to Hailey. "It's obvious that you really care and want everything to be perfect here."

Hailey smiled at the other woman, stunned that Phoebe was the one defending her. "Thanks."

"Phoebe isn't the only one," Tessa said. "A lot of people agree that Hailey takes her job seriously and they trust that she's always working to make things better."

Well, that was nice.

"They're just intimidated to *talk* to you about any of it," Tess said.

And then there was that.

"Ninety-two percent of people wish there could be a

way to make Hailey and Ty both mayor?" Lauren asked Tessa, reading from the paper. "What's that mean?"

"Well, it's a small sample size," Tess said. "That came from about six people at the Come Again, three at the Stop and three at the grocery store, but, yeah. They said that both candidates bring great things to the table, but neither of them has it all."

Lauren studied Hailey at that, her wheels clearly turning.

"No candidate ever has it all," Hailey said.

"Except, one here does," Lauren said.

That made Hailey nervous. "What are you thinking?"

"I'm thinking that you're serious and smart and everyone knows you're a hard worker who had this town's best interest at heart all the time. But I'm also thinking that you're funny and that you've seen all of the *Back to the Future* movies a dozen times and you make amazing spaghetti sauce and you swear like a sailor when you've been drinking Booze and you give a ton of money to the local animal shelter."

Hailey stared at Lauren. Lauren knew some things about her, that was true, but she'd trusted Lauren to keep Hailey's soft side to herself. "So what?"

"So you're like the rest of us. Probably funnier and nicer than some of us. And I think that this town needs to get to know you."

Hailey was shaking her head by the time Lauren finished. "They've elected me twice—heck, I went to school with most of the town, so they've been electing me for things for *years*—exactly as I am. They want a tough leader to take on their problems for them. They might think they want to sit down and hash it all out, but really they want someone who will fight the fights for them."

At that, Lauren did the most astonishing thing. She reached out and took Hailey's hand.

"Hailey," she said sincerely. "You're right. They like

seeing you tough and fighting for them. But I can tell you from personal experience, that seeing this other side of you makes you being tough and confident and brave enough to lead this town even *more* amazing."

"What other side?" Hailey asked hesitantly.

Lauren smiled. "The side that eats half a roll of cookie dough one day and then eats nothing but salad the next, the side that can't turn off a Harry Potter movie on TV no matter what else is going on, the side that hates getting stuck behind the tractors on the highway but who doesn't want to lose the sidewalk to the park more. Because all of that makes you like the rest of us. It makes you *one* of us. Instead of this powerhouse who was born to be in charge, I see a woman who has accomplished her goal of being in charge in spite of not feeling good enough and *not* being a natural at interacting and relating to people. And that is more amazing. People will love that."

Hailey felt tears stinging her eyes and she blinked rapidly. She had no idea what to say to all of that. She was overwhelmed.

"And I see a person who isn't used to people telling her nice things about herself except that she's beautiful," Lauren said, squeezing her hand. "But there is so much more to you, Hailey. And I think *you* need to see that as much as the people in this town do."

Hailey sniffed and Tessa handed her a napkin. "Why do you care about this so much?" she asked Lauren.

"Because I want you to invite me over for spaghetti and to watch the entire boxed set of *The Wonder Years* that I know you have in your entertainment center."

Hailey's eyes widened and she smiled. "Anytime."

"And," Lauren said, her tone and expression softening, "no one should hide who they really are in order to get approval from anyone else." She squeezed Hailey's hand again. "Especially not the man they love."

Hailey was surprised. But she wasn't as surprised as she

would have expected to be.

Strangely.

Phoebe looked from Hailey to Lauren. "Is it Ty?"

Now Hailey was really surprised. "How did you know?"

"I knew it!" Tessa said. "That is amazing. Does he know? If so, why he's running against you? If not, why haven't you told him?"

Hailey just smiled, surprise and a touch of panic fighting for attention in her mind.

"Haven't told who what?" Adrianne asked, coming out of the kitchen with scones.

"The man she's in love with," Tessa said with a grin.

"It's Ty, right?" Adrianne asked. "I've had a feeling about you two."

Hailey had to laugh at that. "You all suspected?"

"The heat between the two of you has been so obvious," Phoebe said.

"And he would be so good for you," Adrianne said, setting the scones down and pulling up another chair. "You would balance each other out."

"Because he's laid-back and I'm not?" Hailey asked. What did she bring to the equation? Yes, Ty helped her kick back, but it wasn't as if she could keep him on track or even really motivate him. He was very self-driven, self-motivated, and now he was ready to give up on his training and goals no matter what she said.

But Adrianne shook her head. "No, because he can handle the organization and scheduling and stuff. You can be the one thing that makes him realize he doesn't have to travel to Rio de Janeiro and win a gold medal to be happy."

Hailey stared at Adrianne. And she wasn't the only one. Phoebe, Tess and Lauren were looking at her with the same stunned expression.

Adrianne looked around at them. "What?"

"How do you know all of that?" Phoebe asked.

Adrianne shrugged. "Isn't it obvious? Ty's a driven professional athlete. Obviously, he has to be used to schedules and regimens and being organized in everything from his workouts to his diet. Hailey, on the other hand, has found fulfillment and happiness in her tiny hometown in Nebraska and delights in things like strawberry festivals. Ty can keep Hailey on track and she can show him an appreciation for the simpler, smaller things in life."

Lauren nodded, clearly impressed. "And they say Mason's the genius."

Adrianne laughed. "You all know Mason doesn't know much about interpersonal relationships. But I make up for that with him. That's how *we* fit. Every couple has a way of bringing out the best in one another."

Hailey was reeling with all of this. Adrianne was completely right. And maybe Hailey needed to get off Ty's case about moving home and starting a new career.

"And this town needs to see that side of you, Hailey," Lauren said, getting back to their conversation.

"But if they see the organized, driven side of Ty, they'll be impressed by that too," Hailey said. "He really is amazing. He's a hard worker, pushes and inspires the people around him. He's got more than he's showing too."

"Well, *you're* not his campaign manager, so keep that to yourself," Lauren said. "And it won't matter. You're it, babe. You're the one who should be mayor."

Hailey appreciated the support of these women and knew that she had to give the rest of the campaign her all, if nothing else to show that having them on her side mattered to her. "Okay, tell me what to do."

Lauren smiled. "Show up at the gazebo tomorrow night at six. And Phoebe, you're in charge of dressing her like a typical everyday Sapphire Falls girl."

Phoebe lit up. "You've got it."

Hailey managed not to groan. Out loud anyway.

CHAPTER SEVEN

Ty's grin grew wider and wider as he approached the middle of the town square. In front of the gazebo were hay bales arranged to resemble two couches—a bale on the bottom to sit on and one behind to lean against. They were covered with blankets to avoid hay stabbing their occupants in unpleasant places. There was a makeshift coffee table in front of the couches as well, made of another bale with wooden planks on top. There was an arrangement of wild flowers in a mason jar on the table along with mason jars of lemonade.

Other hay bales had been pulled up, covered with blankets and arranged in a semicircle three rows deep, facing the gazebo for people to sit on during the Q&A session he and Hailey were holding tonight.

White twinkle lights had been suspended from the tree branches throughout the square and around the gazebo. Situated around the area were more bales with coolers on top, filled with ice and mason jars of lemonade, fruit punch and iced tea.

The whole thing was very inviting, and Ty had to admit that Hailey's camp had come up with a great idea for the Q&A, as well as making the setting casual and comfortable.

A lot of people were already showing up, milling around and chatting. Everyone was dressed casually and seemed happy and relaxed.

After the debate, Ty had been worried about Hailey. She'd annihilated him. As expected. It had been his fault he didn't know anything about the policies in town or the issues Hailey and the town council had been dealing with, and the town knew they were now competitors. But Sapphire Falls didn't like to see one of their own *humiliated.*

This was going to be good. A relaxed atmosphere, a more casual conversation with him and Hailey with the goal of letting the town get to know them both better, rather than an actual debate about issues.

Besides, there hadn't been much debate in their debate. It wasn't as if he didn't agree with her regarding the issues and how to solve them.

"You ready?"

Ty turned to smile at Travis. "Sure. Of course."

"Okay, well, don't hold back tonight," Trav said with a frown.

"Hold back? Why would I do that?"

"Didn't you the other night at the debate?" Travis asked. "You looked like a moron up there."

Ty laughed. "Did I? Well, I'm the first to admit that I don't know much about the issues in town."

"Yeah, you should probably brush up on that. You're a lot of fun, but that won't win this election."

Ty peered at his brother. "What's with you?"

"I'm supporting you because you're my brother. While my wife is the campaign manager for your opposition. What do you *think* is with me?"

"You and Lauren are arguing?" Ty asked. He hated that idea. This wasn't supposed to be serious.

"Not arguing," Travis said. "It's...tense."

"Because we're not getting laid."

Ty glanced at Tucker as he joined them. "*What?*"

Tucker looked annoyed too. "Lauren has convinced Delaney to defect."

"Defect?"

"To the Hailey camp. Girl Power. Women building each other up. The Bennetts shouldn't get everything just because we're good-looking, sexy, intelligent, funny and sweet. That kind of stuff."

Ty laughed. "She said that we get everything because we're good-looking, sexy, intelligent, funny and sweet?"

"She implied it," Tucker said.

"But she didn't *say* any of those things?"

"Well, she did say that you shouldn't be able to waltz in here and take over just because you want to."

Ty turned to face Tucker fully. "Wait a second. Did Delaney, by chance, say that *I* was good-looking, sexy, intelligent, funny and sweet?" he asked, with a huge grin he couldn't hide.

Tucker's eyes narrowed. "Doesn't matter."

Oh, but it did. Because it was bugging his big brother. Ty grinned. "Got it. I totally see where Delaney is coming from."

"She *doesn't* want you to win," Tucker said. "You got that part, right?"

"And the part about how she's cut you off for supporting me," Ty said with a nod.

"Well, it's more that Lauren has had her down at their headquarters until damned near midnight the last few nights," Tucker said.

"On purpose, I swear," Travis said. "Because I can tell you that Lauren *is* punishing me for supporting you."

"But we're family," Ty pointed out. He was enjoying all of this far more than he should. But if *he* wasn't getting any because of the campaign, then at least he had brothers to share his sorrow with.

"And she thinks that's even more reason that I should be talking you *out* of running," Travis said.

"Why's that?"

"Because you'll be a terrible mayor," Travis said bluntly.

Ty lifted an eyebrow. "You think so?"

Travis gave him an unamused look. "You looked like an idiot at the debate. You show up two weeks before the election to campaign? Obviously, this is a last-minute decision you didn't think through very well."

Then maybe they wouldn't vote for him and everything

would be fine.

"Looks like you're getting your way," TJ commented as he joined them.

"How so?" Ty asked.

TJ looked around. "This and the debate the other night? You're pulling Hailey out of her shell, that's for sure."

"What do you mean? Those were both her ideas," Ty said with a frown. Pulling her out of her shell sounded like it could be a good thing, but again, Ty hadn't realized she *had* a shell. The woman he'd always thought of when he thought of Hailey was absolutely the type to get up on stage and tell everyone everything she knew and make anyone who dared think they could keep up regret it quickly. "She likes the spotlight the way I do. She likes having people's attention."

"She doesn't, actually," TJ said.

Dammit.

"She would rather do her job and take care of things that need taking care of and enjoy the festivities she organizes and never have another town-council meeting or a town-hall meeting where she has to hear about problems or justify her thoughts and actions," TJ said.

Ty felt the knots from his shoulders slide down into his gut. Fuck. Hearing his brother confirm that he knew nothing didn't help his state of mind at all.

When Ty didn't respond, TJ went on. "You want her to be like you, because you don't understand *not* wanting the spotlight and the glory of competition. But trust me, falling in love with someone different from you can be incredible."

Ty stared at TJ. The sudden transformation in his brother's face, the way his expression and voice softened, took Ty a minute to adjust to.

"True story," Travis said. "Lauren and I are pretty different in a lot of ways too. Maybe not as different as TJ and Hope, but, yeah, the trick is finding the things you do have in common and then appreciating and learning from the things that make you different."

Ty blew out a breath. "Not sure this is the time or place for a big lesson on relationships, guys."

"It's the perfect time and place," TJ said. "It's amazing loving someone different, if you *let them* be different. You shouldn't try to change her."

"And you think that's what I'm doing?"

"I think you're bored," TJ said bluntly. "Things with your career aren't going your way, so you move home and stir everything up here because you don't know what to do with yourself. But you're stirring other people's lives up too, Ty."

Ty frowned at him. "I'm not—" But he *was* stirring Hailey up. Because he liked her stirred up. "Fuck," he muttered.

"Yeah," TJ said.

"How do you know all this about Hailey anyway?" he asked his brother.

"It's amazing what you can learn when you're not totally wrapped up in yourself," TJ said. "I know a lot about all of the women my brothers have fallen in love with."

Travis and Tucker's eyes widened at that, but Ty jumped in before they could say anything.

"How did you know I was in love with Hailey all this time?"

TJ gave him a slow smile. "Hope says it's because I'm very insightful."

Before Ty could respond to *that*, he heard Lauren calling for everyone to take a seat.

His mood about this whole thing had definitely soured a bit. He was fucking tired of everyone claiming that he was only thinking about himself and that he didn't know Hailey.

He was *really* fucking tired of fearing they were right.

Ty stomped toward the hay bales where he and Hailey were clearly supposed to sit.

She wasn't in her seat yet, so he chose first. He noticed there was also a PA system set up. The setting wasn't huge, but they were outside and they wanted to be sure that everyone could hear everything. The crowd had already filled the bales set up for seats and there were still at least fifty people standing.

He was the first to see Hailey. He was sitting facing the crowd and she came up behind them and started weaving between the bales of people, smiling and greeting them as she went.

But he couldn't take his eyes off her. Or rather, her outfit. And how she looked in it.

He hadn't seen Hailey Conner in cut-off jeans since high school, and the sight back then had almost stopped his heart. Now, a woman not a girl, who had grown into her long legs and had curves everywhere she was supposed to, approached him. And his heart did stop for a moment. He was sure of it.

He knew this woman intimately. He knew what that denim and that fitted sleeveless shirt covered. He knew how it all looked, felt and tasted. And he knew the sounds she made when he looked, felt and tasted it.

Ty shifted on the hay bale, itching with the desire to surge out of his seat, sweep her up into his arms and head right back out of there.

But he wouldn't. Because whatever she was doing was important. Hailey wouldn't show up at a town meeting, something TJ claimed she hated, in cut-off jeans unless there was a good reason.

Finally, she made it to the front and her eyes met his. She faltered in her sure steps for a split second—her sure steps in cowboy boots no less, which also made him hard— then she gave him a smile and took her seat.

TJ thought Ty was trying to make Hailey into something she wasn't, pushing her to be what *he* wanted instead of seeing who she was. His mother thought there was more to Hailey too, deeper, softer stuff that she didn't want anyone to see.

He'd started all of this to show Hailey that she could be number one, then he'd kept with it so she could see the woman he saw. But right now, right here, with everyone in the damned town watching, *he* wanted to know her. Not to prove that he already did. But because he realized that he didn't.

Lauren took the mic from the stand in front of the coffee table and greeted the crowd.

"Good evening, everyone, thanks for coming. As you know, we have two very interesting candidates who are vying for the position of mayor. We, Mayor Conner's team, invited Ty and his team here tonight so that you could all get to know them both better. Tonight isn't about what they will do about the highway expansion or what they think about the gas tax. Tonight is about them, as people and citizens of Sapphire Falls. Ask them anything—within reason, of course." She paused for the expected laughter to fade. "And let's make it fun."

"I have a question." Phoebe Sherwood bounced out of her seat and took the mic from Lauren. "Hailey, since you've been mayor you've organized a number of festivals, fundraisers and charity events and, of course, headed the efforts to build Sapphire Hills. What are you most proud of?"

Ty rolled his eyes. He was certain Lauren had come up with a number of questions ahead of time and had planted them with various people. And it was probably a great idea. One that his team hadn't thought of. But the question annoyed him. Everyone knew Hailey was amazing at her job. While pointing that out over and over again was absolutely her campaign manager's first priority, it wasn't what he wanted to hear. He wanted to get to know *her*.

He waited politely for Hailey to explain why it was hard to choose what she was most proud of when Sapphire

Hills helped the local economy so much but the pet adoption and spay-and-neuter program was important in its own right.

No, this was not how the evening was going to go.

"I have a question," he said, pushing off the hay-bale couch and reaching for the microphone when Phoebe tried to hand it off to Delaney.

Phoebe brought it to him, eyes wide. She glanced at Lauren, who was frowning at Ty.

Ty didn't care.

"I have a question for Hailey," he said, turning to face her. "What is your best childhood memory of Sapphire Falls?"

She was clearly stunned. She glanced at the crowd, all of whom were watching her intently. Then she looked at Lauren, who shrugged. Finally, she focused back on Ty.

He gave her an encouraging smile. He wanted her to trust him here. To go with the questions and be honest and be herself.

"Summertime," she finally said. "Everything about it. Spending the days at the pool and then riding my bike around town with my friends. Buying popsicles at the Stop. Catching lightning bugs after dark. The movies they'd show on the side of city hall. The annual festival and going on the rides and watching the fireworks." She was quiet for a moment and then added, "I think it's those memories that make me want to work to keep this town as wonderful for everyone as it always has been for me."

Someone in the audience coughed, and Hailey shook her head, almost as if she'd gotten caught up and forgotten the nearly hundred people listening in.

She smiled, clearly a little embarrassed. "Everything about summertime."

Ty had to clear his throat before he said, "I have another question."

Lauren had been on her way over to him, but she

stopped after only a few steps. She looked at Hailey.

But Hailey was looking at Ty. "Okay," she said.

"Everyone knows you love your job. But what do you like *best* about being mayor? And you can only pick one thing," he added.

She smiled. "That's easy. Seeing people move back after leaving home for a while, or when new people come to visit and end up staying. I love knowing that people want to be *here* over everywhere else they could be."

Ty felt like her answer was just for him. It wasn't, of course. There were a number of people who had left and come home, like Mason, and there were even more who had come to town for some other reason but ended up staying—Lauren, Adrianne, Joe, Levi, Kate, Hope and Delaney were only a few.

But the way Hailey was looking right at him as she answered made him think that maybe she was especially happy he was in that group after all.

"So you plan to spend your life here?" he asked her.

"Yes."

"And you hope to have a family? Get married? Raise your kids here?" With each question, Ty felt his chest getting tighter and tighter.

He wanted those things. He wanted to get married and have kids right here in Sapphire Falls. He wanted his kids to have what he'd had growing up—the sense of community, the safety of the small town, the joy of having family all around. He'd love to see his kids playing in the park where he'd played and running through the fields with his brothers' kids. He'd love to gather at his mom's place for birthdays and holiday celebrations. He felt it to his bones.

She swallowed hard before answering. But she gave a nod. "I think about that all the time," she finally said. "A part of me would love that. Sapphire Falls is made for families. But…"

She trailed off and Ty took a step toward her without meaning to. "But?"

"I'm hard to live with," she said with a light laugh.

But he could see there was some true regret in her eyes.

"I don't know if I'd be a good mom or wife," she said truthfully. "So I've focused on making this town good for all of the other families."

She glanced away from him, her gaze landing on the crowd gathered—the very quiet and attentive crowd—and blushed a deep red.

"My favorite childhood memory is summer too," Ty said, pulling the audience's attention back to himself and off her sudden discomfort. "Summer at the pool meant girls in swimming suits."

Everyone laughed, and Ty felt a wave of relief that he'd been able to divert the attention and lighten the tone. He hadn't meant to make Hailey uncomfortable. He supposed he hadn't expected her to be so honest about not believing she'd be good at being married or parenting.

"Oh, Ty," Hailey said. "You shouldn't joke about that. You were at the pool to train. I remember you being ticked off when the kids would get into the lap lane and mess up your stroke. And you were out biking and running all the time. When did you start that? You were young."

He blinked at her. Turning the questioning back on him? Positively?

Okay.

"I've loved to run, bike and swim as long as I can remember. My brothers were responsible for my competitive streak." He glanced at the three men who had pushed him since he was born. "Since I was the youngest, it was about keeping up with them. And they didn't make it easy." Travis, Tucker and TJ all grinned at that and Ty affectionately rolled his eyes. None of *them* had an Olympic medal.

"And how did that all turn into triathlons?" Hailey

asked.

She knew this story. She'd asked him before.

"When I was fourteen, triathlon was a part of the Olympics for the first time and I remember watching it with my dad."

Thomas Bennett was in the front row next to Kathy and he smiled and nodded at the memory.

"You have a wonderful family," she said.

No one else probably heard anything but a sincere compliment, but Ty saw the wistfulness in her eyes and heard the longing. He'd thought he knew about her family and how she'd grown up, but his mother had turned that all around the other morning.

"Tell me about your family," he said before he could think better of it.

He didn't want to make this embarrassing or painful, but there were things about Hailey that people needed to understand. Family made a person who they were in so many ways. And he would suspect that if Kathy Bennett knew some of the truth, others did too.

Hailey looked at him for a long moment and Ty held his breath. He gave her a single nod.

Then her chin lifted, and he breathed.

"My dad has always been very caught up in his work. Being a politician means a lot to him," she said. Her eyes stayed on Ty, as if they were having a conversation just between the two of them.

And Ty wished they were. Or that they had. They'd talked, of course, but thinking back on their time together over the past few years, it seemed their conversations had stayed in the present tense. They hadn't talked about the past much and rarely mentioned the future beyond the few weeks directly in front of them. He wished he'd asked her these questions, and many more, before this.

"He's a workaholic, but not in the negative way a lot of people say that," Hailey went on. "He truly loves being a public servant, and there isn't anything more important to him." She took a deep breath. "I had a wonderful role model for true dedication to an elected office and public service. He said that it's the epitome of trust for people to put you in charge of things."

It seemed that the audience agreed with her assessment of her father. Ty didn't know Stan well at all, but his impression was that he was an honest, hardworking man, and Ty knew his own father had voted for Stan for state Senate. That was all the stamp of approval Ty really needed.

"What about your mom?" Ty pressed.

Hailey took a deep breath. "My mother was a waitress at my dad's favorite café before he moved back to Sapphire Falls. They had a brief affair, she got pregnant and then was killed in a car accident when I was two months old."

There was a collective gasp. So Ty wasn't the only one who hadn't known all of that.

"Angela was my stepmother. She doesn't like me very much," Hailey said with a wobbly smile. "And she loved to point out the things I did wrong. My flaws."

"You don't have any flaws, Madam Mayor," Ty said, his voice gruffer. She was opening up and he knew what that took from her. God, he was proud of her.

She laughed and the strain in her eyes eased a little. "Of course, I do. We all do."

She took another deep breath and lifted her chin in that way that never failed to make Ty confident that she was determined about something.

"I was easily distracted. I was always losing things, forgetting things, running late. And Angela loved to point my mistakes out to my dad. She told me I was an airhead, ditzy, a dreamer, unorganized, impossible—lots of different variations of that. She would say things like I was a true blond. Just like my mom. And what did he expect from the daughter of a waitress? A rocket scientist?"

Hailey stopped and looked around the crowd. "And she wasn't wrong about me," she said. "I *was* unorganized. I *did* have a hard time focusing and keeping track of things. I still do. And it causes a lot of anxiety in my life. I'm obsessive about things now—I triple-check things and write things down in three places and I sometimes redo things two or three times until they're perfect. I sometimes have to get up and go to the office in the middle of the night because something will occur to me and I can't sleep until I take care of it. I'm completely addicted to sticky notes, I have three different planners, and I have to read very slowly and methodically to absorb and understand what I'm reading."

Ty frowned. He hadn't meant for her to spill her guts entirely. He didn't consider her an airhead or unorganized at all. What was she doing?

"And," Hailey went on, "it wasn't until I was in college and really struggling to keep up that I learned that I *wasn't* dumb or slow or ditzy, and it had nothing to do with my blond hair. They diagnosed me with ADHD, attention deficit hyperactive disorder."

She paused to let the murmur go through the crowd and Ty crossed to his hay bale to sit. He hadn't known *any* of this. She'd hid it well. Which made sense, he supposed. She hid a lot of things well.

But it also meant she hadn't trusted him enough to share.

Hailey continued. "Yes, that's typically something you hear about kids having and sometimes growing out of, but no one tested me, and I struggled all the way through school. I got good at covering it up because I hated giving Angela things to comment on," she said. "It was such a relief when I finally found out that it wasn't my fault. Once I talked with someone who really understood it, she was able to give me study techniques and other things to keep me more on track and focused, and learning became easier.

But I still get frustrated with it—with myself—on almost a daily basis. No matter how organized I try to be or how many techniques I learn, I can't get over it completely, and I'm obviously not going to grow out of it."

Hailey stopped and took a breath. "So if your child is struggling at all, don't make assumptions or place blame. Talk to someone and see if there's a way you can help him or her."

Ty knew he was staring, but damn. That was easily the most transparent moment he'd ever experienced with Hailey. And he was experiencing it with a huge group of people. Not in the bedroom, not during a quiet moment between the two of them. She wasn't even really telling *him*.

This was one more obvious example of how he *didn't* know the real Hailey.

And yet he was fascinated.

"There's medicine for ADHD, isn't there?" he asked without really thinking.

She glanced at him for the first time during her reveal. She nodded. "But it has side effects, and for me the headaches were too much. Instead, I work with other behavior modifications, watch what I eat because sugar makes a big difference—in a bad way—and exercise really helps work off some of my excess energy and helps me focus."

He shook his head. Well, it made sense why she'd loved all of the physical activity in Colorado.

She turned back to the crowd. "I haven't ever talked about this openly. It's been hard for me to admit that I have some struggles. But I promise you that I work hard to not let this affect my job, and I have wonderful friends and a fantastic assistant." She smiled at the women clustered off to the side near the front.

Lauren, Adrianne, Phoebe and Tessa were all standing there, looking surprised but pleased. They hadn't expected all of this to come out perhaps, but Ty could tell that they weren't shocked by what she was saying. They knew. They knew about Hailey's issues.

Which meant she did share it. With people she felt close to and trusted.

Ty felt his gut knot and he worked not to scowl in front of everyone.

"My friends keep me from freaking out," Hailey said with a smile to the audience. "They put up with my quirks and my overuse of highlighters and my being late. So be patient with the people in your lives. Especially the kids. You never know what they might be struggling with."

Ty agreed. And his current struggle was that the woman he was in love with had struggles he didn't know about. That she had shared with other people. That she had not only *not* shared with him, but that she'd actively hidden from him. She had techniques she had to use to stay focused and on track? He'd never noticed a thing.

Was that a commentary on what a great actress she was or how unobservant he was? TJ said Ty had been wrapped up in his own stuff to the point of not paying attention to what was going on with Hailey and what she wanted and needed.

He'd moved in next door to her because *he* wanted to, without thinking that maybe her irritation would go beyond the initial surprise of it. He'd moved his life here, changed their entire relationship, without talking with her about it. Without even really considering how it might affect her.

No, that wasn't it. He'd considered it. He just hadn't worried that it would be a problem. He'd trusted that he'd be able to win her over.

"Ty?"

He shook his head and realized that Hailey was looking at him.

"Uh, yeah?"

"I asked what you would change about yourself if you

could change anything?"

Ty felt his jaw tighten. He'd change the fact that his girlfriend couldn't be honest with him. He'd change the fact that there was anything to change in the first place.

Dammit.

He wasn't good with things not being exactly as he wanted them to be. When he didn't hit the time he wanted, he pushed harder. When the weather was crap, he worked through it. When he wasn't feeling well, he worked out anyway and upped his fluid and vitamin intake. When he had an equipment issue, he got it fixed or bought something new.

Things didn't always go his way, but he could always do something about it.

But how could he change this? He hated that Hailey didn't feel like she was the woman he'd spent years adoring. Yes, he wanted her to be that woman—that woman was perfect for him. He wanted her to be confident and proud of herself, not have any leftover insecurities from her childhood, and not feel as if she had to defend herself to the town she'd served for six years.

But as conflicted as he was about all of this and how it affected him—typical of a guy who was used to everything revolving around him, he supposed—he also admired what she'd done tonight.

Pure honesty and vulnerability were the themes of the night? Okay, he could do that.

"I'd change the fact that I'm not someone the woman I love can trust with all her secrets and fears."

Hailey's smile fell instantly and a strange hush surrounded them.

She looked like he'd slapped her, and Ty couldn't quite figure out why. She knew that she hadn't shared everything with him. She'd been very purposeful about it. So was she surprised that he was hurt by it? Was she simply surprised that he'd said it publicly?

The silence stretched long, with no one even shifting on their hay bales.

Finally, Lauren stepped in. "Okay, let's take some more questions from the audience."

Ty kept his eyes on her as he took his seat. Hailey, on the other hand, avoided looking at him completely.

๛๏๛

Hailey went through the rest of the Q&A session with only half her mind on what was happening. She avoided looking at Ty, but she could feel his gaze boring into her at various times. She could practically feel the waves of tension coming at her across the space between them.

They answered a few questions each about their favorite books, how they spent their down time, favorite Sapphire Falls festival or activity, favorite thing to order at Dottie's and at Adrianne's, and Hailey was grateful for the easy questions that required almost no thought.

Ty was pissed. Because she hadn't told him about the ADHD. But how could he not understand why she hadn't told him? *He* was the one who constantly talked about how great it felt to have won her over, how tough she'd been to get and how hard she'd made him work and how much he loved making her give in in the bedroom.

Most people who knew them both on the surface would have never believed they worked as a couple. It seemed that they both liked to hog the spotlight. But she was relieved to give it over, to let people focus on Ty when they were together. She could let go and not worry about keeping up the pretense of being queen bee. Everyone assumed she liked being in charge and that she'd sought the mayor's office as a way of bossing everyone around. The truth was she'd gone after the office because it made her father proud and it was the most direct way to take care of her hometown.

If there was another way to be involved and make Sapphire Falls great, she'd do it.

And, yes, she needed to get over the need to seek her father's approval. She knew that. She and Lena were working on it. But lifelong habits were tough to break.

Finally, they finished the session and everyone was encouraged to help themselves to the ice cream sundae bar set up on the other side of the gazebo.

"You were amazing," Adrianne said, giving Hailey a hug. "Wow."

"That was ballsy," Lauren told her. "I didn't expect you to open up about everything."

Hailey shrugged. "It felt right. Maybe it's the denim shorts, but I felt more comfortable telling everyone." She tipped her head to the side. "You don't seem surprised about the ADHD."

Lauren shook her head. "Not surprised. I knew there was something going on with you."

"You never asked."

"Not my business unless you chose to tell me."

Hailey glanced to where Ty had disappeared across the square. "You're not upset I didn't tell you?" she asked. "You're not hurt that I didn't confide in you?"

Lauren also glanced to where Ty had walked off. "No. But I haven't been sleeping with you for almost four years."

"He told you?" Hailey *was* surprised by that. Kind of. It depended on the circumstances of their conversation. "How? When?"

"At his mom's the other day. Right after he announced he was running. He thought maybe he'd screwed up."

Yeah, okay, surprised was right. "Ty never admits when he's screwed up."

Lauren nodded. "It must have really mattered to him."

"Were you surprised about me and Ty?" Hailey asked.

"Not really. You seem like the perfect couple."

Perfect. There was that word.

"We *seem* like the perfect couple?"

"Beautiful, successful, big plans and lots of talent," Lauren said. "And Ty loves a challenge. You've been a challenge to him."

"Ty likes to win," Hailey said, feeling her heart aching. "He's done this whole thing with this election because he didn't want me to have an empty victory, but I told him that our whole relationship has been an empty victory for him."

Phoebe frowned. "What does that mean?"

"He thinks that I'm this perfect woman that he had to win over and impress. When the truth is I'm far from perfect, and getting me wasn't hard because I haven't given him a real relationship." She took a deep breath. "And I've loved it. I've loved how things have been between us. In little bits."

Phoebe looked sad. "You don't want him full time? Just in bits and pieces?"

"That's what I can handle," Hailey told her. "I can be the perfect girlfriend for two days at a time. Not full time."

That felt horrible. She'd known it for a long time, but she had never said it out loud to someone else.

"I think you're selling yourself short," Adrianne said. "Full-time relationships take more work than weekend flings, but you've had full-time relationships with all of us."

"But you know me," Hailey said. "You know I'm not perfect."

"Because you let us in. You told us what was going on with you. You didn't do that with Ty."

Hailey felt the tears threatening. "Because Ty had this idea about me already built up, and I couldn't bring myself to tell him the truth. I loved having his attention, spending time with him. I—"

"Didn't trust him," Lauren filled in. "And he knows that now."

Hailey nodded. "I didn't mean to hurt him."

"I think the fact that it *did* hurt him should tell you something," Lauren said.

Hailey thought about that. Maybe. Maybe Ty wanted to know her better. Maybe it bothered him that there were things he didn't know. But she was more afraid that he was mad she'd been deceiving him—and wasting his time.

"Hailey, honey." Kathy Bennett was suddenly there, enfolding Hailey in a big hug. She rubbed her hand up and down Hailey's back. "That was so wonderful."

Kathy was an expert hugger. Hailey felt so much more than just the other woman's arms around her. She felt surrounded by support and love. And she absorbed it all like she was a sponge tossed into the ocean. Or like she was still the little girl who could do nothing right in her stepmother's eyes.

The tears did more than threaten this time. When Hailey pulled back and saw Kathy's smile and the affection in her eyes, they spilled over.

"Oh, honey, don't cry." Kathy brushed a hand over Hailey's cheek. "Think of all the kids you helped by showing them that this amazing woman they've looked up to had to overcome some struggles. Think of all the women that have looked at you and seen how put together you are and how you seem to do everything right who can now relate to you and accept that they don't have to be perfect."

That made Hailey cry harder.

Lauren stepped forward and put a hand on Kathy's shoulder. "I agree. You did something awesome tonight," she said to Hailey. "And if not everyone sees it that way, that's their problem."

Unless, of course, it was the man Hailey was in love with. Then it was her problem too. She could lose him. She'd always known it, and had known on some level that he'd eventually find out that she wasn't the perfect woman he saw, but she'd had no idea that losing him would hurt this much.

Kathy scowled. "Who doesn't see it that way? Did someone say something to you?"

Hailey caught Lauren's eye and she shook her head. She couldn't tell on Ty to his mom.

But Lauren said, "Ty."

Kathy looked from Lauren to Hailey. "What do you mean?"

"Ty's upset because Hailey didn't tell him all of this before tonight."

Oh, so Lauren was going to tell Ty's mother on *Hailey*.

"Why not, honey?" Kathy asked, her scowl gone and her tone gentler now.

Hailey swallowed hard. "I liked being his perfect woman."

Kathy's eyes lit with understanding. "And you think the ADHD and your anxiety makes you imperfect."

"It does," Hailey said. "Trust me. I mess things up all the time. Things that take someone else an hour to do can take me all afternoon."

"We *all* mess things up," Kathy said. "But you've been made to think that it makes you a bad person."

"Ty doesn't mess things up," Hailey said. She smiled at Kathy. "Okay, here and there, but he's the most organized person I've ever met. He likes things a certain way. He thinks everything through and plans it out. I know he comes across as this laid-back, spontaneous guy, but that's an act. Underneath, he's so on top of things." She paused and shrugged. "If he learned local policy and got up-to-date on current issues, he could be a really good mayor."

"Being a good mayor is about a lot more than being organized," Kathy said. "It takes passion and love for the community."

"Ty has that."

"No one has it like you do," Kathy said. "I've lived here all my life, and listening to you talk makes me love this place even more each time."

Hailey felt a tiny heart flip at that, but she asked, "Listening to me tonight?"

"Anytime," Kathy said. "You have an enthusiasm in your tone that always makes me look around and think this town really is amazing. And tonight, finding out what you really have to do to be so good at your job, makes me admire you all the more."

Now her heart did a full three-sixty flip. Kathy Bennett had listened to her and been positively affected. Kathy admired *her*.

"It's all stuff I *have* to do," Hailey said, trying to resist the urge to throw her arms around Kathy again.

"No, honey. You want to. Or you wouldn't put yourself through all of that," Kathy said. "You love this town enough to triple-check things and come down in the middle of the night to make sure everything is done right. If you didn't, you would have found another job that caused you a lot less stress and anxiety. I'm sure every time you have to prepare for a meeting or read a report or any of the other things that are difficult for you, you're reminded all over again of Angela pointing out your shortcomings and that feeling of not being quite good enough. And I am so sorry you had to go through that growing up."

Hailey pressed her lips together and nodded. Kathy had nailed it. There wasn't a day that went by that Hailey wasn't reminded she would never get it all right or do a great job. So she overcompensated and did four times the work. And never felt fully satisfied with it.

"And if Tyler makes you feel that way," Kathy said, her eyebrows pulling together over blue eyes that looked exactly like her youngest son's, "then you're better off without him."

Hailey stared at the other woman. She was admitting Ty might have done something wrong? And she thought Hailey would be better without him?

He'd openly adored her for fourteen years. He'd actually been a balm on the wounds that Angela's constant criticism had caused.

That was why Hailey had kept stringing him along for so long. Because if anyone or anything made her feel unworthy or like a screw-up, all she had to do was bump into Ty in the hallway and he'd give her a big grin that said clearly he was happy to see her, and a compliment that would make her smile for hours.

The years she'd been away at college, she'd been eager to run into him in town over her breaks or weekends home. And the years after he went to Colorado and before they reconnected had been long and noticeably less happy than when she was seeing him from time to time.

She'd fallen easily into his bed—or onto his desk, more accurately—because she'd missed how much he liked her.

Hailey blew out a breath. "It's not Ty," she told his mother. "He's never made me feel anything but like he thinks I'm perfect and amazing."

"Good." Kathy actually seemed truly relieved by that.

"But that's made me really work on being that perfect woman," Hailey said. "I'll drive him crazy if we're together all the time."

"Your sticky notes haven't driven him crazy yet," Kathy pointed out. "Your need to triple-check everything hasn't bothered him, right?"

"He doesn't know about all of that. Or, he didn't," she said, realizing it was all blown wide open now. "He's never seen my sticky notes."

Kathy nodded. "And why is that?"

"I've hidden all of that from him. It's silly, I suppose, but the things that keep me on track and organized—the planners and sticky notes and highlighters—are also constant reminders that I need all of that to be effective, and they make me feel bad. So I leave them behind when I visit Ty."

"But you don't need them when you're with Ty?" Kathy asked.

"No. He takes care of everything when we're together."

Kathy didn't respond at first. She just watched Hailey's face.

The words replayed in her mind. Ty took care of everything when they were together. Which was true. She let go of a lot of her anxiety when she was with him because she knew he was in charge.

"I want to be his partner, not someone he needs to take care of," she said softly.

"And that right there is probably the only mistake you've really made in all of this," Kathy said.

"What is?"

"Not letting people take care of you."

Hailey glanced at the three women standing behind Kathy watching their exchange. Adrianne, Phoebe and Lauren. They had always been there. They'd loved her in spite of her being scattered or bitchy.

And they had jumped in to take over the campaign for her. She hadn't had to worry about a single detail at all. She'd shown up where they'd told her to and done what they'd told her to do. It had all worked beautifully.

But she'd never asked them for help with anything else.

"When people love you, they *want* to take care of you, Hailey," Kathy told her. "Yes, Ty will want you to be an equal partner in the relationship. But being an equal partner doesn't mean you don't lean on the other person—it means that you're there for them to lean on when they need it too."

Hailey took a deep breath and then blew it out.

People didn't lean on her, didn't ask her for help outside the help that a mayor needed to give. Adrianne, Phoebe and Lauren hadn't. Ty hadn't.

And, yes, that had hurt. She would have gladly been there to visit him in the hospital or to help him out around his house when he'd first gone home.

She hadn't given it a lot of thought until now, but thinking about Ty hobbling around his house, hurting, frustrated and scared and worried about his future in competition made her heart clench.

She definitely would have been there if he'd told her. But he hadn't.

"I need to go talk to him," Hailey said. "Thank you so much," she told Kathy. She stepped back and lifted her eyes to her friends. "Thank you all too."

"Believe it or not," Adrianne said. "You can be quite lovable."

Hailey smiled and turned away before she started crying again. She wasn't used to hearing that kind of stuff, and it was going to take some work—and some sessions with Lena, no doubt—to get over the knee-jerk urge to deny it.

But Ty Bennett had loved her for fourteen years. At least part of her. The idea of her.

Maybe she *could* be quite lovable.

CHAPTER EIGHT

Ty threw his cap against the kitchen table as he banged into his house. But the cap hitting the wood wasn't nearly satisfying enough. He picked up a half-empty bottle of water and threw it against the lower cupboards across from him. That too was less than satisfying. So he stomped into the living room. But other than lamps and books, there wasn't really much to throw around.

It wasn't like he left plates and beer bottles lying around.

Now *that* would feel good—to heave a beer bottle against his stone fireplace.

But he wouldn't do that. That would be a damned mess to clean up after.

But that didn't mean he couldn't drink one.

He stalked back into the kitchen, yanked the fridge door open and grabbed two. He put the lip of one cap against the counter and banged the top with his hand, flipping the bottle cap off and sending it skittering across the wood floor.

He tipped the beer back, swallowing three times before lowering it.

Then he thought back to the moment when he realized that he'd been having a fake relationship with a fake woman for the past almost four years.

Two beers weren't going to be enough.

He grabbed a third from the fridge and headed back into the living room.

He stood in the middle of the room and turned a slow circle.

The living room he now owned because he'd packed up his imperfect, fucked-up life in Colorado to come to Sapphire Falls and have the perfect life with the perfect woman in the perfect town.

All of which was fake.

Well, the town wasn't fake. But, hell, maybe it wasn't perfect either. That was pure blasphemy to even *think*, of course. Everyone who lived here thought Sapphire Falls was as perfect a place a guy could be while still on earth. But what did he know about it? He knew Colorado had skiing and better enchiladas. That's what he knew. He hadn't lived here in eleven years, and he wouldn't be here now if his knee hadn't crapped out on him.

It was that thought that made him slump onto his couch and drain the rest of beer number one.

He'd had the perfect life. For a while.

Everything had been mapped out. He'd had a *plan*, dammit. He'd known what he was working for and had daily, weekly and monthly goals. He'd known how long he was going to compete, who his sponsors would be, when he would move into coaching instead and settle down.

The training center had been his plan, but just…not yet.

He'd played with the idea of putting the center here. But not yet.

He'd planned to get married and settle down and have a family. Just not yet.

But nothing was going according to that plan anymore.

He'd had an amazing career, been at the top of his game, on track for the gold. The fucking Olympic gold medal. His lifelong dream.

And he'd had Hailey. The perfect woman—gorgeous, smart, sharp, sassy. She didn't let men close easily, didn't date them for long, didn't rearrange her schedule and travel eight hours to see anyone. Except him. *That* had felt perfect. Everything from her hair to her ass to her toes was perfect.

He'd had Bryan—coaching him and pushing him and telling him when he was slacking and when he wasn't being realistic. Or when he was plain being an ass. Bryan definitely kept Ty's jackass tendencies in check. That had been the perfect setup too. Lord knew, he needed someone keeping his jackass under control.

Now his knee was messed-up, his relationship was messed-up, Bryan was messed-up.

And the jackass who was never far from the surface was starting to rear his head a lot more regularly.

But Bryan *was* messed-up and couldn't focus on Ty and tell him when he was veering way off course. Bryan couldn't make Ty the center of his attention anymore. So he'd come to Sapphire Falls to Hailey.

He tipped his head back and stared at the ceiling.

Fuck, was that really what he'd done?

Yes. Ty couldn't deny that was how it felt. He'd had his entourage in Colorado, and when the leader of the band was out of commission, it hadn't been the same.

But when in Sapphire Falls, Hailey couldn't revolve around him either.

And when had he become the ass who expected all of that anyway? About the time he'd moved to Colorado and no longer been *one* of the Bennett Boys, the younger brother of three great men who everyone liked.

He'd liked having the spotlight. There was no denying that.

So, yeah, he'd come to Sapphire Falls looking for a spotlight. Not even a big one. He'd wanted one woman to make him the center of her time, energy and attention like she did when she came to Colorado. Hailey not only relaxed and had fun in Colorado, but when she let him dictate every minute of their time together, that made him feel as though he was the center of her universe, and he really liked being there. That wasn't realistic for Sapphire Falls. She was in charge here. Other things were priorities to her and had to have her attention. Her *full* attention, according to what she'd spilled tonight. She didn't have time or energy for anything else—or *anyone* else—demanding attention in Sapphire Falls.

Denver had worked for them. It had worked *well*.
Things had been perfect.

Ty pushed himself off the couch.

He needed to go to Colorado. He needed to see Bryan.
He should have been checking in as it was, but he'd gotten
wrapped up in his own stuff—typical—and hadn't called in
days. And now he could use an eight-hour drive alone to
think things through.

But one thing was already clear.

He wanted Hailey, and things between them back to
when she'd been excited to see him and he'd made her
happy.

He wanted the laughing, relaxed, sassy woman who
would cheat when they played checkers by putting lotion
on her legs while he was trying to concentrate, and who
could make drinking a strawberry malt pure erotic torture
with her moans and sighs and tongue and lip action. He
wanted the woman he loved making chocolate-chip
pancakes for because she acted like he'd lassoed the moon
when he did it. He wanted the woman who had gotten him
hooked on the show *Parks and Recreation* and who had
introduced him to the music of Brett Eldredge.

He wanted what they'd always had. He missed her—
not just the sex they hadn't been having, but the feeling he
got when he first saw her after weeks apart. And the way
her eyes lit up when he got her a gift. And the way she
snorted when she got to laughing really hard. He missed the
things she yelled at referees and umpires during ballgames
and the way she wiggled and danced after getting past the
third screen in Pac-Man on his vintage videogame console.

As he climbed the stairs and threw clothes into a duffle,
something else became clear.

If he wanted things to be the way they'd always been
with Hailey, he was going to have to *move* back to Denver.

Things had been good with them when he'd lived in
Colorado. He didn't get to see her as often as he wanted to,

but he'd rather see her happy for two days at a time than see her stressed and unhappy because he'd forced her into a lifestyle she didn't want by moving in next door.

His duffle full, Ty grabbed his keys and phone from the dresser and headed back downstairs. He needed to find her before he left, but he wasn't sure if he should tell her he was going to visit Bryan or if he should tell her what he was feeling about them.

He was in love with her, and so far he'd done a shitty job of showing it. It had been all about him since he'd opened his front door to her and her brownies.

Hell, it was no wonder she didn't tell him everything.

He'd shown up next door without talking with her about it. He'd pushed her into a campaign she never should have had to run. The campaign had forced her to open up about things she'd kept to herself all her life.

He was causing her trouble and pain here.

He needed to leave her alone and be thrilled with the two days every four to six weeks they had.

Ty was reaching for the knob when the doorbell rang.

He pulled the door open, expecting a brother to be on his doorstep.

But it was Hailey.

"Hi."

"Hi."

His whole body ached with the need to pull her into his arms.

"We should talk," she said.

"Yeah. We should. Okay." He stepped back to let her in.

Her eyes landed on the bag in his hand. "What's that?"

"Clothes and stuff for a couple of days. I need to go check on Bryan." He dropped the bag behind the door. "But I can talk first. I want to talk first."

She stopped in the arched doorway to the living room and turned to him with her arms crossed. "Is Bryan okay?"

"I don't know, actually. I haven't checked on him the way I should have. I need to go and spend a couple of days."

Ty didn't know exactly what kind of talk this was going to be. He slid his hands into his front pockets and kept the five feet of space between them. He'd been hurt to learn there were things she hadn't felt she could share with him, but like his conversation a few days ago with Lauren, Ty realized this was on both of them. No, Hailey hadn't shared. But he hadn't asked. He hadn't dug into her motivations, into the things that made her tick. He'd thought he knew her and had been content with what he thought he knew. She had been the woman he wanted and he'd been happy with the fantasy he'd built up in his mind.

"Okay, so maybe we should talk later. Or never." She took a step toward the door.

He moved in front of her. "Hold on. Not never. We should talk."

"About how I'm not the perfect woman that you want anymore."

"I never thought you were perfect." Not literally. Completely. Fuck, he was a jackass.

"You thought I was perfect for *you* though," she said.

"Yes," he said sincerely. "Absolutely."

"But I'm not. You've been realizing that ever since you got here. I'm not confident and in charge. And now you know that I'm not organized and on task and goal-oriented like you are. The things you respect and like about me are all fake."

He didn't answer at first. It was true that he'd believed all of those things about her before he'd become her next-door neighbor. It was true that he'd thought one of the things that appealed to him about her was that he had won over the woman with sky-high standards. He'd also believed they had a lot in common—driven, competitive, career-oriented type-A people.

But did the fact that she wasn't any of those things change how he felt?

He wasn't sure.

"I think I got my answer," she said after the silence had stretched too long. She started for the door again.

Ty stepped in front of her. "Hang on. Give me a second."

"You don't need a second," she said. "You know how you feel. You just don't know how to say it."

"Dammit, Hailey, I've been a little blindsided here, okay? Give me a damned minute to process it all."

"What's to process? I've been lying to you and keeping things from you for years. I've made myself into the woman that I knew you wanted, but that's not really me."

He stepped close, towering over her in the boots more than he could in her usual heels. He didn't touch her, but he knew she wasn't going to try to get around him. She knew he'd stop her. And he would. Not to force his will on her, but because he needed some answers and he had some things to say and she wanted to hear them. Somewhere deep down she knew that.

"Why did you try so hard to be who you thought I wanted? Seems like I worked awfully hard for a long time to get you. If you thought I wouldn't like the real you, why not just show her to me from the beginning?"

He saw the sparkle of tears in her eyes. Oh no, she couldn't cry. He couldn't handle her tears.

"No crying and getting my sympathies that way, babe," he said softly. "I need to know this stuff, and if you cry, I'll want to hug you, and if I hug you in those shorts, it's going to be a long time until either of us can catch our breath enough to talk again."

That did the trick. Heat and affection flared in her eyes instead, and Ty was comforted knowing that he still knew her on some level. Maybe a more important level than knowing about her ADHD.

Still, that was a big deal. It clearly affected how she lived her life. He needed to know about it if they were going to have a future.

"So you never thought there would be any long-term for us?" he asked, realizing it only a moment before he asked. "Because if you had, you would have realized that you needed to tell me about the sticky notes and anxiety."

She pressed her lips together and nodded.

"Yes, what?"

"I did realize that," she said. "I wanted long-term, but I didn't think it would happen. I thought I was safe—I was mayor here, so you'd never expect me to move to Denver. And your life was there, your training and everything, and I knew nothing else would be that important and you'd never move here."

He kind of hated the nothing-else-would-be-that-important bit, but he wasn't sure he could effectively argue against it. Chasing the gold had consumed his last eleven years. Having her in his life had been a break from the pressure and the pain of going after something that stayed beyond his reach.

"I was crazy about you because as I was training for the medal that just wouldn't fucking come, I had you. I had this woman who was my dream girl—and many men's dream girl—in my bed, in my life. I could make you go weak and beg and want me. You'd drive eight hours to be with me. That made me feel like a king."

"And that's why I kept it all up," she said. "I knew that dream girl mattered to you and if I wasn't her, someone else would be. For real. And I'd lose you."

He moved in even closer, until the toes of his boots touched the toes of hers. "You didn't want to lose me?"

She shook her head.

"Because of the sex?"

She shook her head. Then she nodded. Then she wiggled it side to side. "That was some of it. Sex with you is amazing."

He gave her a half grin. It definitely was. "Because of my Olympic medal or the hopes of another?"

She shook her head.

"Then why? The chocolate-chip pancakes?"

"Okay, those are amazing too," she said. But then her expression grew serious. She took a deep breath. "Honestly?"

"God, *yes*," he said. "Please."

"It's because you were the only person to ever come after me, to want to be with me. You made me feel special and wanted and cherished. I hadn't ever had that before."

He finally couldn't resist. He lifted a hand and cupped her cheek. Ty felt the tension through his whole body. The ache to make things better for her, to make up for what she'd been missing, the urge to hurt those people who'd hurt her. But there was also a surge of satisfaction upon hearing that he'd given her something no one else had.

"I want to keep making you feel that way," he said.

"Thank you."

She smiled and it reached her eyes in a way that made Ty breathe easier. He did that to her. For her. He made her feel special and important for something other than being pretty or being mayor. That made *him* feel important.

"I'm going to take my house in Denver off the market. Tomorrow, as soon as the office opens."

She pulled her face away from his hand. "What?"

"I'll move back to Denver. I shouldn't have moved here without talking to you about it anyway. But things were good when you came to Denver. Let's go back to that."

She stared up at him, a myriad of emotions flashing across her face. "What about your training center?"

"I can open it there. It will be okay." He'd loved the idea of having it here where he'd started his journey, but Denver made sense.

She stepped back and he dropped his hand. "And what

if you win the election?"

"I'll step down. Hand it over to you. Whatever I need to do. I never wanted to win, Hails."

"It's not that easy. You can't say, 'Oh, I've changed my mind.'"

"Then I'll have Travis lead a campaign to have me impeached or something. I'll embezzle some money or something."

"And go to prison." She crossed her arms again.

"We'll figure it out. And if I'm not here for these next few days, maybe no one will vote for me anyway."

"We can only hope," she muttered.

He stepped toward her. "Running was a dumb idea. I'm sorry."

She shrugged and studied her boots. "It wasn't so bad. It made me realize some things too. No one's wanting or waiting for me to fail."

"Of course not."

"And I have some really good friends. In spite of everything."

"You do." He'd liked Adrianne, Phoebe and Lauren as long as he'd known them, but he was now also grateful for their support of Hailey. "I'm glad you were able to open up to them."

She studied his eyes. "Really? Even though I didn't open up to you?"

"Of course. I love the idea of being important to you." He reached out and took her upper arms and brought her forward. "I *love* the idea of being important to you. But I'm glad you know you're important to other people too."

She pressed her lips together, strangely quiet after that.

Finally, she said, "I thought you'd like the shorts."

So they weren't going to talk more about their feelings. Good.

He could definitely deal with cut-off denim shorts that showed long, smooth legs he wanted wrapped around his waist.

Emotions, on the other hand… Yeah, they should stick with the shorts.

"Those shorts are the hottest fucking thing I've seen besides your bare pussy on the edge of your *cherry*-wood desk," he said bluntly.

Heat flared in her eyes and she sucked in a breath.

"But I'm not happy that you wore them for the whole town. Just like you confessed all your secrets for the town. For the votes." He needed her riled up. "While all the women were admiring how honest and strong you were to tell about your ADHD, all the guys were admiring the sweetest thighs and ass in Nebraska."

He needed her riled up because the soft Hailey made him want to wrap her in a fuzzy blanket and stay in Sapphire Falls and take care of her. And that was the last thing she wanted or needed. She didn't need to be taken care of. She needed to be respected and supported. That was different. He knew that. He just wasn't really sure how to do the support thing.

He needed to go to Denver, get some distance, get his house off the market. Talk to Bryan.

There was a knowing look in her eyes. She knew what he was doing. "I wore the shorts for you. Not for the votes."

"No, you were trying to look like one of the girls."

She took his hand and put it on her right butt cheek. "Do I look like one of the girls to you, Ty?"

He couldn't help it. He squeezed the firm curve of her ass. "Not a bit."

"I wore the boots for the town. I wore the shorts for you. I was trying to distract you from being too charming and smooth tonight during the Q&A."

He couldn't help it. He laughed. And put both hands on her ass, drawing her up against him. "I think it worked. You were the one in the spotlight tonight."

"I confessed because of you too," she said, wrapping her arms around his neck. "You led me into that with your questions. You made me open up."

"I'm not sorry."

"You're mad that I didn't trust you enough to tell you."

"That's on both of us." He took a deep breath. "I liked my dream girl just as she was. I didn't delve into anything deeper. I didn't want to rock the boat. That's my fault too."

"I can be the dream girl, Ty. If that's what you want. You go back to Denver and I'll show up as your fantasy like always, and we'll both have what we want."

His gut churned at that. That *was* what he wanted. Wasn't it?

"I want you to be happy," he said honestly.

Her smile softened at that. "I want the same for you."

"I don't know if I'd be a good twenty-four-seven boyfriend."

"I don't know if I'd be a good twenty-four-seven girlfriend." She lifted a shoulder.

"So, me back in Denver, right?" If she told him that was what she wanted too, then he'd feel better…and less like he was bailing.

Hailey swallowed hard. "I do miss those enchiladas."

Okay. That was that.

Enchiladas, skiing and his dream girl once a month or so. Who could complain about that?

And why wouldn't his stomach stop cramping?

He brought her up onto her tiptoes and kissed her. Kissing Hailey never failed to make things better.

She arched against him, kissing him back hungrily. As if she also realized that this would be one of the last times in Sapphire Falls.

But a thought occurred to him and he pulled back. "But we can be together now when I come home to visit, right?" he asked. "I can hold your hand downtown and kiss you in the gazebo and we can make out at river parties?"

She grinned. "Yeah, for a weekend or so, it can work. You'll distract me, but I can probably let things go for a couple of days here and there."

Ty recognized that what she'd said was big. "I'll help keep you on track while I'm here if you have anything going on."

She kissed him, then whispered, "Thank you," against his lips.

He deepened the kiss, sweeping his tongue over her bottom lip and then taking her mouth fully when she sighed. Her breasts pressed into his chest and her belly pressed into his rock-hard cock.

Ty dragged his mouth to her ear. "You know, my dream girl would let me bend her over that couch."

"I want to be your dream girl, Ty," she said softly.

He walked her backward until the couch was right behind her. "Then turn around."

She spun in his arms, bracing her hands on the back of the couch.

"Damn, I do really like these shorts," he said, running his hands over the denim-covered curve of her ass.

She wiggled under his touch.

"And I love this T-shirt," he said. He slid his hands around to her stomach, rubbing back and forth across the soft cotton before moving up to cup her breasts. Her nipples were already hard, and he took his time playing with her through the shirt.

She pressed her butt back into his groin. "More, Ty."

His cock throbbed at her plea. "Yes, ma'am."

He pulled her shirt up and one side of her bra down to expose the firm flesh and hard tip while he unbuttoned and unsnapped her shorts with the other hand. The denim parted and he was able to get his hand underneath the silk of her panties and against the wet heat he craved.

Hailey ground against his hand, seeking pressure against her clit, and she gave a soft whimper that fired his blood. But he wasn't ready to give her what she wanted just yet. Instead, he slipped two fingers into her pussy, feeling the muscles tighten around him and relishing her groan.

She widened her stance and her head dropped forward.

He squeezed her nipple while pumping his fingers deep. "I don't care where we are," he said against her neck. "I love making you come apart. Over and over."

Her muscles clenched and she whimpered again. "Ty."

"And that. I fucking love hearing you helpless for what only I can give you." He stroked in and out of her again.

"Yes. God," she panted.

"I can't stop touching you for even a second," he told her gruffly. "Push your shorts and panties off."

She moved swiftly, shoving the shorts and her tiny thong to her ankles.

"I had a few fantasies of you exactly like this in high school," he told her, leaning back to take in the sight of her undressed only enough that he could get to where she really needed him.

She looked damn good like this—shorts bunched on top of her boots, T-shirt shoved up, body bent over and at his mercy.

"If I'd ever come over to your house after school, this is how it would have ended up," she told him breathlessly.

He squeezed her nipple. "Yeah?" Even if she was just saying it, her words fed the fantasy and he felt almost lightheaded as more blood surged to his cock.

"I had a hard enough time holding back from you at school and in public. If you'd ever gotten me alone, I would have jumped you."

He chuckled softly. Even at age twenty-nine, having had her in every position and several locations over a long period of time, he really wanted to believe what she was saying.

"I would have made you beg for it," he told her.

She wiggled against his hand. "I would have gladly

begged. God, if I'd known that you would take over and take *me*, I would have found a reason to get you alone long before the river."

He moved his fingers faster inside her, making her gasp and moan.

"You didn't think I could take care of you?" he asked.

"I didn't know. I guess I thought that since I was older and more experienced that I'd have to initiate things," she confessed.

"But you still didn't."

"I didn't want to disappoint you."

She said it almost too softly to hear. He paused and she whimpered at the loss of motion.

"Fucking you on that riverbank after graduation was one of the best nights of my life," he told her sincerely. "You were every fantasy come to life."

"You had me up on a pretty high pedestal. I was so afraid of falling off," she said.

"You were like a goddess to me, and that night blew my mind."

"But you took charge," she reminded him. "I kissed you and then you took over."

"I couldn't hold back. That was four years of lust all coming out."

She laughed. "It was so good."

He had to chuckle at that. "No, it wasn't. It was over way too fast. I had no control."

"I loved that. That was the best part. No one had ever wanted me like you did. It was like you were a kid, I was a candy store and someone told you I was all yours. You didn't know where to touch first, what to do first, you tried to do everything at once and you couldn't get enough."

He rested his forehead on her shoulder and admitted, "That was exactly what it was like. And then you were gone the next morning and I felt sick—like I'd eaten too much candy too fast."

She laughed. "I couldn't believe how good it had been and I didn't know how to face you. After all the years of thinking I was somehow in control of our relationship and then to lose myself in you like that."

Ty moved his fingers, getting a heartfelt moan from her. "Do you know how badly I wanted everything to be perfect, mind-blowing and amazing for you the next time we were together?" When she'd shown up in person in Denver, he'd known he needed a redo of the night at the river.

"That was when I knew I'd never get enough of you," she said hoarsely.

He rewarded her words by brushing his thumb over her clit. The spot was swollen and sensitive and she cried out from even that light touch.

"You're still like my candy store, dream girl." He went to his knees and pushed her forward over the back of the couch. He put his mouth to her pussy, flicking his tongue against her clit, his hands holding her hips as she squirmed. "Better than candy," he murmured. He licked over her clit again, dragged his tongue over her slick heat and then returned to her clit and sucked.

She gasped his name and pressed back.

He looked up to see her digging her fingers into the back of the couch. She was close. He licked over the nub again, increasing the pressure slowly until finally, when he sucked again, she went over the edge calling his name.

Ty was on his feet, his fly undone seconds later.

He grasped her hips and pulled her toward him as he thrust, sliding into her fully. She arched her neck, and he ran his hand up and down her back as she took him.

"Yes, Hailey, move with me."

She leaned forward, then back, sliding along his length, and he shuddered with the wave of pleasure that washed over him.

And in that hot, erotic moment, it hit him how truly

amazing this all was. She had doubted herself, hidden so much of herself from everyone, been taught that things she couldn't control made her flawed and not good enough, and yet she'd still let him close. She'd turned her body and her pleasure over to him completely when they were together. She might not have trusted him fully with her secrets, but she'd trusted him with intimate knowledge about her body and her fantasies and what fueled and satisfied her passion, and that was something. Something big. Something he could cling to.

He grasped her shoulders as he drove forward, embedding himself as deep as he could get.

"You're amazing," he told her sincerely. "More amazing than I ever imagined."

He felt her body clamp down on his and he thrust again, hard and deep, and a few minutes later, they went careening into an orgasm together.

After a shower together and making love again on the bed, he kissed her and got in his car to head to Denver, and saw that saying goodbye was hard on her too. He was going to cling to that as well.

❦

Thursday night, five days before the next mayoral term began, Hailey sat in the Come Again—Ty's campaign headquarters—and allowed Phoebe to fill her margarita glass for the third time.

The campaign was almost over.

And having Ty as a next-door neighbor was over.

And keeping secrets from her friends, town and boyfriend was over.

And she was miserable.

"I can't believe he isn't planning to vote in the election," Phoebe said with a grin. "Ty better hope he doesn't lose by one."

"He'll lose by a hell of a lot more than one," Lauren assured them all. "Hailey's got this."

Hailey just drank.

The election was tomorrow, the votes would be counted over the weekend and the winner posted on Monday.

She didn't care about the election. That was a startling truth that she'd only realized when she'd watched Ty's taillights disappear around the corner as he headed back to Denver. The place she'd never wanted him to leave in the first place.

Typical.

He'd come to town and stirred her up. As always. This time he'd stayed longer though, and *really* messed around in her life, so it made sense that she felt more annoyed than usual.

But that didn't explain the aching in her heart.

She hadn't *missed* him before. Or she hadn't let herself anyway. She'd believed that she wanted him to stay in Denver, far from her life in Sapphire Falls. So when he left after a visit, she usually felt relief.

Or that's what she'd told herself she felt.

Now it seemed that the being-honest-with-everyone thing was extending even to herself. And if she was honest, she'd admit that she missed him now that he was gone.

Dammit.

"Tell me again why he went back to Denver," Adrianne said.

The women were clustered around one table while their husbands, Ty's campaign team, sat at another. But they were really only divided because the guys were closer to the television, where they were watching the end of a baseball game. The women had to sit away from the TV so they could talk.

The exception was Adrianne's husband, Mason, who sat next to his wife. But he was completely absorbed in whatever he was doing on his tablet, and Hailey knew from experience he heard nothing that was going on around him. When Mason Riley was in work mode, the only person who could get his attention was Adrianne. And he was often in work mode.

"He had to go back and check on Bryan."

"But he'll be here Monday, right? To see who wins?" Phoebe asked.

Hailey had no idea. That wasn't new either. Ty never told her when he was coming to Sapphire Falls for a visit. But suddenly that seemed...wrong. Too detached. Too casual and emotionless.

She took another big drink. After she swallowed, she shook her head. "I'm not sure. He's..." She debated telling everyone Ty's plans to move back to Colorado. They wouldn't understand. "He's taking his house off the market and moving back there," she said anyway.

Because over the course of Ty being in town and her campaign for mayor, she'd realized that talking things out and letting people close wasn't so bad.

In fact, it was kind of nice.

Phoebe set her glass down hard and stared at her. "What?"

Hailey nodded. "He decided...we decided...that things were great when he lived in Denver, and that maybe this was all too much and we'd be better off if he moved back."

And she ignored the pang of doubt that arose every time she thought about the fact he hadn't decided to move back to Denver until he'd heard her public declaration of all her many flaws.

She'd been his dream girl for fourteen years, and finding out that not only did she have multiple *quirks* but that they weren't going away had obviously spooked him.

If it hadn't been for the sex before he left, she'd think maybe this was all over. But the sex had been...different. He'd been his usual domineering self, but there had been a sweetness and something else, almost like reverence as he'd touched her. For some reason, she'd been taken back to the night at the river after his graduation, and she'd remembered that having his lips and hands on her had felt like such a huge *relief*. Probably a strange word for it, but she'd felt as though she'd been waiting for him to touch her, to kiss her, to take care of her for so long. Which was crazy. Had felt crazy even then. He hadn't even been quite nineteen. She'd been with older, more-experienced guys. He'd been sexy and charming, and yet he'd been so…greedy. That was the best word. It had been exactly as she'd said—as if he'd been given free rein in a candy store that held every treat he'd ever dreamed of.

Last night had been like that. As if he was truly amazed to be with her.

Which made no sense, considering he'd found out how screwed up she was. She didn't believe her ADHD made her screwed up. It was that she couldn't admit to it and she couldn't get past wanting her father's approval—well, wanting the approval of everyone she admired really—and that she couldn't stop hearing Angela's voice in her head telling her she would never be good enough to deserve her busy, important father's attention.

And, no, she hadn't wanted Ty because of his medals and fame. But knowing that a man like him, who could have any woman he wanted, had wanted *her*, had made her feel equal parts amazing and determined to continue to be the girl of his dreams.

"You're not serious, are you?" Phoebe asked. "You really think you'll be happier if Ty's in Denver permanently?"

Part of her thought that. It would be easier in a lot of ways. There would be less pressure to be perfect, to be the fantasy he wanted all the time. But part of her thought it really sucked.

"It's better than having him here and slowly driving him crazy," she said. "I'd rather have him for a little bit than not at all."

"This is because of all these flaws you think you have, right?" Lauren asked, leaning in, her expression almost angry.

"Quirks," Hailey told her. "I prefer the term quirks."

"Quirks, flaws, deficiencies, imperfections, mistakes, limitations, failures—"

"Okay," Hailey broke in. "You're familiar with the thesaurus app on your phone."

"Another word for all of it is bullshit," Lauren said.

"Excuse me?"

"Bullshit," she repeated. "You forget stuff and get distracted and write things down a million times, and the fact that you're hyperaware of it makes you jumpy and anxious and slightly obsessive compulsive. So what? We've all got stuff. None of that makes you a bad person. It makes your stepmom a bitch."

Hailey huffed out a surprised laugh. "Well, she is that."

"She is. You don't like her either. So why do you care what she thinks?"

Hailey sighed. "It's not that I care what she thinks. I just can't get her voice out of my head."

"That totally offends me," Lauren told her, sitting back in her chair and crossing her arms and legs.

"Why?"

"Because *I* tell you things like you're sweet and kind and funny. And you make great marinara and have excellent taste in television. And yet it's *her* voice you hear."

"Maybe you should say it all really low and sexy," Phoebe said with a grin.

Lauren winked at the redhead. "If you want me to talk sexy to you, Red, all you have to do is ask. But we're talking about what *Hailey* wants to hear. And she's super straight."

Phoebe's cheeks turned a dark red to match her hair.

"I'm super straight."

Lauren patted her hand. "Okay, honey."

Lauren's bisexuality and her penchant for redheads had been a long-standing joke, and Hailey couldn't help but laugh. Even though Phoebe was straight and Lauren was happily married to a man who did *not* share, Lauren could always make Phoebe blush.

"The truth is," Hailey said. "I wanted Angela to like me for so long. I wanted to be like her."

Phoebe wrinkled her nose. "I remember her. She was so cold and so standoffish."

Hailey lifted an eyebrow and waited for the three beats it took for Phoebe's eyes to widen.

"You were cool and kept everyone at arm's length because of *her*?" she asked. "Because you wanted to be like her?"

Hailey shrugged. "Well, I learned how to do it from her. I know that she kept me at arm's length, and I know that it made me feel intimidated and fascinated at the same time." She looked around the table at the women who were all frowning. "Hey, I was a little kid. One who thought Angela was her mother until I was old enough to understand stepmothers. And believe me, Angela explained it early on."

Lauren shook her head. "And she was your only mother figure. I get it."

"She was beautiful, put together from head to toe, a gourmet cook. She could talk politics and strategy with my dad." Hailey thought back to the early days of trying on Angela's makeup and shoes when Angela wasn't around, begging to help in the kitchen, sitting in the same room with the two of them as they talked and laughed but never being included in the conversations. "My dad had cheated on her. Looking back, I think she overcompensated after that so it wouldn't happen again. And my dad was impressed by her. Of course I wanted to be like her. And then, as I got older and was trying to cover up my quirks and compensate for my ADHD, I modeled my behavior after how she treated me—let them close enough they notice the good things but not close enough that they really *know* you."

Several seconds passed without anyone saying anything.

Finally, Lauren said, "You need to get over that woman."

Hailey nodded. "Working on it."

"Maybe I could help." This came from Hope. She was standing behind Hailey, drink in hand and a sincere smile on her face.

Hailey glanced toward the guys' table and noticed TJ had pulled up a chair. It was nice Hope was over here. Hailey knew their group could be intimidating because they'd all known each other forever. But Hope didn't seem to get hung up on things like being the new girl.

And the woman had introduced Hailey to the world of essential oils. Hailey's feet and back had never felt better than after Hope had worked on them. Hailey was a fan.

She pivoted on her chair. "What do you have?"

"Positive affirmations. Meditation. My mom worked with people on doing affirmations while they were falling asleep. Things like that."

Phoebe pulled an empty chair up to their table and Hope took a seat.

"You're talking about falling asleep to those tapes that tell you over and over 'I'm a good person', 'I'm smart and successful'. That kind of thing?" Hailey asked.

Hope nodded. "Or making your own recording. Sometimes your own voice is even more powerful."

"There's been some research done that indicates self-affirmations can actually reinforce negative thoughts and feelings."

Everyone looked over at Mason, who was still looking

down at his tablet.

"Why do they feel the affirmations reinforce negative thoughts?" Hope asked him, apparently unfazed by the fact that the man could look completely absorbed in what he was doing and still catch every detail of a conversation.

"Positive statements to people with low self-esteem and habitual negative thoughts will sometimes focus them on the negative instead."

"If you tell someone they are lovable, they would instead focus on the fact that they're *not* lovable?" Hope asked.

"Yes. Their subconscious will reject the positives as an untruth."

Hope looked intrigued. "That's fascinating. Have you done a lot of reading on the topic?"

Mason looked up. "I've done a lot of reading on a lot of topics."

"I'd love to hear more about this. My mother used affirmations all the time, but I don't know as much about it as I'd like."

Mason nodded. "You can stop by the greenhouse tomorrow. I can find some of the articles and we can discuss after you've read them."

"That would be great."

Hailey watched the exchange with a baffled amusement. Mason Riley and Hope Daniels couldn't be more different, and yet here they were, finding something to talk about.

Adrianne laughed. "I'll warn you, all conversations with Mason eventually end up on the topic of plants. Especially if he gets you out to his greenhouse."

"I love plants," Hope said enthusiastically. "In fact, I was thinking about talking with you about some of the herbs I'd like to start growing. But I didn't know if that was something you'd be willing to give me some help with. I know you're working on much more important things."

Mason put his tablet on the table and fully focused on Hope.

The women all exchanged looks. That was impressive.

"I'd be happy to discuss anything you need."

Adrianne shook her head. "This is awesome. Between Tucker and Delaney's boys and now Hope, *I* won't have to hear about growing cycles and soil hydrogen levels for a long time."

Mason leaned and draped his arm around his wife's chair, pulled her close and whispered something in her ear. Adrianne blushed and giggled.

Hailey marveled at that. Mason Riley, boy genius, geeky outcast, had managed to make soil hydrogen levels sexy and snare the heart of one of the best women Hailey had ever known.

She felt her eyes get misty and she picked up her margarita glass for a huge chug.

She missed Ty.

"Hailey," Adrianne said, her expression still happy but more composed again. "I think I've realized something that will help you get over your hang-ups about your quirks."

Hailey was all ears. "Do tell."

"*Everyone* has quirks. Your stepmother used yours to belittle you. But that's like telling someone they're making a mistake every time they sneeze. You can't help them and we all have them. *And* when someone loves you, they don't just love you *in spite* of the quirks, often they'll love you more *because* of them." Adrianne smiled at Mason. "For instance, my husband loves to play in the dirt and gets excited about soil hydrogen levels and routinely uses words like rhizome and pistil."

"You know it turns me on when you start talking about pistils," Mason said with a grin.

God, they were cute. Hailey hated them a little in that moment.

Adrianne was grinning as well. "But I love him for all

his dorkiness and plant talk. And I'm sure there are things about me that he would rather he *didn't* have to live with. But he loves me anyway."

Hailey propped her elbow on the table and leaned her chin on her hand. It was abundantly clear that Mason was deeply, madly in love with his wife and would be forever. Hailey wanted that with Ty. Was it possible that he could not only tolerate living with her quirks but that he could love them? "Okay, like what?"

Adrianne looked at her husband. "What are some things you'd change about living with me if you could?"

Mason seemed to be thinking hard.

Several seconds ticked by.

Finally, Adrianne said, "Oh come on, there has to be *one* thing."

"Of course," Mason said easily, brow still furrowed. "I'm trying to decide if I should list the things in descending order of most annoying to least or from least to most."

Adrianne's mouth dropped open and the rest of the table burst into laughter.

Adrianne rolled her eyes at Hailey. "Well, you get the idea."

"Oh, no, I want to hear this list," Phoebe said. "In order from least to most if you please."

"That's not—"

"She buys smelly soap."

Adrianne frowned. "What?"

"The hand soaps that you put in the guest bathroom on the first floor. You buy strange scents."

"Strange?" Adrianne looked at Hope. "Lavender and rose petal and lemon."

Hope couldn't hide her smile. "I could make you some that have a more natural, softer scent."

"No scents," Mason said. "Soap doesn't need to smell like anything but soap."

Adrianne muttered something under her breath.

"What else?" Phoebe asked, leaning both elbows on the table. "What else is on perfect Adrianne's drive-Mason-nuts list?"

"You don't think Joe has a list about you?" Adrianne asked.

"Oh, I *know* Joe has a list," Phoebe said. "He shares it with me sometimes."

"What's on your list?" Hailey asked.

"I get up too early. I can't *not* talk for more than five minutes at a time. I like kiwi. I like to have sex in the laundry room."

"How is liking to have sex in *any* room annoying?" Mason asked.

"We just did it one day spontaneously," Phoebe said with a grin. "But the dryer is exactly the right height. Now I want to have sex in there all the time."

"So?" Mason asked. "I'm still not seeing a problem."

Phoebe nodded. "I know, right? But Joe prefers a bed. Or the front seat of his truck."

"How is liking kiwi a problem?" Lauren wanted to know.

"He thinks they're creepy. It's the fuzzy brown outside," Phoebe told her.

"Joe is weird," Lauren said.

"Well, and I eat like ten kiwi at a time," Phoebe said. "That's a lot of fuzzy brown peeling lying around."

"Lying around?" Adrianne asked. "As in lying on the counter or something?"

Phoebe seemed to be thinking about it. "Huh, maybe *that's* the problem."

Hailey snorted at that and realized she'd had *a lot* to drink. "I want to hear Travis's list on Lauren," she said.

Lauren grinned and got out of her chair. "Me too."

They all headed across the room to the table where the guys were clustered.

TJ pulled Hope onto his lap and Lauren propped her butt on the edge of the table next to Travis, facing him. The rest dragged extra chairs around the table, blocking any possible escape for Travis, Tucker, TJ and Joe. The guys all looked nervous.

"What's up?" Travis asked.

"We're wondering if there are any quirks about living with me that you would change if you could," Lauren said.

Travis started to laugh and then turned it into a cough and shook his head. "Of course not."

Lauren laughed. "You're so full of shit. We're trying to show Hailey that Ty can want to live with her even if she's not perfect."

Travis looked at Hailey, his eyes not exactly sympathetic, but understanding. "The first thing you need to know is that Ty is completely full of himself and that he's kind of an ass sometimes."

Tucker and TJ nodded, and Hailey smiled. "I'm actually aware of that. Turns out, I'm kind of an ass sometimes too."

Travis grinned at that. "Okay, so Lauren's flaws."

"We prefer the term quirks," Hailey said.

"Got it. Quirks. How many do you want?"

Lauren kicked him in the shin. "Two or three is fine."

"Oh, I have a lot more than that," Hailey said, fighting her own grin. "I think the more I hear of yours, the better I'll feel."

Travis nodded sagely. "I agree. Okay, number one— when she tells me about news stories or things going on at work in the lab or in DC, she dumbs it all down for me."

Lauren frowned. "That's not on the list."

"It is."

"I was thinking you were going to say that you hate how I eat ranch dressing on everything."

Travis looked at Hailey and nodded. "Oh, that's on there too. I mean, who puts ranch dressing on grilled cheese? That's not right."

"You think I dumb stuff down for you?" Lauren asked.

"Don't you?" he asked.

She sighed. "I wouldn't put it quite that way."

"But you do make it simpler for me."

She nodded reluctantly. "Maybe a little."

"But do you actually know what a pistil is?" Adrianne asked him, a tiny smile curling her mouth.

Travis narrowed his eyes. "No."

Mason looked at Hailey. "Another important lesson is compromise—meeting somewhere in the middle of scientific and political terminology and..." He trailed off and looked at Travis.

Travis lifted an eyebrow. "Is dumb farmer the term you were looking for?"

They all laughed and Lauren slid onto Travis's lap. His hands cupped her butt and he nuzzled her neck. "At least we don't have to have a glossary for *every* conversation we have," he said. "In the bedroom, we both understand what we're saying perfectly, don't we?"

Lauren kissed his temple. "And in the kitchen and the laundry room."

Phoebe blushed and Joe laughed. "I see we've already covered Phoebe's list."

"Really, man?" Mason asked. "How can you not like sex in the laundry room?"

"I like sex in *any* room," Joe said. "But there are things I like to do that don't work as well on top of a dryer."

Hailey was overcome by jealousy and longing and she hated them all even as she realized that she really, truly loved them all.

"You guys suck," she muttered. She'd left her margarita glass behind on their table. Because it had been empty. She reached out and snagged a beer glass from the table and took a long swig.

"Yeah, I was thinking I should head home," Tucker

said, stretching to his feet. "Delaney's probably about done with the project she wanted to finish up tonight."

"Don't forget to pick the boys up from mom's first," TJ said with a knowing wink.

"Actually, I think Delaney and I need to do some laundry before the boys come home," Tucker said. He clapped Joe on the shoulder. "You're crazy, man."

Hailey finished off the beer and looked at TJ. "Well? Your turn. Does Hope have any quirks?"

TJ stared at her for a long moment. Then he burst into laughter. Laughter like Hailey had never seen from gruff, tough TJ Bennett.

When he was composed again, he said, "Hope is one giant quirk, Hailey."

Hope hugged him as if it was the greatest compliment anyone had ever given her.

"You don't go crazy living with her? Don't want to change her into your perfect dream girl?" Hailey asked.

"Living with her makes me crazy sometimes," TJ admitted. "But living *without* her would be worse. And she's my perfect dream girl because of her quirks and making me crazy."

Hope looked completely serene and satisfied perched on TJ's lap. As if his words not only made her happy, but they didn't surprise her a bit.

Hailey frowned. She wanted a little bit of that serene-and-satisfied stuff. Just a little.

"Making you crazy makes her perfect for you?" Hailey asked.

TJ nodded. "If someone doesn't make you kind of crazy, they must not matter much. And being crazy once in a while keeps things interesting."

"Well, Ty must find me *fascinating* then," Hailey muttered.

"He does," TJ agreed.

She hadn't meant for anyone to actually respond to that.

"I don't know. He's back in Colorado now that he knows I'm *not* the woman he thought I was and wanted."

"He's back in Colorado because things aren't going according to his plan," Travis said. "Ty likes control, and finding out that not every aspect of his life will always go exactly the way he wants is taking some getting used to."

Hailey thought about that. It was true that his career wasn't going as planned. And with her...well, she wasn't who he'd thought she was. But she still loved when he took control. That wasn't a problem. That had never been a problem.

Even in high school, when she'd thought she was the one dictating how their relationship would go, or not go, she'd been fooling herself. She'd lived for those stolen moments in the hallway or at her locker. She'd anticipated him approaching her at dances and ballgames, and when he didn't right away, she'd put herself in his path. When she was feeling down because a boyfriend had upset her or because Angela had said something mean or because her dad was ignoring her, she'd thought about Ty and the things he said to her, the way he smiled at her, the way he went out of his way to give her attention. And the moment she'd stepped into his office in his house in Denver, she'd been all his.

"He's planning the training center because it puts him back in control of his career," she said.

His brothers nodded.

"He doesn't do well with unpredictability," TJ said. "Rather than take a risk on rehab and competing again, he's taking the safe route."

"Except that I didn't go along with his plan and jump for joy that he was moving here and starting the training program," Hailey said.

"And thank God for that," TJ said. "Ty needs to learn that just because something isn't on his list of goals, that doesn't make it a bad thing, and just because something is written in his planner, it doesn't mean it has to happen exactly as scheduled."

Hailey felt her heart thump hard at that.

She used her planner to stay on track and to tone down the flakiness. She needed more organization and structure in her life. But Ty was the king of structure. Maybe he needed to be a little flaky once in a while.

Maybe they could be good for each other.

And maybe Denver was too far away from Sapphire Falls for that to happen. Maybe they'd fallen into their roles when they were together—him the leader, her the follower—because it was comfortable and easy, and anything else would have taken more time than they really had together.

But something she had learned over the past several days was that getting uncomfortable and doing something new and scary—like actually *running* for mayor and being vulnerable and open—could be a really good thing.

She looked around the table. She felt closer to these people than she ever had. They loved her and were here for her in spite of the things she'd shared, the things that had held her back. She hadn't been only concentrating on being Ty's dream girl—she'd wanted to be everyone's dream girl. Or a dream mayor at least.

But she didn't have to do that. They knew she had quirks but they loved her anyway. Maybe even because of them.

And Ty could too.

She suddenly stood and her chair skittered back across the wood floor. Eight pairs of wide eyes looked up at her.

"I need to go."

"Go where?" Phoebe asked.

"Halfway to Denver."

TJ nodded. "Halfway. I like that."

She didn't know exactly what was halfway, but she'd find out.

"You can't leave," Phoebe protested. "The vote is on Friday. You need to campaign."

"I might be back by Friday. Or I might be in Denver by Friday. I don't know. But this is more important than being mayor."

She could feel the jolt of surprise that went through the group, and she smiled. "I know. I never thought I'd say that either. A dream mayor would never say that. But a dream girlfriend would. I don't have to be perfect to be right for Ty. I have a lot of experience with things not going according to my plans. I can help him with this."

Phoebe gave her a big grin and swiped at her eye. "Wow, our little mayor is growing up."

TJ seemed most pleased of all for some reason. "Our mom always says that falling in love changes you for the better."

Hailey took a deep breath and let it out, letting the realization sink in that she really was getting over some things.

She was getting over the fact that she made mistakes. She was getting over the idea that letting people close made her vulnerable—it actually made her stronger. She was getting over the idea that being mayor meant she had to be perfect. And she was definitely getting over the idea that being with Ty meant she had to be perfect.

She might even be getting over having three planners and five highlighters within reach at any given moment.

She *might* even be able to give up her sticky notes...

But that was where she stopped herself. She couldn't go too crazy here. She would never give up her sticky notes.

CHAPTER NINE

Bryan pulled himself up off the sofa, propped himself on one crutch and made his way to the wheelchair a few feet away. Ty made himself watch, even though it felt like someone was punching him in the stomach as he did.

Bryan was getting around much easier than the last time Ty had seen him, and that made Ty feel good, but damn. Bryan wasn't supposed to hobble around. He wasn't supposed to need to be propped up.

Bryan was a go-getter. If people thought Ty had trouble sitting still and that he pushed himself to nearly breaking, they'd never seen Bryan go at it. Of course, their motivations had been different. Ty had been training, doing it all for the glory. Bryan had been doing it for the adrenaline and fun.

But that was over. And it pissed Ty off.

"Quit looking at me like that," Bryan said, lifting his left foot up onto the wheelchair footrest with his hands. His leg muscles and control were improving, but he still couldn't lift his leg enough to get it onto the chair or into bed.

Ty scowled at him. "Like what?"

"Like you're about to hug me. Or puke," Bryan said.

"I'm not about to do either thing." Though his stomach was definitely in knots. "You want a hug from me you're gonna have to do more than roll down a hill."

Bryan gave him a grin. "Fuck you. That *mountain* tried to take me down, but it never had a chance."

Ty forced a smile past the holy-shit-he-could-have-died thought that hit him at random moments.

"Yeah, yeah, you're a big tough guy," Ty said.

Bantering with Bryan had always come easily. The first time they'd met, they'd been five. Ty had been talking to Tessa Sheridan, a girl who would become one of his favorite classmates and, recently, Hailey's assistant.

Bryan had walked up to them both, told Tessa he liked her hair and asked Ty to be his best friend. Ty had asked if Bryan could ride a dirt bike, Bryan had said yes. Bryan had asked if Ty had a skateboard, Ty had said yes. They'd been best friends ever since.

And when they'd been in high school, Bryan had admitted that if Ty hadn't been with Tess, Bryan probably would have decided to be best friends with Marc Larson. Marc had a Teenage Mutant Ninja Turtle backpack. Thankfully, he'd liked Tess more than the turtles.

They'd hung out all through high school and college. The first time they'd been apart had been when Ty had moved to Denver.

And then, a month later, Bryan had walked up to Ty at a race, looked him up and down and said, "Not every guy is comfortable wearing pink."

It had been a marathon for breast cancer awareness and research and everyone had been wearing pink T-shirts.

"Everyone's got one," Ty had told him, hiding his surprise and pleasure at seeing his friend.

"Yeah. I'm just saying not everyone is comfortable in them. You, on the other hand, look like you're made for wearing pink."

"It's not the T-shirt that's important. It's what you do in it," Ty had said, putting as much cockiness into his tone as he could.

The truth was, he'd been nervous about the race. He couldn't explain it. It had been his first race after college. It had been his first race against the next level of competitive marathoners. It had been his first race in Denver. He hadn't known what all had been going on, but he'd been wound tight.

Seeing his friend and trading insults as if it was any other day had taken his mind off the race and relaxed him. He'd set a personal best that day.

Bryan was kind of like the clown in the rodeo of Ty's life. He made Ty laugh, made him not take everything so seriously, he diverted and diffused a lot of the pressure around Ty and had, in Ty's opinion, kept Ty competitive for so long. He would have burned out a long time ago without Bryan there.

Now Ty was feeling the pressure building. Bryan couldn't do his thing for Ty because he had a lot of his own stuff going on. The pressure wasn't about racing now, though. It was about bigger issues, life-altering issues, issues Ty had absolutely no clue about.

And there wasn't a thing he could say about any of it because being partially paralyzed and in a wheelchair was pretty fucking life-altering, and Ty's questions and issues were nothing next to that.

"You look like your best friend just ended up in a wheelchair. What's up?"

Ty's head came up and he focused on Bryan. "*What*?"

"People say, 'You look like your dog died', but you don't have a dog, so I went with something else shitty that's happened."

Ty frowned. "It's not funny."

"You think I don't fucking know it's not funny?" Bryan asked. "My ass hurts from sitting around all the time. But then I'm happy that it hurts because it means I can feel it. There was a chance I might not have been able to *feel my ass*, Ty. And you're looking all miserable and pissed off. Knock it off."

Ty started to respond and then decided that being honest was the only way to go. He scrubbed a hand over his face and sighed. "I don't know what to say to you. I don't know if I should help or let you do things yourself. I don't know if I should ask the questions I've got. I don't know how to have a best friend in a wheelchair, okay? But I'm figuring out that I'm a jackass, so that doesn't really surprise me."

"What you don't know is how to be there and build somebody else up," Bryan said bluntly. "It's not about the wheelchair, so let yourself off that hook. If I'd broken my arm or ended up in jail or decided to quit our scene and start painting landscapes in the countryside, you wouldn't have known what to say either."

Ty blinked at him. "Jesus, Bry, have you always thought I was the biggest asshole you've ever met?"

"You have to make *everything* a competition, don't you? You're actually *not* the biggest asshole I've ever met," Bryan said. "Sorry, man. You'll have to try harder to get that number one spot."

Ty slumped back against the couch. "The two most important people in my life need me to step up, and it turns out that I suck at it. I hate sucking at things."

"Assuming I'm one of those two people, I'm not super thrilled that you suck at stepping up either," Bryan said.

Ty scowled at him. "Thanks. That's really helpful."

Bryan laughed. "You want *me* to give *you* a pep talk about you giving pep talks to me? That's messed-up."

Agitated, Ty sat forward, leaning his arms on his thighs. He pinned Bryan with a direct look. "I'm used to people coaching me and cheering *me* on. I haven't been on the other side of it. That doesn't mean I don't want to be, okay? I just don't know what the hell I'm doing."

"Bullshit." Bryan rolled his chair closer. He leaned forward, his arms on his thighs too, and met Ty's gaze. "You know all about it. Your family and friends— including me—are awesome at that shit. We're always there, we're always supportive, and you know that. So you know everything you need to know about coaching and cheerleading. You're scared that you won't do it right or be enough. And *that*, my friend, is your problem."

Ty stared at him.

Damn.

All the years of riding and running and swimming next

to this guy, having Bryan spotting him in the gym, blowing off steam with him with women and liquor and parties, Ty hadn't realized that they'd actually gotten to *know* each other.

But Bryan was exactly right.

"I hate not being good at something," Ty finally said. "I *really* hate *almost* being good at something."

The things he wasn't good at—baseball, accounting, saying the right thing at the right time to help someone—he either avoided or paid someone else to do. The things he was *almost* good at—winning the big race, for instance— he kept torturing himself over.

"You've avoided being a supportive friend and boyfriend because you don't want to have it not work," Bryan said. "You came to the hospital after my rehab was over for the day and you came to my house early in the day when you knew I'd be up on crutches and not tired enough for the wheelchair yet, because that way you can say encouraging things and not have to see me struggle and your magic words not work immediately."

That all sounded terrible.

And accurate.

He nodded miserably. "Yeah. I can't make it better and that kills me."

"But it's not about you."

Bryan's words hit Ty hard, directly in the chest. For a second, it was difficult to breathe.

But then, slowly, he nodded. "Yeah. I've been making it about me."

"You have. *You* want to be the good friend, the best cheerleader, the biggest support. Because you have to be the best and the biggest at everything," Bryan said. "You want to see that what you're doing and saying produces a measurable outcome. But you know what, Ty? Stuff doesn't work like that all the time. You don't get a medal every time you do something hard. You don't always get a spotlight shined on doing something good. And not every challenge is measured by miles or minutes."

Ty sat looking at the guy he'd seen jump off a bridge on a bungee cord, take a bike up and over a ramp, flip it twice in the air and land on one tire, down more tequila in one sitting than anyone he knew and coax a girl into an airplane bathroom only twenty minutes after her best friend had been in there with him.

How the hell had *Bryan* gotten so wise and insightful?

"So how do I know when I'm doing the best-friend thing right?" Ty finally asked.

"When you're the one I call when I need someone to talk to," Bryan said simply. "When you're the one I tell the not-pretty, not-fun, scared-and-pissed-off stuff to. Anyone can listen to the good stuff, you know?"

Ty swallowed hard. He was not going to get all teared up here. He'd never hear the end of it. He nodded. "Okay. I'm that guy. From now on."

Bryan gave him a grin. "I promise to tell you the good stuff too."

"Good." Ty looked at him closer and noted the twinkle in Bryan's eye. "For instance?"

"Two words—hot nurses," Bryan said. His grin grew. "Two more words—sponge baths."

Ty couldn't help by laugh. "Jesus. You're seducing nurses?"

"Well, not anymore," Bryan said. "I've moved on to physical therapists."

"So you can…" Ty asked.

"Well, up against a wall is out, but yeah, I can," Bryan confirmed.

Ty laughed again and felt the tension drain from his body. This was Bryan. The same guy he'd always been. His legs didn't work exactly the way they used to, but the main stuff, the big stuff, was still the same. And the new stuff—the adjusting to the stuff—wasn't about Ty. It was whatever Bryan made of it, and Ty just had to love him.

That wasn't actually a challenge at all.

And as for Hailey...

"How do I know when I'm doing the boyfriend thing right?" he asked Bryan.

He'd filled Bryan in on everything that had happened in Sapphire Falls and between him and Hailey. Including the fact that Hailey wasn't his perfect dream girl after all.

"I'm guessing the same way," Bryan said. "When you're the one she wants beside her for all the stuff—not just the good, happy, fun times."

That didn't make him feel better. "I don't know if that's going to happen," he admitted. "She already has people who are there for the...other stuff."

"That's because Hailey's like me," Bryan said. "You weren't the only one who got used to *you* being the one that needed the coaching and taking care of. Hailey and I put you at the center of things a long time ago."

Ty frowned. "She took care of me?"

"Didn't she?" Bryan said. "That girl let you lead the way, make the decisions, feel like the king. That's Care and Feeding of Ty Bennett's Ego 101."

"She *liked* me leading the way."

"Sure. Because she's in love with you. She let you have your way in all things, and believe that things were perfect because *you* made them perfect, because she loves you and knows that's what you needed."

Ty felt his head spinning. "You think she's in love with me?"

"Why else would she do things your way for so long?"

"Because she *liked* my way," Ty insisted.

"I'm not saying she didn't get anything out of it," Bryan said. "It was obvious she loved coming out here for a lot of reasons. But do you really think she didn't want to also tell you all these secrets she kept? You don't think she wanted to talk about her stepmother being a bitch—because if you think that's ended now that Hailey's grown up, you don't know bitchy stepmothers very well—or talk about her job and the things she was stressed about? When you two were together, it was like rainbows appeared overhead and there were unicorns prancing in your backyard and everything smelled like cupcakes. It was kind of sickening really."

Ty let all of that sink in and realized Bryan wasn't just insightful—he was actually better at this than even TJ.

"You saw all of that and knew that the rainbows and unicorns and cupcakes were going to disappear when I went back to Sapphire Falls and you didn't say anything?" Ty asked. "What kind of best friend were *you*?" But he didn't mean it. Bryan was the best.

"The best friend who, like Hailey, protected your fantasy bubble for you because I cared about you and knew that you wanted your full focus on the gold."

"Were you ever going to point all of this out?"

"When it mattered. And when you were ready to hear it," Bryan said. "Like now."

Ty let it all roll around in his head. "I'm right to give up the training and the gold and focus on the center and put things back to the way they were with Hailey?"

Bryan laughed. "No."

"No? To which part?"

"All of it."

Ty sighed.

"You need to work your knee, get back into shape and race in Rio," Bryan said. "You need to put the center in Sapphire Falls and you need to live there. With Hailey. Without the unicorns."

That was what he wanted. Hearing it out loud from Bryan made a resounding *yes* shoot through him.

He focused on his friend again. "If you come to Sapphire Falls with me, I promise to be the best friend you've ever had."

Bryan chuckled. "Glad to hear it. The movers are coming next week."

Ty shook his head. "You were supposed to say that I'm *already* the best friend you've ever had."

Bryan rolled his eyes.

"Wait," Ty said. "You were already planning the move?"

"Yeah. It's time to go home. And," he said, "it would be tough running the Come Again from here."

"You're going to work at the Come Again?" Ty asked.

"I'm buying it. Tex and Mary are retiring."

Ty's eyes widened. "But—"

Bryan laughed. "Mary's still going to make Booze and sell it. They'll still run the liquor store. They don't want the hours and headaches of the bar anymore."

Ty shook his head again. "You really don't talk to me about stuff in your life."

"I didn't have much of a life outside of your life," Bryan said with a shrug. "I realized that while I was lying in that hospital bed. My life was revolving around you. I was going through all of that testing and rehab and everything to get back a life that wasn't even really mine. So I'm getting a life. I'm going home, I'm going to run the Come Again and I'm going to find some thrills that don't involve throwing myself into the air—or off a mountain."

He gave Ty a grin that was almost sheepish. If Ty didn't know Bryan better.

An hour later, Bryan was going through his rehab workout—the first one Ty had seen—and flirting shamelessly with his therapist, and Ty was feeling good. About his friend's situation, his prognosis and their friendship, as well as the future in Sapphire Falls.

Ty would have gone back without Bryan, but the idea that his friend would be in town, making a life, his *own* life but with the support of family and friends, felt good.

There was just one more puzzle piece. Hailey.

Ty opened an internet window on his phone and typed in *ADHD in adults*.

Almost forty minutes later, Bryan rolled to a stop in front of Ty's chair. "Hey, I'm done."

Ty looked up. "Oh, good. Sorry. Got caught up in something."

Bryan waved that off. "No big deal. I'm glad you came with me."

"You were doing great."

"It's getting better," Bryan agreed. "It might be a while before I can do a full work shift on my feet, but I can modify behind the bar so I can reach everything from my chair."

"Tucker's girl, Delaney, could probably come up with something amazing for you," Ty said, stretching to his feet.

"I'll have to talk to her," Bryan agreed. They started down the hall but got about halfway to the doors when Bryan stopped.

"What's up?" Ty asked.

"She worked the piss out of my arms," Bryan said, shaking both arms out. "Would you mind pushing me out the rest of the way?"

Ty froze.

Bryan had never asked Ty for help with anything that he could recall. Nothing major, anyway. A lift to or from football practice in high school. Maybe a few bucks at the Stop for pizza. Maybe to be his wingman at the bar in college. But never for real *help*.

"You put your hands on those things sticking out of the back of the chair and push," Bryan said after a moment.

Ty took a breath, nodded, forced a grin and stepped behind the chair.

Pushing Bryan out to the car in his wheelchair did something to Ty. Something unexpected. It felt good to help. Even when he ran the footrests into the car door and tangled his feet with Bryan's when he helped him into the car. He didn't know what he was doing, really, but it felt good to do *something*.

Ty was lost in thought as they drove back to Bryan's house. He hadn't realized how humbling it could be, being asked for help. Especially from someone who didn't often need it and who could have pushed through on his own or could have covered up the need by flirting one of the women into helping him.

But Ty completely admired Bryan for being able to ask for help. Being strong didn't always mean doing it on your own, pushing when you wanted to quit or not letting people see your need. Being strong could also mean being humble, putting your pride aside and letting someone do something for you because it mattered to *them*.

Hailey had been doing that. For him. He'd thought of her as strong, and it turned out she absolutely was. She'd been strong enough to put him and what she thought he needed ahead of *her* needs. She'd been his dream girl and let him have his way because he mattered to her. She'd wanted him to be happy. And she'd let him make her happy—at least in some ways—because that also made *him* happy.

She'd understood him and given him what he needed.

And now he wanted to do the same for her.

He didn't need any more unicorns. He needed the real stuff. With her.

"Did you know that adults with ADHD have a hard time with relationships because people think their inability to focus and pay attention is them being self-centered and not caring about what the other person is saying?" Ty asked Bryan.

Bryan looked up from what he'd been texting. "Uh, no, Ty, I don't think that's *your* problem, if that's what you're asking. You *are* self-centered."

Yeah, he was. "I'm talking about Hailey."

"You did some reading, I see."

"Yeah, and you know what? I noticed a lot of these things about her over the years even though she was trying to cover them up."

"Things like what?"

"She doesn't sit still very well. She constantly has to be doing something with her hands. Even if we're watching a movie or something, she'll be flipping through a magazine or playing games on her phone. It's like she can't *not* multitask."

"That comes from the ADHD?" Bryan asked.

"Yeah. Guess so. So does the thrill-seeking," Ty said. "I thought she was like us and liked the adrenaline, and I felt lucky to have a girlfriend who liked zip-lining and stuff. Turns out, that kind of high-energy activity is really good for her. Lots of adults with ADHD turn to other stimulating activities like drugs and gambling."

"You sound like you memorized that webpage," Bryan said with a grin.

"It all makes so much sense now," Ty said. "She loses things all the time. And she loves when I say I'll take care of stuff. That's like this aphrodisiac, I swear. I thought it was the high demand of her job and that she liked kicking back when she came here to visit, but turns out that ADHD makes it hard for her to focus on details and finish all the little things. That's why her assistant is so important to her. She said the other day that she's been good at surrounding herself with good people."

"Tessa's still her assistant, right?" Bryan asked.

His tone was casual, but Bryan asked Ty about Tessa after every visit Ty made to Sapphire Falls.

"She is," Ty said. "And she looks really good. And is still single."

Bryan grinned at that.

"Anyway," Ty said, not feeling bad about making *this* conversation about him. Because it was also about Hailey. "I've noticed all these things over the years, and they don't bother me."

"Why would they bother you?" Bryan asked.

"Exactly. Hailey thinks she's hard to live with and that a goal-oriented planner like me would go crazy with her. But those things don't bother me, and besides, the article said she *needs* someone like me around to keep her on track and help with those details she hates."

"Well, then you need to convince her of that."

Ty thought about that. "I should probably head back to Sapphire Falls for the election. Maybe I'll make a big public speech about how she should be mayor and that I love her or something."

Bryan chuckled. "Dude—big public speech, stage, spotlight...no. Stop already. Do something nice and quiet and private and meaningful that puts all the attention on her and shows her that you've been really thinking about this."

Quiet and private and meaningful.

Not words Ty was all that familiar with.

"I, um, might need some help with that."

Bryan laughed. "You got it."

Not that quiet or private were really Bryan's forte either.

They pulled into Bryan's drive and Ty got out to pull the wheelchair out of the trunk. His phone rang just as he'd set it down.

It was Hailey.

He answered immediately. "Hails."

"Hi."

God, the sound of her voice actually made his knees weak. Not just the banged-up one either. He'd never tell his brothers or Bryan, but he had a suspicion that his brothers might know what he was talking about. And he hoped Bryan would someday.

He and Hailey never talked on the phone for more than a few minutes when they were making plans, and now he realized why.

He'd missed her when they'd been apart, but they'd both compartmentalized their relationship. It was a once-in-a while thing and they both had a lot going on when they weren't together. Phone calls made it more like a relationship.

And with one simple word from her, Ty missed her with an ache that stunned him with its intensity.

"I miss you," he said. They needed to get better about communicating and honesty.

That seemed to surprise her, if the moment of silence was anything to go by. "I miss you too," she finally said.

Ty let out a long breath. He felt like he was back in high school, unsure about what to say to the girl he liked now that he had her on the phone. But with Hailey, he'd never felt that way even when he'd been *in* high school. His blatant flirtations had been over-the-top but had kept them both smiling and hadn't left room for nerves. That and the fact that he hadn't *actually* thought he'd ever have a real chance with her. He'd never gotten too anxious because it had been one big game.

It was no longer a game. This was as real as it got.

"I'm coming home," he said. "Tonight."

Bryan shot him a grin from where he was maneuvering out of the car with his crutches.

Okay, so Ty had just decided he was going back to Sapphire Falls tonight. But as soon as he'd heard her voice, he'd mentally left Denver anyway.

"No!"

And that was *not* the reaction he'd been expecting. Or wanting. "No?"

"I mean, I'm not in Sapphire Falls," she said quickly. "I was hoping you'd meet me partway."

He held on to the wheelchair while Bryan settled into it, but Ty's attention was definitely not on Bryan. "Partway? You mean between here and there?"

"Yes. I'm on the road already. I really want to see you,

and if we both start driving toward one another, it will be sooner rather than later."

Bryan rolled into the house but Ty was riveted where he was. "You're already on your way?"

"Yeah." Her voice got quieter. "Is that okay?" She sounded worried.

Was it okay? Was it okay that she wanted to see him? That she already wanted to see him after only three days apart?

"Hell yeah, it's okay," he said sincerely. "Always, Hailey. I *always* want to see you."

She laughed softly, sounding relieved. "Ditto. Will you meet me? Ogallala is about halfway."

"Of course." He mentally calculated that it would be about three hours from there. "How close are you?"

"I'll be there first. I'll get a room and text you the details," she said.

"Great." He was still stunned by this, but it actually seemed perfect. Neutral territory to say all the things he needed to say and to convince her that he was in this for good. Forever. "I'll get on the road right away."

"Thank you."

"For what? Wanting to see you so badly I'm wondering if I should tell you to stop driving and I'll *fly* to wherever you are?" he asked with a grin, heading for the house to pack up his stuff.

"For that," she said. "I knew when I called that you'd do this. It's an amazing feeling knowing for sure that all I have to do is ask and you'll be there."

He stopped halfway up the stairs. "Always," he said again, his voice gruff. "*Always.*"

He pictured her face and knew that she was smiling with tears in her eyes.

"I don't want you to move back to Colorado. At least not without me," she said. "I was going to wait and tell you that in person, but…I really want you to know that."

"You can't move to Colorado," he said lightly, continuing on to the guest room for his bag. "You can't be mayor of Sapphire Falls and live in Denver."

"I don't care about being mayor."

He could hear the sincerity in her voice even as he shook his head. "Yes, you do."

"No. Not if it means not having you. You're more important than being mayor, Ty. There, I said it. Finally, after all these years, I'm admitting that you are the most important thing to me."

He had to swallow hard before he could reply. He really had waited a long-ass time to hear that. But for so long it had truly been about winning, about conquering his greatest challenge—Hailey Conner's stubborn insistence that she didn't want him. But now he knew, somewhere along the way, he'd fallen in love with her, and he wouldn't be happy with anything less than her love in return.

"Well, it's about damned time," he said softly.

"I'll see you in Ogallala," she said.

"I'll be there."

They disconnected, he threw his clothes in his bag, threw his bag over his shoulder, then said goodbye to Bryan and that they'd talk soon about the details for Bryan's move.

On his way out, Ty grabbed one last thing off the table by Bryan's front door—a pad of sticky notes.

Hailey had never been this nervous to see Ty.

Of course, she'd never known when he was coming to see her. She could guess around the time of a family member's birthday, a holiday or a town celebration, but she was never *sure* when she'd run into him. When she'd been going to see him, she had time to prepare…and had been looking forward to the enchiladas and zip lining too.

Now she was in a tiny hotel room in Ogallala, Nebraska. She had no idea if there were enchiladas in this town, and she wasn't sure when Ty would get here exactly. Or what he'd be thinking or feeling when he showed up.

This wasn't about a fun weekend fling with great food and fun activities. This was about their future.

Ty had left Sapphire Falls after finding out her secrets and quirks.

Those weren't gone. They never would be. Would he still want to be with her?

He'd said he missed her on the phone though. And he'd immediately agreed to meet her. That had to mean something.

Hailey replayed the warmth that had rushed through her when he'd said he'd missed her and wanted to see her, and the tone in his voice when she'd told him, finally, that he was more important to her than being mayor.

She'd realized that being mayor had originally been about taking care of Sapphire Falls and keeping people at arm's length, but over the past three years, as she'd fallen more and more in love with Ty, being mayor had turned into an excuse to keep from getting closer to him—and getting hurt.

That was still a possibility, she knew. Ty had as much to learn about being close to people and being there for them as she did. But he was worth the risk.

It was that final thought that made Hailey finish writing on the sticky notes she'd brought.

She really hoped Ty didn't think this gesture was stupid.

She heard her phone ding with a text message and her heart leapt. It had been over three hours since she'd talked to him. She lunged for the phone on the bedside table.

"I'm here."

Her heart hammered hard in her chest and she pulled in a long breath. Then typed, *"Get a key from the front desk and come on up. Room 302."*

She put the phone back on the table and hastily arranged herself on the bed. She felt completely exposed and a little silly and a lot cold.

But it was worth it.

She hoped.

Her palms were sweating and she was forcing long, deep breaths when she heard the sound of the keycard in the door.

A moment later, the door swung open and Ty strode into the room. He wasn't treading carefully, he wasn't hanging back to judge a reaction from her. He came into the room like a man on a mission.

But when he saw her on the bed, he stopped in his tracks and stared.

The door swung shut behind him.

"Hi," she finally said.

He swallowed hard. "Holy shit."

Okay, she'd take that reaction.

He threw his duffle bag to the side and started toward the bed. "What's this?" His gaze was roaming over her and in his expression she saw surprise and confusion and amusement. And affection, if she wasn't mistaken.

She took a deep breath. "I have a sticky-note fetish."

"I see." He put one knee on the mattress, leaned in and reached for her shoulder.

He pulled a sticky note from her skin and held it up. "I never bake cookies, but I make a lot of cookie dough," he read out loud.

His eyes found hers again. "What is this, Hailey?"

She looked down. She was naked except for the pink sticky notes she'd stuck all over her body. She'd used up a pad of fifty—well, minus the three she'd used to make actual reminder notes to herself about other things. Each note was something else that she wanted Ty to know about her. As he pulled them off her, she would become more and more naked and exposed…literally and figuratively.

"This is a symbol," she told him. "I use sticky notes to remind me of important things. Now I'm using them to tell you things about me. Things I haven't told you before."

His mouth curled and she felt her cheeks flush.

"It's stupid, right?"

She started to get up, but Ty quickly covered her body with his. The notes crinkled between them, one came off of her hip and the corner of a couple jabbed her, but she wouldn't have moved a muscle for anything. The look in Ty's eyes took her breath away and glued her to the bed.

As if his two hundred and twenty pounds of pure muscle on top of her wasn't enough.

He propped his elbows beside her ears. "This is the most un-stupid thing either of us has ever done," he told her sincerely. "You've amazed me beyond words or even the ability to do anything but *be* here with you. I can barely remember how to do anything or feel anything but love for you."

"I'm glad you—" She stopped and stared into his eyes. "You love me?"

"I love you so damn much I'm not really sure what to do about it."

Her heart squeezed and she felt tears stinging. She'd never almost cried as much as she had in the past few weeks. "You haven't read all the sticky notes yet. You might find something you won't love."

He started to shake his head but then caught himself. "Okay, maybe. *Maybe.* But that won't mean that I'll love *you* any less."

She wanted to believe that. So much. And she could feel herself grab for that truth rather than pushing it away as she always had before. She was getting closer to being able to accept that.

"I still want you to read these notes," she said.

"I want to read every one of them," he said. "And I

have a few notes I want you to read as well."

"You do?"

He rolled to the side and pulled something from his front jean's pocket.

It was another pad of sticky notes. These were a bright fluorescent green.

She started to sit up, but he pushed her back onto the pillows. "Relax," he told her with a grin.

He peeled a pink note from her stomach and read, "I can't sit still and watch a movie without doing something else at the same time." He looked up at her. "I already knew this one actually."

Then he tossed the pink note aside and pulled a green one from his pad. He held it up and she saw he'd written something on it.

"I remember the first time I heard you laugh."

She looked from the note to Ty's face.

He stuck the note where the pink one had left an open spot. "You were standing by your locker and your friend Kristie had said something I couldn't hear, but I heard you laugh. And I thought my heart and my cock were both going to explode," he told her.

Hailey felt her mouth drop open, then her grin spread. "What are you doing?"

"This pad of sticky notes holds thirty-three things that I remember, know and love about you," he said. He lifted a shoulder. "It's Bryan's, so it wasn't a full pad. But the idea came to me while I was packing to come here and I grabbed it on my way out. That's why I'm late. I thought about all of these things as I drove and stopped about six times to write them all down."

Hailey felt the tear that ran down her cheek but she couldn't stop smiling. "That's...amazing."

"See, we're pretty in sync after all this time together," he said. He looked up and down her body. "For everything you want to tell me that you think might scare me off, I've got something that will assure you that won't happen."

She reached for her right thigh, pulled a note free and held it up. "I would have never tried zip lining if it wasn't for the grin on your face when you talked about wanting to take me".

She tossed the note away and put her hand against his cheek. "They're not all things that might scare you off. They're things I've never said to you that I should have."

She thought she saw a shine in his eyes too, but Ty turned his face to press his lips against the palm of her hand before she could be sure.

"Are any of them dirty?" he asked with a grin that wiped any shine of tears from either of their eyes.

"You mean like the one that says I love the way you grab my hair when I'm giving you a blowjob?" she asked with a mischievous grin of her own.

He winked at her. "I already knew that too."

She laughed. "Okay, but I never *told* you that."

He looked down the length of her body. "Where's that one?"

"You'll have to find it," she said with a shrug. "Along with the one that says we don't do the reverse cowgirl enough."

He held up his pad of sticky notes. "'I love you in the reverse cowgirl position' is in here too."

She laughed and wrapped her arms around him, pulling him down for a kiss. "We really are in sync."

Ty kissed her deeply and it was hot and sweet, like always, but this time it felt like *more*. Like everything they'd each written on the notes was being poured into the kiss.

It took them almost an hour to go over every note they'd each written—especially because Ty kept kissing the spots he revealed under the pink notes before covering them back up with a green one, and sometimes those kisses took a while.

But as they made love on top of pink and green sticky notes, Hailey realized that her only true flaw had been fighting her love for this man for so long.

ᔆᕦ

"We should go straight to city hall and see the results, right?" Ty asked.

Since they'd each had a car in Ogallala, they'd driven back to Sapphire Falls separately.

She'd been relieved when he'd pulled over at the park before they'd gotten into town. They were now leaning side by side against her car. They had their hands in their pockets and were studying the edge of the river as it ran under the little white wooden bridge.

"Yeah, we probably should," she agreed.

She didn't really want to see the results. Either she'd won—and she wasn't so sure how she felt about that now, strangely—or she'd lost, which wouldn't feel so great either.

The win would be nice since she'd finally opened up about everything and it would mean that people were accepting her in spite of all of that. It would mean that they didn't feel as though they needed a kick-ass, put-together mayor making all of their decisions for them so they wouldn't be bothered.

But a loss would mean she could relax. No more boring reports and meetings where she'd struggle to pay attention long beyond her ability. No more second-guessing and over-worrying and stressing about being on time. That was big. She wouldn't have to set three alarm clocks and ask Tess to call to be sure she was up. She wouldn't have to read through her own presentations four times to be sure she hadn't skipped any important details. She wouldn't have to spend her day in a sterile office so she wouldn't get distracted.

She wasn't sure what she *would* do, but she had some ideas. Her degree was actually in marketing, and she'd done a hell of a job and enjoyed developing Sapphire Hills. Maybe she could talk to Levi Spencer, their resident millionaire, about hiring her to help him develop some business investments in the area.

But even if she went to work baking for Adrianne or helping Delaney on renovation projects or helping Hope set up her shop, Hailey could still help Ty with the pieces of local government he'd need assistance on. And that would be helping make Sapphire Falls the great place she wanted it to be, and that would be enough. The idea of being more behind the scenes was appealing.

"I'm going to be okay either way," she told Ty honestly. She could tell he was worried about her.

"I really don't want it," he said. "I mean it. If I win, you have to work to impeach me or something."

She laughed. "Oh no. It's all yours, Mr. Mayor. But I promise to come debase your new desk as soon as I can."

"New desk? I don't get to keep the cherry one?"

She grinned. "You can if you want to. But you get to redo the office however you want it."

"Well, I'm partial to that desk." Ty sighed. "I want to start training again."

She looked over at him. "Yeah?"

He nodded. "The chances of medaling are almost zero. I'll probably be only a silver medalist forever, but I'll regret it if I don't compete in Rio," he said. "There are other reasons to race. Even if I don't win."

Her heart expanded and she turned to him. "That's amazing. And I love you and am proud of you no matter what."

He pulled one hand from his pocket and held it out. She put her hand in his.

"It's going to kind of suck at first. My knee needs a lot of work. And I'm on a tight timeline."

"I'll do whatever I can."

"Take over as mayor for me if I win?"

She laughed. "Except that. But I'll help."

He smiled and nodded. "We'll figure it out."

She squeezed his hand. "Of course we will. Together."

He pulled her in for a kiss and then wrapped his arms around her. "I'm still going to call you Madam Mayor in the bedroom."

"You better."

"Okay, let's go see what the next three years of our lives are going to look like," he said.

She hugged him tight and then leaned back. "I already know what I need to know about the next three years, Ty. We'll be together. That's all that matters."

He kissed the top of her head. "Good answer."

Five minutes later, they'd parked along the edge of the town square and approached the steps of the city hall.

They could see that the chalkboard was propped on the easel at the top but couldn't read the result.

It was three o'clock in the afternoon, so most of the town had already been by and knew who their new mayor was. There were a few people in the square and the usual foot traffic along Main Street, but it was only the two of them on the city hall steps.

"Okay, come on," Ty said after they'd paused at the bottom for nearly a minute.

She nodded. Butterflies were swooping in her stomach, but she had no idea if they were excited or worried butterflies.

Probably equal amounts of each.

They climbed the steps hand in hand and stood in front of the chalkboard.

"*TJ Bennett*?" they said at the same time.

They turned to each other.

"TJ?" Hailey asked.

"Did they get the letters wrong?" Ty asked.

"Mistakenly put a J instead of a Y?"

"I have no idea." She looked at the board again.

But it most definitely did *not* say Hailey Conner.

And she was so okay with that.

She felt a grin spread, the butterflies did a big happy swoop and she felt a huge weight lift off her shoulders. "But it's not me!" She turned to Ty and threw her arms around him. "Congratulations!"

"Hey, that's *my* congratulatory hug," a voice said from behind them.

They turned to find TJ and Hope climbing the steps.

"What?" Ty asked. "They got the letters right?"

TJ stopped in front of his brother. "They sure did."

"You're the new mayor?" Hailey asked.

Hope smiled and squeezed TJ's arm. "He is."

"But...*how*?" Hailey asked.

"*Why*?" Ty added.

TJ shrugged. "I started a write-in campaign. Apparently, the town feels that I have the right combination of things—I'm smart and tough and love this town like Hailey, but I'm approachable and fresh like Ty."

Ty lifted an eyebrow. "*You're* approachable and fresh?"

TJ clapped him on the shoulder. "And I know the answers to all the questions and issues brought up at the debate."

"You did all of this in the last couple of days while we were gone?" Hailey asked.

It hadn't fully sunk in, but if she'd been pressed to answer if TJ would make a good mayor or not, she would have said yes.

"I've been doing it since Ty announced he was running," TJ said. "Turns out you can *talk* to people one on one rather than having big debates and parties."

Hailey and Ty looked at one another. They grinned and nodded. That didn't really surprise them at all.

"I never knew you had political aspirations," Ty said to

his oldest brother. "But congrats."

"Thanks. And I didn't," TJ told him.

"Then why?" Ty asked. "You thought we were going to screw it all up?"

"Because *you* need to be training for Rio," TJ said. "You need to quit hiding out and filling that spot in with other things that don't mean as much."

Hailey looked up at Ty. He looked stunned but touched.

"I was planning on resuming my training," he said. "But here. Not Colorado."

"Good," TJ said with a nod. "This was where you started and where your biggest fans are. That makes a lot of sense."

Hailey really loved Ty's brother in that moment.

"And you," TJ said, looking at her. "You've done a great job, but this isn't where you belong."

She lifted her chin. "I'm not leaving Sapphire Falls."

"Of course not," TJ said. "I meant your office in city hall. You need a chance to do the things you're *really* good at and love."

She swallowed. "And what's that?"

"Director of Business Development and Tourism for the town of Sapphire Falls," TJ said.

She frowned. "There's no such thing."

"There is now. Or there will be as of tomorrow morning when I take office," TJ said. "It's my first official act. I still intend to farm and I've got Hope, so I can't give myself to this job twenty-four-seven. You did, but it was because you were doing it *all*. Now, instead of the mayor taking care of every tiny detail in this town, I'm going to *hire* someone to take care of a lot of it. You. You can do all the stuff you love and shine at, and I'll take care of the meetings and reports."

Hailey blinked at him. He thought she shone at some things? And she wasn't going to have to read any more reports?

Now she *really* loved Ty's brother.

"What about the highway expansion proposal?" she asked.

TJ smiled. "I have a plan."

"What?"

He shook his head. "Not your worry anymore."

That sounded nice too. Except...

"But if I'm going to develop—"

"The job sounds perfect," Ty said, hugging her against his side. "The town needs you to do that, Hails. Starting on *Tuesday*."

She looked up at him and then at TJ. She sighed. She was going to have to let go of some more things. "Okay, I accept."

"Of course you do. You're a very bright woman," TJ said. "Who only lost to me by three votes, by the way."

And she decided TJ was absolutely her favorite someday-brother-in-law.

"We're going over to the Come Again to celebrate," Hope said. "Come with us."

They turned and started down the steps.

Hailey looked up at Ty. "Can your training wait one more day?"

He grinned down at her. "Doesn't even really matter," he told her. "I have the only gold medal that matters right here in my arms."

Her heart thumped hard at that. "I love you, Tyler Bennett."

"I love you, Hailey Conner."

He lowered his head to kiss her, but Hope called, "Oh, I forgot to give you this."

She came back up the steps and handed Hailey a small plastic container.

"She said you two were supposed to share this," Hope said with a grin.

"She?" Hailey asked.

"Kathy."

"My mom?" Ty pulled off the lid. And immediately started laughing.

Hailey looked in and saw a huge piece of German chocolate cake.

"Is that what I think it is?" she asked.

He nodded. "Kathy Bennett's famous engagement cake."

Everyone in town knew that Kathy made German chocolate cake for all engagements and anniversaries in town.

Ty dipped a finger into the frosting and lifted it to Hailey's lips.

She leaned in and sucked it clean.

His eyes heated. "Now we're officially engaged, you know."

"I know."

The heat was intensified by a look of love that made Hailey catch her breath

Ty glanced in the direction of the Come Again. "So I was wondering…"

"Yes?"

"Bryan said that I should be better about making things quiet and private and meaningful."

She shook her head but was already smiling. "But you'd like to get up at the Come Again and make a big public announcement and steal the spotlight from your big brother, right?"

Ty shrugged, but his grin gave him away. "Maybe a little."

She laughed. "Well, they don't put big billboards up on the edge of town of people who shy away from making a spectacle of themselves," she said.

"I'll take that as a yes. To the spectacle *and* to the proposal."

"It's a definite yes," she said. "To both."

And as she hugged him, Hailey relished the fact that no matter how much they'd both changed, some things would always stay the same. Like Ty's love, his support and his honesty. And his ego.

And the fact that she was never, ever going to get over him.

ABOUT THE AUTHOR

Erin Nicholas is the author of sexy contemporary romances. Her stories have been described as toe-curling, enchanting, steamy and fun. She loves to write about reluctant heroes, imperfect heroines and happily ever afters. She lives in the Midwest with her husband, who only wants to read the sex scenes in her books; her kids, who will never read the sex scenes in her books; and family and friends, who say they're shocked by the sex scenes in her books (yeah, right!).

You can find Erin on the Web at www.ErinNicholas.com, on Twitter (http://twitter.com/ErinNicholas) and on Facebook (https://www.facebook.com/ErinNicholasBooks)

Look for these titles by Erin Nicholas

Now Available at all book retailers!

Sapphire Falls
Getting Out of Hand (book 1)
Getting Worked Up (book 2)
Getting Dirty (book 3)
Getting In the Spirit, Christmas novella
Getting In the Mood, Valentine's Day novella
Getting It All (book 4)
Getting Lucky (book 5)
Getting Over It (book 6)
Getting to Her (book 6 companion novella)

The Bradfords
Just Right (book 1)
Just Like That (book 2)
Just My Type (book 3)
Just the Way I Like It (short story, 3.5)
Just for Fun (book 4)
Just a Kiss (book 5)
Just What I Need: The Epilogue (novella, book 6)

Anything & Everything
Anything You Want
Everything You've Got

Counting On Love
Just Count on Me (prequel)
She's the One
It Takes Two
Best of Three
Going for Four
Up by Five

The Billionaire Bargains
No Matter What
What Matters Most
All That Matters

Single titles
Hotblooded

Promise Harbor Wedding
Hitched
(book 4 in the series)

Boys of Fall
Out of Bounds, Erin Nicholas
Going Long, Cari Quinn
Free Agent, Mari Carr
Illegal Motion, Erin Nicholas
Going Deep, Cari Quinn
Red Zone, Mari Carr

And don't miss how it all began with Hailey and Ty in
Getting to Her,
the companion novella out now!

by Erin Nicholas

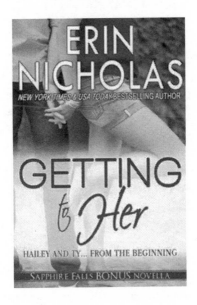

Excerpt

SAPPHIRE FALLS HIGH SCHOOL
Fourteen years ago

"You know the word 'secret' in secret admirer is kind of a keyword." Hailey Conner slammed her locker shut and turned to face him. "It's supposed to be a *secret*."

Tyler Bennett grinned at her. "I signed it TB. There are at least three others."

All of his brothers shared those same initials.

"Mark is going to kick your ass, TB," Hailey said with

257

a little shrug. "Guess he doesn't care if he gets the right TB or not."

Ty only grinned wider. Mark Andrews, Hailey's boyfriend, wasn't going to kick his ass. Mark was no doubt going to talk about it all over school all day long, but it was never going to happen. Mark didn't want to risk hurting his shooting hand before the big basketball game on Friday, and everyone knew the Bennett boys had hard heads.

"Don't worry, I'll pretend to be scared of him and sorry," Ty said. "Nothing will happen."

Hailey crossed both arms over the short stack of books she carried. "If you didn't sign it at all, it would be a secret and you wouldn't *have* to be sorry." She said it almost as if she truly was puzzled about why Ty insisted on putting his initials on his secret admirer notes.

"I said I would *pretend* to be sorry," Ty corrected. "And if it was a complete mystery, how would you know who to have a little crush on because he's so sweet and romantic?"

"I would still know it was you," she said. Then frowned. "I mean, I would still know the notes were from you. I don't have a crush."

But Ty didn't believe her. She always pretended to be exasperated by his attention and flirtation, but she never told him to stop. Maybe she didn't have a crush on par with his—he wasn't sure Romeo's crush on Juliet had been on par with Ty's feelings for Hailey—but she liked being on the pedestal he'd put her on.

That was why they worked.

Hailey loved to be adored and Ty was a competitor.

To the core. He loved to win. He *lived* to win. He had to be number one. He had three older brothers who were good at absolutely everything and Ty had been competing against their grades, their reputations and their records since he was born. But Hailey was the biggest, most difficult challenge Ty had faced.

He hadn't won her over. He wasn't the most important

thing in her life. He wasn't the center of her universe.

Yet.

Hailey flipped her silky blond hair over her shoulder and turned to head down the hallway to history class. Ty fell into step beside her.

"So what has Mark given you this week?" he asked.

He knew the answer. Nothing.

It was Valentine's Day week. The Sweetheart Dance was on Saturday and the big day was on Sunday. Everyone was taking advantage of the upcoming holiday to buy cards and candy and stuffed animals for the ones they loved. Or the ones they wanted to love.

There was something about Valentine's Day that made people braver, more willing to go over the top and make a spectacle. And Ty loved it.

He had been making a spectacle of himself over Hailey Conner for the past four months. It was nice to have some comrades this week.

The hallways of Sapphire Falls High School were filled with pink and red and white balloons, notes taped to lockers, guys approaching girls with roses, girls approaching guys with roses.

It was awesome.

"Mark is waiting until it's actually Valentine's Day to give me my gift," Hailey said, her chin up, her tone haughty. "He doesn't need all this showing off for me to know how he feels."

Ty would much rather Mark *not* wow Hailey with romantic words and gestures, but the team captain's complete lack of attention to his girlfriend made Ty burn.

He kind of hoped Mark did pick a fight with him. Mark would make him hurt, no doubt, but Ty would get in a few good punches before he was down for the count. He'd fought with his brothers—his three older, *bigger* brothers—his whole life. He was no lightweight.

"You know you're too good for him, right?" Ty asked

with a sigh as they stopped outside Hailey's classroom.

Her eyes narrowed, but not before Ty saw a flicker of affection.

He didn't know what Mark said or didn't say, did or didn't do, when he and Hailey were alone but he knew that *his* attention mattered to her. And that wouldn't be the case if Mark was treating her the way she deserved.

"You barely know me, Ty," she said.

He gave a single nod of acknowledgement. That wasn't completely untrue. Hailey was a senior and he was only a sophomore. The only time they spent together was in the hallways of the high school like this, or in the few minutes she gave him when he approached her at ball games, dances or downtown.

But he paid attention to her. He couldn't help it.

She was gorgeous—long legs, silky blond hair, big blue eyes. She was also sharp and witty, president of everything, bossy and bitchy. He loved everything about her.

She was *the* girl to get. The girl everyone wanted. Every guy wanted to date her and every girl wanted to be her.

If Ty wanted to go for the big prize, get the un-gettable, win the un-winnable, Hailey was it.

Her legs, breasts and ass were only a part of his attraction. Though they were absolutely part of it. The other girls in the school couldn't begin to compare with Hailey as far as beauty went. But he was also attracted to the fact that she was the boss; the take-charge, get-it-done, I'm-always-right ruler of the school.

Someday he intended to win an Olympic Gold medal in the triathlon.

Hailey was the Gold medal of Sapphire Falls High.

"Here's what I do know." He moved in closer and looked down at her. Even though he was not quite sixteen and she was about to turn eighteen, Ty still had a couple of inches on her, even in her cowboy boots. "I know that if you were my girlfriend, Valentine's Day or not, you would know that I think about you all the time and that I love making you smile and that I would do everything in my power to make you happy."

Ty felt satisfaction course through him as Hailey stared up at him and sucked in a quick breath.

Damn right.

"Hey, back off, Bennett."

Mark Andrews. Right on cue. Ty knew Mark was in this class with Hailey. But when a guy had a chance to stand this close to a girl who smelled like sweet coconut and who filled out a pair of jeans the way Hailey Ann Conner did, he took it.

He gave Hailey a wink and turned to face Mark. "Hey, Mark."

"What the hell are you doing?" Mark's gaze flickered between Ty and Hailey.

"Just wishing Hailey a happy Valentine's Day," Ty said easily. "It's this weekend."

"I know it's this weekend," Mark said with a frown.

"Oh, I wasn't sure. Since you haven't given her anything yet."

Mark's eyebrows shot up. "I don't think you need to worry about Hailey."

Ty shook his head. "It's not Hailey I'm worried about."

"Oh really? You worried about yourself, since I'm going to kick your ass if you don't back up from my girlfriend?" Mark moved in closer.

Ty sighed. "No, I'm worried about *you*, Mark."

"And why is that?"

"Ty, stop," Hailey said from behind him. "Don't."

"Why are you worried about me?" Mark demanded, scowling at them both.

Ty felt Hailey's hand on his arm. "Because your girlfriend is going to be thinking about *me* all day and the whole school's going to be talking about what a romantic I am. That's gonna be tough on your ego."

Mark frowned at Hailey. "Why would she be thinking about you?"

"Because *this* is going to be hard to forget."

Ty turned, took Hailey's face in his hands and kissed her.

And he *kissed* her. It was a full-on movie-quality lip lock, complete with the sounds of her books thudding to the floor and people gasping around them and the feel of her hands grabbing the front of his shirt.

It was the best twenty seconds of his life.

Followed by some of the most painful.

Mark grabbed him, spun him around and punched him in the face.

That was all he did, fortunately, because Ty's older brother Travis walked up just then.

"What the fuck?" Travis pulled Mark back and glared at the two guys with him. "Step back, Andrews."

"He deserved it," Mark said.

"I'm sure," Travis said. "That doesn't mean I'm going to stand here and let you beat him."

Which was also why Ty had chosen this moment and this place. Travis was taking history this period too.

Ty rubbed his jaw and shrugged at Mark. "Like I said— thinking about me all day."

Mark lunged for him, but Travis held him back.

Travis looked over his shoulder at Ty. "Shut the hell up, Ty. Get lost."

Yeah, okay. Ty bent to pick up Hailey's books and handed them to her, giving her a little wink. "Totally worth it."

She was staring at him with wide eyes, her cheeks flushed, lip gloss smudged.

Ty wiped his thumb over his bottom lip where the gloss had been transferred. "Love this flavor."

Mark jerked forward, but Ty sauntered off down the

hall.

Hailey deserved to be kissed by a guy who thought she walked on water, and she deserved to have two guys fighting over her.